THE BODY IN THE LIGHTHOUSE

KATE HARDY

Storm

Ebook ISBN: 978-1-80508-750-2
Paperback ISBN: 978-1-80508-751-9

Cover design by: Lisa Brewster
Cover images by: Shutterstock, Depositphotos

Published by Storm Publishing.
For further information, visit:
www.stormpublishing.co

ALSO BY KATE HARDY

A Georgina Drake Mystery

The Body at Rookery Barn

The Body in the Ice House

The Body Under the Stage

The Body at the Roman Baths

The Body at the Windmill

For my big sister Jackie, with love

ONE

Georgina Drake walked into the churchyard at Little Wenborough and placed the pink carnations in the flower vase on Doris and Harrison's grave. The headstone had been removed so Harrison's name could be added, but it would be another couple of months until the stone could be replaced.

Today – the fifty-third anniversary of Doris's death, and Georgina's own fifty-third birthday – she wanted to bring flowers.

'I miss you, Doris,' she said softly.

It had been odd to hear a voice through her hearing aids when Doris had first introduced herself as the girl who'd died in Georgina's house on Valentine's Day 1971, but it felt even stranger not to hear Doris anymore. Since Harrison's funeral, Georgina hadn't heard from Doris at all.

Now they were together, the restless spirit was clearly at peace.

But Georgina missed chatting with her friend about books and music. Missed sharing their love of Shakespeare, and capping each other's quotes. Missed Doris's wry chuckle and her delight in technology. Missed working with her to unravel the truth about unexplained deaths in the past.

Bert missed Doris, too. Right now he was lying on the grass, his chin on his spotty front paws, his golden-brown eyes as mournful as only a springer spaniel's could look.

Georgina shook herself. Today wasn't a day to be maudlin. The only other people who knew that she could communicate with Doris were Doris's younger brother, Jack, and his wife, Tracey, and it had been hard enough to convince them of the truth. Now Doris had gone silent, it looked as if Georgina would never have to explain the situation to the other people in her life who didn't believe in ghosts, and would probably think she'd gone utterly mad.

'I hope you're both happy, now you're together again. I'll play a bit of George Harrison in your honour, later today,' she said.

Though, right now, she had a date. She glanced at her watch. There was just enough time to walk back to Rookery Farm before Colin arrived.

Five minutes after she'd got home, she heard the gravel outside crunch and then Colin knocked at the kitchen door before walking in.

'Happy birthday, Georgie,' he said, kissing her and handing her a bunch of pink, purple and cream stocks – her absolute favourites.

'Thank you. These are lovely.' She kissed him back and breathed in the clove-like scent before filling her favourite duck-egg blue china jug with water and slotting the flowers in. 'As we're meeting the Musketeers' – her nickname for her closest friends in the village, Sybbie, Francesca and Jodie – 'at the farm shop café before going to see the snowdrops at Walsingham, shall we take my car?'

'I honestly don't mind getting dog hair – or mud – in mine,' he said with a grin. 'Not when it comes with this beautiful beastie.' He made a fuss of Bert.

'You might not mind; though, if you get called out, your passengers might object,' she said. Despite Colin booking three days off to spend with her, she knew that if a case came into the local CID he'd need to cancel their plans and go in to work. 'It's probably less hassle if we use mine.'

She secured Bert's harness to the seat belt in the back of her car, then drove them all to the farm shop at Little Wenborough Manor, on the opposite side of the village.

'Here she is: the birthday girl!' Francesca, the owner of the farm shop, called as Georgie, Colin and Bert entered the café area. As usual, the café was full of people who'd popped into the farm shop to pick up vegetables and deli goods, but had been unable to resist the lure one of Francesca's amazing cakes. Francesca had clearly reserved a table for the five of them and Bert, because there was a cake with a single candle in the middle of one of the tables, and a cupcake on a plate next to it.

As Georgina reached the table, Sybbie stood up to give her a hug and one of her trademark wide smiles. 'Happiest of birthdays, dear girl.'

Georgina hugged her back. 'Thank you.'

'Happy birthday, Georgie. Sit down. I'm just making your usual – and Colin's,' Jodie called over from the coffee machine.

'Thank you,' Georgina said, smiling.

Francesca hugged her. '*Buon compleanno, bella.*'

'*Grazie,* Cesca.' Georgina grinned, knowing that Francesca was hamming up her Italian heritage for Colin's benefit. She gestured to the cakes. 'I really appreciate this, but isn't having two birthday cakes a tiny bit – well, greedy?'

'The little one's actually a "pupcake",' Francesca explained. 'For Bert. It's the Battersea Dogs' Home recipe, made with bananas, though I didn't have time to do the mashed potato "icing". Max and Jet' – Sybbie's black Labradors – 'taste-tested a couple earlier and gave their seal of approval.'

Bert, hearing his name and clearly working out that a treat was in his very near future, wagged his tail, sat down and offered a polite paw, then happily munched a piece of 'pupcake' that Georgina broke off for him.

'Make a wish,' Sybbie said, lighting the candle and launching into 'Happy Birthday to You', along with Colin, Francesca, Jodie, and everyone else within earshot.

'There's only one candle,' Francesca said. 'I didn't want to risk setting off the smoke alarm if I used one for every year.'

Georgina laughed. 'The *cheek* of you! But that looks like lemon cake, so I'll forgive you.'

'Of course it's lemon,' Cesca said. 'What else would I make for your birthday but your favourite cake? It's a new recipe, though – there's home-made lemon curd icing on the top.'

Georgina blew out the candles, Cesca served the cake, and Jodie brought over the remaining mugs of coffee.

'What are you doing today?' Sybbie asked.

'We're going to see the snowdrops at Walsingham,' Colin said, 'followed by fish and chips on the quay at Wells, and a gig in Norwich tonight.'

'We're not having dinner out,' Georgina added, 'because it's Valentine's Day.'

'And you'd rather have your birthday dinner when you can choose what you like and not be stuck with a set menu of steak and chips, followed by heart-shaped strawberry cheesecake,' Francesca said, nodding sagely. 'Very wise.'

'We've got a table booked tomorrow night at the Feathers instead,' Georgina said. 'During the day we're taking Bert out somewhere; and then on Friday I've got a commission in Summerstrand, photographing the lighthouse and the man who's renovating it.'

'I'll be checking the new guests into Rookery Barn on Friday, after I've cleaned it,' Jodie said. 'Though I don't think you'll enjoy your photo session very much, Georgie.'

Georgina frowned at the younger woman. 'Why not?'

'You know Vicky Evans, who teaches at Little Wenborough Primary School?' Jodie asked.

'And whose little boy is your Harry's best friend?' Georgina asked.

Jodie nodded. 'Eliot Manson – the guy renovating the lighthouse – is her ex-husband.'

It sounded as if Jodie was about to impart some village gossip. Part of Georgina felt awkward, as if she shouldn't be listening; on the other hand, this was all part and parcel of living in a small community. Everyone knew nearly everyone else – and also knew almost everything about them.

'He cheated on her. More than once,' Jodie said, an expression of outrage on her face. 'That's bad enough – but, when she left him and fell in love with someone else, he got himself a really fancy lawyer who made out the break-up was all her fault. Manson took Vicky for every penny; then her new bloke died when she was six months' pregnant, and she ended up having to move in with her mum and stepdad. That's Sally and Ben, who run the Feathers,' Jodie added. 'If you see them tomorrow, I probably wouldn't mention your plans.'

Georgina winced. Poor Vicky. It sounded as if she'd had a rough time, with a divorce, a bereavement and coping with a baby on her own. 'I feel a bit guilty for doing the photos and interview, now. I was under the impression I'd be talking to a builder who was restoring the old lighthouse and turning it into his dream home.'

'Which will be a nightmare,' Sybbie said dryly, 'if it's anything like that massive pile he owns in Great Wenborough.'

'The one with the over-the-top gold gates?' Colin asked.

'That's the one – rubbing in how much money he has. And poor Vicky has to pass it every day on her way to work.' Jodie pulled a face. 'I feel a bit guilty, too, because one of my clients, Tara, moved in with Manson six months ago when she got engaged to him. Which means I'm sort of working for him, too.'

'You don't have to like your clients,' Cesca said, patting Jodie's hand. 'Though I could always give you an extra shift here in the café, if you want to stop working for Tara.'

'I can't drop her. She's my best friend's sister,' Jodie said, looking miserable. 'And I don't want to upset my best mate. I mean, Bethany always stood by me when people were nasty about me being pregnant with Harry so young.'

'Tricky,' Sybbie commiserated. 'But I'm sure Vicky understands you're working for Tara, not him.'

'We all think Tara's mad, being with *him*,' Jodie said. 'Even if you ignore him being a good fifteen years older than her, and his looks – he's shorter than Tara, he's got a chubby face, and designer stubble doesn't look great when you're bald – it's his personality that's the problem. He throws his money about, snaps his fingers and expects people to jump, and makes out he's best mates with some gangsters. Why would you want to marry someone like that?' She grimaced. 'Bethany can't stand him. But Tara's convinced that he loves her and he'll change for her.'

'Ouch,' Sybbie said. 'A lot of women have made that mistake.'

'Manson's barred from the Feathers,' Jodie said. 'And from Ben's other pub, in Summerstrand. When Manson found out Sally was going to buy the lighthouse, he gazumped her. And he crowed about getting it – obviously because he thought it'd twist the knife for Vicky if he was the one who ruined her mum's plans.'

'Why did Sally want the lighthouse?' Georgina asked, puzzled. 'She's the village doctor a couple of days a week, as well as running the pub. A lighthouse doesn't seem to fit in with either the pub or the surgery.' She clearly hadn't gone anywhere near deep enough with her preliminary research into the lighthouse – or Eliot Manson.

'Her dad used to be the lighthouse keeper in the 1960s and 1970s,' Jodie said, 'and I think Sally wanted to turn the place into a museum. Instead, Manson's going to make it into some flashy holiday home he'll rent out for a fortune.' She pulled a face. 'Everyone hates him in Summerstrand, too. Vicky said that Manson's planning to build all these new houses on the edge of the village, but nobody local can afford one.'

'That makes me feel even more guilty about doing this commission.' Georgina winced. 'Though I can't let the magazine down at the last minute. That wouldn't be fair.'

'Don't feel bad about it. It's work,' Jodie said. 'Like me cleaning for Tara and doing her ironing.' She grimaced. 'I'd better not say any more.'

'Thank you for the warning,' Georgina said. 'All the background work I did was on Manson's professional life rather than his private life. I'll know to be careful what I ask him on Friday.'

'Be careful, full stop. And that's enough about him. We're meant to be celebrating your birthday, not talking about *him*,' Jodie said. She lifted her mug. 'Happy birthday!'

When they'd all finished their cake and coffee, and Georgina had opened her birthday cards and the presents her friends had insisted on buying her, she drove Colin and Bert out to Little Walsingham and found a space in the car park. Colin hadn't visited the quaint little village before; its narrow medieval streets were lined with half-timbered houses with white-painted sash windows and grey-tiled roofs. Pubs and cafés sat cheek by jowl with curiosity shops, bookshops and craft shops. In the middle of the marketplace, surrounded by cobbles, was a small, squat octagonal brick building with a weathered stone roof and a pillar on top, capped by an iron basket.

'What's that?' Colin asked.

'The old pump house,' Georgina said. 'The beacon on top is lit on special occasions, according to Sybbie.'

'It's like a glimpse into another world – into the past,' Colin said softly.

He couldn't quite read Georgina's expression when she asked, 'Do you believe there are other worlds?'

'I'm not sure,' he answered honestly. 'I don't believe in little green men – but we can't be the only inhabited planet in an infinite universe.'

'What about people who've slipped back into the past, or seen a ghost?' she asked.

Colin thought about it for a moment. It wasn't the first time Georgina had mentioned ghosts. 'They might genuinely believe it happened,' he said at last, 'but there's always a rational explanation.'

'Maybe,' she said.

Before he could pin her down to explain more, she nudged him. 'That's where we're going.'

In front of them on the main street was a massive flint wall and a square tower, with a huge arch set into it.

'That's the old priory's gateway,' she continued. 'Though there isn't much left of the priory itself now – mainly the big arch of the old East Window, though that's pretty impressive.'

'I take it you've photographed this place before?' Colin asked.

'Not officially. I came here last year with Sybbie to see the snowdrops,' Georgina said. 'They're amazing – like a bluebell carpet, only white, and they stretch as far as you can see.'

'Right,' Colin said, humouring her.

She raised an eyebrow. 'Prepare to be stunned, city boy. I certainly was.'

Colin just about stopped himself saying that she was stunning enough for him. That would be way too cheesy. And he was aware that she was much better-read than he was, so quoting poetry at her was out of the question. Though he'd look up Shakespeare on the internet later, to see if he could find a quote about snowdrops; he knew how much she loved Shakespeare.

Instead, he took her free hand – the other was holding Bert's lead – and strolled through the archway with her. He paid the entrance fee for them both, muttering, 'Birthday treat – don't argue,' when Georgina tried to go halves. In front of them was a small garden full of snowdrops.

'They're all named varieties,' she said.

He blinked at her. 'There's more than one variety of snowdrop?'

'Loads,' she said. 'And it's hard to identify them because they vary so much. Two clumps of snowdrops from the same variety might look completely different, depending on the weather, the growing conditions, whether it's the first time it's flowered or if the clump's recently been split.'

Colin was about to ask how she knew so much about snowdrops when she wasn't a gardener; then he remembered her saying who she'd come here with, last year. 'Sybbie?'

'Yup. She knows as much about snowdrops as she does about azaleas, and she taught me everything I know as well as quite a bit I've forgotten,' Georgina said with a smile. 'Apparently this man called Heyrick Greatorex – what a name! – bred double snowdrops, and he named a lot of them after Shakespearean characters. Sybbie insisted on buying me a couple of pots in the abbey shop to plant in my garden. Sadly, there isn't a Beatrice – I mean, how cute would it be to have a snowdrop named after my daughter? – but she found me a *Galanthus* White Swan, which she thinks is probably a reference to Shakespeare himself, and a *Galanthus* Jacquenetta. Young Tom planted them for me under the trees, and they look gorgeous this year.'

They rounded the corner and Colin stopped dead as he saw the ruined stone arch of the priory and what lay beyond. 'I thought you were exaggerating,' he admitted. 'But there must be hundreds of thousands of snowdrops here. Millions, even.' He bent to ruffle the top of Bert's head. 'No digging up any bodies here, OK?'

The spaniel wuffed gently, as if promising to behave.

Colin and Georgina wandered through the grounds, holding hands. The sky was a pale but rich blue, and the snow-drops in the dell glittered like drifts of snow under the wintry sun. Colin couldn't resist taking some snaps of the 'snowdrop carpet' to send to his daughter, and some of Georgina with Bert. 'Shall we take a selfie?' he asked. 'I'm getting better at this sort of thing, thanks to you.'

'You're the one putting in the practice,' she reminded him with a smile.

They sat on a horizontal tree-trunk, Bert between them, and when Colin checked the snap he was gratified to see that he'd managed to get some of the snowdrops in the background, too.

When they'd had their fill of the snowdrops, Georgina drove them to the beach, and Bert thoroughly enjoyed a run on the sand before they queued up for fish and chips at the quay-side and sat on the wall, looking out at the salt marshes and the boats moored in the harbour. Colin saved some of his cod for Bert, cutting it into chunks to let it cool enough for the spaniel to enjoy.

'You spoil him,' Georgie said.

Colin coughed and looked pointedly at the matching chunks of cod cooling in her cardboard box; she simply laughed. 'This is the perfect day, Colin.'

'Definitely one to remember,' he agreed.

And it stayed that way, because thankfully he wasn't called

back to the station to deal with something urgent. He could just enjoy spending time with Georgina, a day full of sunshine and sea and snowdrops, followed by an evening watching a blues guitarist on the stage of the tiny city venue with his arms wrapped around Georgina. And, best of all, staying overnight at Rookery Farm so he could go to sleep with her in his arms.

TWO

It had rained heavily overnight, but the clouds cleared over breakfast and it looked like it was turning into another sunny day. Georgina and Colin took Bert on a snowdrop walk at a country house not far from Little Wenborough, where there was a pop-up tea tent serving cheese scones and cake – and, to Bert's delight, sausage rolls. Although the house and gardens were pretty and he enjoyed the walk, Colin thought the incredible spread of the snowdrops at Walsingham Abbey had ruined him for seeing any others.

Later that evening, when Georgina and Colin arrived at the Feathers in Great Wenborough, Bert lay peacefully next to their feet as they ate, knowing that he'd get some special treats in a doggy bag later because Hannah the chef adored him.

'Happy birthday for yesterday, Georgie,' Sally called as she brought over their coffee and a plate of petits fours with a birthday candle stuck in one of them and the words 'happy birthday' written in chocolate on the plate. 'Make a wish!'

Georgina smiled and blew out the candle. 'Thanks, Sally. I hoped I'd see you, actually; I wasn't sure if you were doing Pilates tonight or working.'

Pilates was Georgina's usual Thursday night class with Sybbie, Jodie and Francesca, Colin remembered; but tonight she was skipping it to celebrate her birthday with him.

'Normally it'd be Pilates, but we're short-staffed tonight as Molly's gone down with a virus, and it would've been unfair to leave Ben all on his own,' Sally said. 'What did you want to see me about?'

Colin could understand Sally's slightly cagey expression; she was the village's part-time GP as well as co-owner of the pub, so people tended to ask her about their health whenever they saw her.

'I wanted to apologise to you,' Georgina said. 'You've probably heard on the village grapevine that I've been commissioned to take photos of the lighthouse at Summerstrand tomorrow.'

'And of *him*.' Sally grimaced. 'Don't worry, it's not your fault. I wouldn't expect you to turn down work.'

'Just so you know, if I'd realised who he was,' Georgina said, 'I would have turned it down when they asked me. I only found out yesterday, but I think it'd be unprofessional now to let the magazine down at the very last minute.'

'You're right. But thank you for – well, being thoughtful.' Sally sighed. 'I probably shouldn't say this in front of you, Colin, but when I think about what that man's done to my daughter, and what he's going to do to the home I grew up in, I wish I could hire a hit man. Or that he'd just drop dead. I sometimes hope that he forgets to take his blood pressure tablets and has a heart attack, when he's on his own and his mobile phone's out of charge so he can't call for help. And that nobody finds him until it's too late.'

Colin's first thought was for Georgina; she'd told him confidentially a while back that she'd been the one to find Stephen, her late husband, when he'd died after a heart attack. Alone. Everyone in Little Wenborough and Great Wenborough knew she was a widow, but she clearly hadn't shared the details or Sally wouldn't have said something so crass.

He glanced at Georgina, seeing the way her face was carefully blank, and pressed the side of his foot against hers in a gesture of comfort. The grateful look in her eyes told him she knew that he understood and was supporting her.

And then he thought about what Sally had just said. Doctors took the Hippocratic Oath when they qualified, to do the best by their patients, but Sally's feelings towards Manson were clearly pushing her towards breaking that oath. 'That's pretty much malice aforethought, you know,' he said lightly. 'If Manson's ever found dead after an unexpected illness' – the heart attack Sally had suggested, but he wouldn't be so cruel as to say that in front of Georgina – 'someone would need to interview you.'

'If he was my patient, believe me, I'd be tempted to prescribe him arsenic, or make some personal tweaks to his medication,' Sally said grimly. 'Luckily for both of us, being his ex-mother-in-law means that he counts as being related to me and needs to be registered with a different GP. I'd be forced to treat him in an emergency, but otherwise I don't have to deal with him.'

'It's a difficult situation for you,' Colin said sympathetically.

'I wish Vicky had never married him. God knows what she ever saw in him – or maybe he was all fun and charm until he'd got that wedding ring on her finger, and then he showed his true colours as a cheat and a liar. I always thought he was a Napoleon type. You know, a short man wanting to make himself look big. But I suppose we all have perfect hindsight,' Sally said. 'Anyway, enough of him. Can I get you anything else?'

'This is all perfect,' Georgina said with a smile. 'Please thank Hannah for the petits fours – they're lovely – and for Bert's sausages.'

'The food's always fabulous here,' Colin added. 'Thanks, Sally.'

'Pleasure.' Sally gave them a wry smile. 'If you're still in Summerstrand at lunchtime, go and see Claire – Ben's daughter – at the George and Dragon. She'll look after you.'

'If the food's half as good as it is here, we'll do that,' Colin promised.

'Though we'll have Bert with us,' Georgina said.

'Don't worry – the pub's dog-friendly,' Sally reassured her. 'I'll tell Claire to keep an eye out for you.'

Once Sally had gone back to the kitchen, Colin raised an eyebrow at Georgina. 'Are you all right?'

She nodded. 'Thank you. For not saying anything about the way Stephen died – and for changing the subject to take the heat off me.'

'I'm always on your side, Georgie,' he said gently.

'I know.'

He winced. 'It looks as if tomorrow's going to be a bit tricky.'

'It does,' she agreed. 'I'll need to be tactful what I ask about the lighthouse as well as any personal questions.'

'What do you know about the lighthouse?' Colin asked.

'The editor at the magazine told me it was decommissioned nearly twenty years ago, and the lighthouse and its cottage have been empty ever since,' Georgina said. 'There wasn't much on the internet when I did the background work on the building. I don't know Sally's maiden name, so I had no idea of her connection to the lighthouse until Jodie mentioned it yesterday. Obviously, I didn't do my research on the modern side thoroughly enough.'

'Nobody does a perfect job every single time, Georgie,' Colin reminded her. 'If the lighthouse has been empty for the best part of two decades, it's probably not in great repair. Why wasn't it sold earlier?'

'I couldn't quite get to the bottom of that, but there seemed to be some kind of legal wrangles,' Georgina said. 'Anyway, it finally came up for sale last year. Manson bought it and he's developing the site. The magazine told me it was his dream home – and I have to admit, I love the idea of having a tower overlooking the sea, with glass walls in a sitting room at the top so I can see the sunrise, the sunset and the stars.' She smiled. 'And, on a very lucky night, the aurora borealis.'

'I thought Rookery Farm was your dream house?' Colin asked.

'It is,' Georgina said. 'But it'd be nice to stay in a lighthouse too.'

'A holiday home – which is what Jodie said the lighthouse will become.' Colin blew out a breath. 'I'm not surprised the villagers are upset. Another second home, when none of the kids in the village can afford to buy their first home.'

'And when the owner brings nothing into the local economy and doesn't live there for most of the time,' Georgina agreed. 'Not to mention this new development Jodie talked about. I think I'll need to revamp the session a bit. I'll take photographs of the building, ask him to send in his architect's impression of what it will look like, do some shots of the surroundings, ask him a very innocuous set of questions so I can avoid stirring up painful memories for Vicky and Sally and not make any tension in the village worse, and take his headshot.' She rolled her eyes. 'Which I could've done just as easily at his home. The piece is for an architectural magazine, so it would've been a chance for him to show off his house too. But maybe he sees having the photographs done at the lighthouse as another way of rubbing Sally's face in it, and hurting Vicky.'

'"One may smile and smile and be a villain",' Colin quoted softly. 'Which is what you thought of me when we first met.'

'Handsome, arrogant and throwing your weight around. Which was true. Though you didn't smile. You were grumpy and unapproachable.' She took his hand and squeezed it. 'But I've since learned there's a lot more to you than that. You stand up for people and give them a voice. Actually, I think you might be Henry V. Fair but formidable.'

'Hang on. Didn't he dump all his mates for his crown?' Colin asked, feeling slightly nettled.

'That was when he was Prince Hal, and that's not you. But having those rackety mates when he was young gave him the ability to talk to just about anyone when he became Henry V, not just high society, which is also true of you,' she said.

'Thank you for the compliment. Even though it feels a bit backhanded,' he said.

She chuckled. 'I'll have you know, I have a very soft spot for Henry V. Especially Kenneth Branagh's version. "A good heart... is the sun and the moon; or, rather, the sun and not the moon; for it shines bright and never changes, but keeps his course truly."'

Colin suppressed the pang of disappointment that she clearly no longer thought of him as a potential Benedick, as she'd once hinted; of course the role of Shakespeare's greatest romantic hero would be reserved for Stephen. And Colin would never want Georgina to forget the love of her life. She'd made room for Colin in her life, and he'd made room for her in his. That was enough.

Anyway, he loved it when she quoted Shakespeare at him.

But maybe something of his disappointment showed in his eyes, because she gave him a truly wicked grin. 'Mind you, then there's Lord Wessex in *Shakespeare in Love...*'

Oh, no. He should've guessed there would be a Colin Firth moment waiting in the wings for her to tease him with. And he'd seen that film. It wasn't a compliment. 'Wessex was an utter arse.'

'A pantomime villain. Cute, though.' She raised an eyebrow. 'I can just see you wearing knee-length boots, hose and a doublet. Black velvet, with a bit of silver embroidery. Oh, and a neat little ruff.'

Was that better or worse than Mr Darcy's frilly shirt? Colin wondered, and hoped that none of his former colleagues in London ever got to hear a word of what Georgie was suggesting.

'And a cute little Elizabethan beard.' She leaned forward and traced the shape on his chin. 'I'll let you off the pearl earring, but you definitely need a curl over your forehead.' She twisted her fingers into his fringe, styling it into what he guessed was an Elizabethan-style curl. 'Very, *very* cute.' There was a decided twinkle in her green eyes. She tipped her head to one side and gave a completely over-the-top pout, and he couldn't help chuckling.

How hard he'd fallen for Georgina Drake. She made him laugh, and she made him feel all kinds of things he'd never thought he could feel again, after his divorce. 'I suppose I could buy such a costume,' he deadpanned, 'and wear it as a late birthday present for you.'

'Yes, *please*.' Her eyes glittered. 'You know, with a long day tomorrow, and all the sea air from yesterday' – she gave a very fake yawn – 'I think perhaps we need an early night.'

'Noted. Finish your coffee, birthday girl,' Colin said, aware that his voice had deepened and knowing he was blushing because his face felt hot, 'and I'll sort the bill.'

The next morning, Colin and Georgina, with Bert in the back of the car, headed for Summerstrand. Georgina was dressed for work, in smart black trousers, a black crew-neck sweater, and good trainers, but her walking boots were in a bag in one of the rear footwells. Colin was dressed more casually, in jeans and a long-sleeved polo shirt, because he would be walking Bert while Georgina was at the photo shoot.

'"Very flat, Norfolk",' Colin quoted, when they reached the Acle Straight.

'A lot of it isn't, but this bit of it is, which is probably why the great North Sea flood in 1953 was such a disaster,' Georgina said. They could see for miles across the marshes and the dykes. The landscape was full of church towers and ancient windmills, their sails long gone, and the vast expanse of grey sky was filled with sinister-looking clouds.

The fields had been ploughed and sown; in a month or so, the first green shoots of spring would emerge, but right then the furrows looked as shadowed and ominous as the sky. 'It's bleak,' Colin said, 'but there's a special kind of beauty out here. Since I've moved here, I totally get why people wax lyrical about Norfolk skies. The sunsets and sunrises over the marshes must be amazing.'

'They're pretty amazing anywhere in Norfolk,' Georgina said. 'But I agree.'

There was a massive sign for Manson's new development hammered into a field just before they reached the village; the site had been levelled and a digger was parked, clearly waiting for the site manager to instruct his team to start digging foundation trenches for the houses. Though there were no other vehicles on the site, and nobody was actually working.

Summerstrand itself was a quiet village; picture-postcard flint-and-brick cottages with slate roofs lined the main street, and the front gardens looked as if they would burst with colour in the spring. They could see the lighthouse rising at the far end of the village, the bottom half of the tower painted red and the top half painted white, with a walkway around the glass lantern at the top. As they drew nearer and Georgina's satnav directed them down what looked like a sandy farm track, they realised that the lighthouse was nestled among the marram grass on the edge of the sand dunes, with the white-painted two-storey keeper's cottage attached to one side.

'I was expecting it to be on a huge cliff or something,' Colin said.

'Not on this part of the coast,' Georgina said. 'If there are any cliffs at all, they'll be less than twenty metres tall.'

'If there aren't dangerous cliffs and rocks here, why did they need a lighthouse?' Colin asked.

'To warn of shifting sandbanks near the Yarmouth Roads,' Georgina said. 'Which aren't quite what they sound like – they're a bit of deep water off the coast where ships can anchor safely in a storm. The Navy used the roads as the base for the North Sea fleet during the Napoleonic Wars.'

'I take it that was part of your research for the lighthouse?' Colin asked.

Georgina nodded. 'Daniel Defoe wrote quite a lot about the area. He put Robinson Crusoe's first shipwreck at Winterton Ness, and he also wrote about a real-life disaster one night in the 1690s when four hundred ships were caught in a storm. Most of the ships didn't make it to the safety of the Yarmouth Roads, and a thousand people died in the wrecks.'

'A thousand people on one night? That's grim,' Colin said. 'In that case, surely the lighthouse is still needed?'

'Apparently, with modern navigation, the light floats and light buoys are effective enough nowadays,' Georgina said, 'which is why a lot of lighthouses have been decommissioned or become completely automated.'

There was a shiny black top-of-the-range Range Rover parked on the gravel in front of the lighthouse cottage; the personalised number plate, B16 MAN, pretty much gave it away that the car belonged to Eliot Manson. Georgina parked next to it and exchanged an amused glance with Colin, remembering Sally's comment about Manson being like Napoleon.

'It looks as if he's already here,' Colin said.

'I'll introduce you, and then you can take Bert for his quadruped constitutional while I do the interview and the shoot. Though if you want to stay and Manson doesn't object, that's fine by me. I know Bert will be on his best behaviour for you,' Georgina said. She took her camera bag from the car, and Colin attached Bert's lead to his collar before unclipping the seat belt from his harness.

'The windows on the first two floors are boarded up,' Georgina remarked as they walked across the gravel to the front door.

'I kind of expected that. You said the place has been empty for a long time, so the owners would've wanted to stop people going inside. And if Manson has already started working on the inside of the building and taken the windows out, the boards will keep the place watertight,' Colin pointed out.

She knocked on the door, and they waited.

'I suppose so.' There was no answer to a second knock, either. Shooting a puzzled look at Colin, she tried the handle. 'Locked.'

'Maybe the meeting slipped his mind,' Colin suggested.

'But his car's here,' Georgina said, 'which suggests he remembered.'

From sheer reflex, Colin laid his hand on the car's bonnet. 'It's cold, so it must've been here a while.' He shrugged. 'Maybe he's gone for a walk and lost track of time.'

'I'll try his phone,' Georgina said. She took her phone from her bag, made sure the phone was connected to her hearing aids rather than on loudspeaker, and frowned. 'That's odd. It's gone straight to voicemail. I'll leave a message anyway.' She paused. 'Mr Manson, it's Georgina Drake. We arranged to meet at ten this morning for your interview and photo shoot. I'm currently outside the lighthouse at Summerstrand. Could you call me when you get this message, please?' She ended the call and slid the phone back into her bag. 'It looks as if I spoke too soon and we'll have to wait.'

Five minutes later, Manson still hadn't returned her call;

slightly cross and wanting to get on with things, Georgina frowned. 'I'll see if his office can get hold of him.'

'Good morning, Manson Developments. Phoebe speaking. How can I help?' a cheery voice greeted her.

'Good morning. It's Georgina Drake. I had a meeting arranged with Mr Manson at the lighthouse this morning, but the building appears to be locked. I was wondering if something had happened to change his plans?' Georgina asked.

'I'm so sorry, Mrs Drake. I'm his PA. The meeting's definitely in his diary, and he hasn't said anything to me about cancelling,' Phoebe said.

'His car's here – at least, I presume it's his car. The number plate's B16 MAN.'

'Yes, that's his,' Phoebe said.

'The windows are boarded up and the door's locked,' Georgina said. 'Do any of the neighbours have keys? Then perhaps I can take the location shots now, and rearrange the time and place for the interview and headshots.'

'I'm afraid not,' Phoebe said. 'I have the spare keys here. I can bring them over to you, if you like, but I'm about thirty minutes away.'

'Yes, please,' Georgina said. 'I'd appreciate that.' She relayed the information to Colin when she ended the call. 'Sorry. This is going to drag on a lot longer than I'd intended.'

'Not your fault,' Colin said with a smile. 'I wish we'd brought a flask of coffee, though. Even if there's a kiosk on the beach selling hot drinks, I doubt it'd be open this time of year. There don't seem to be any tourists around.' He glanced up at the sky. 'Though it looks as if we're in for heavy rain, so they're probably waiting indoors.'

'I wonder why the neighbours don't keep his spare keys?' Georgina pondered.

'Maybe he didn't trust them. Or, given that his planned development on the edge of the village is unpopular, and if he's as unpleasant as Jodie and Sally said, maybe they didn't want to help him,' Colin suggested.

'Who knows?' She sighed. 'Well, I might as well take some of the exterior lighthouse shots.'

'Bert and I will walk with you, and I'll carry your bag,' Colin offered.

He obviously wanted to feel as if he was helping, so she didn't reject the offer. 'Thank you.'

She took photographs of the tower, then moved round to the back of the lighthouse cottage. There was a flat rectangle of earth by the back door; a large yellow skip sat next to it, full of carpet, broken furniture and large lumps of aggregate. It looked as if the cottage's interior had been stripped, an old patio had been removed, and the area had been prepared to dig the foundations for an extension to the cottage.

'He's probably going to stick one of those trendy glass boxes on the back of the house to make a combined kitchen, living room and dining room,' Colin remarked.

'It'd have amazing panoramic views of the dunes, the sand and the sea,' Georgina agreed, looking towards the beach. The dunes were low, and behind them was a wide strip of pale golden sand. Right now, the North Sea was slate-coloured and choppy, slamming against the sand with a sullen roar; but on summer mornings you'd see the sun rising, and on winter nights you might even see the Northern Lights dancing far out to sea.

Bert, taking full advantage of the extendable lead, trotted across the flat area by the skip, his plumy tail held out straight and his nose to the ground as if he was scenting something.

Just as the spaniel's paw started to scrape the sandy earth, Georgina heard a voice in her hearing aids – a voice she hadn't heard for a while. 'Georgie, I think we need to talk...'

THREE

Doris.

It had been several months since Georgina had spoken to Doris. Not since Georgina had uncovered the tragic circumstances around her death and Doris had been reunited with her true love, Harrison. The silence after Harrison's funeral had convinced Georgina that the ghost who lived in her house was finally at peace.

Clearly that wasn't the case. Why on earth was the ghost back now? Georgina didn't have a clue what the connection was between Doris and Summerstrand. But right now Georgina couldn't talk to the ghost properly. At least, not without a lot of explanation to Colin that she didn't think he'd believe, and she couldn't even begin to rationalise.

'Did you encourage Bert to dig?' Georgina asked under her breath, turning slightly so that the wind would carry her voice away from Colin.

'Yes.'

Just as she had at Hartington Hall, and in the Regency Theatre in Islington, when they'd solved a mystery from the past together. 'Is there a body buried next to the lighthouse?' Georgina whispered.

'Yes.'

Then she remembered Sally's comments from the previous night: *I sometimes hope that he forgets to take his blood pressure tablets and has a heart attack, when he's on his own and his mobile phone's out of charge so he can't call for help. And that nobody finds him until it's too late.*

Manson's phone had gone straight to voicemail this morning, as if it was out of charge or out of range. What if he'd had a heart attack, been unable to call anyone for help, and died alone?

And, if so... had Sally's words been a coincidence, or had she somehow been involved?

No, that was ridiculous. Sally was a part-time GP who was considering retirement. Of course she wasn't a murderer.

Even so, Georgina dragged in a breath, dreading the answer. 'Is it Manson?'

'No,' Doris said.

That was a huge relief. Georgina had been first on the scene after three deaths, now. It was getting to be a bit of a habit, and one she'd quite like to break. If this was another cold case, like the ones she'd worked on with Doris before, she could handle it.

'We'll talk again in a bit, when Colin's busy,' Doris said gently.

'Got you,' Georgina said, and walked over to her dog just as Bert – who'd ignored Colin's frantic command to stop digging – deepened the hole enough to show off his find.

A bone.

A *human* bone.

'Oh, Christ,' Colin said. 'I think Bert's found a body.'

'Not Manson?' Georgina asked. Even though Doris had already confirmed that, Manson was probably the first person

Colin would think of, given Manson wasn't where he was supposed to be.

'No. It's skeletonised, so it must've been here for at least a year – probably longer,' Colin said. 'Those lumps of aggregate in the skip probably used to be a patio. We need to confirm that with whoever's working on the site, and also find out when it was laid. I'm going to have to call this in.'

'OK. I'll get Bert out of your way,' Georgina said, leaving her camera hanging round her neck by the strap. She took the extendable lead back from Colin and shortened it again, while Bert wagged his tail. 'Good boy, Bert,' she added, reassuring her dog that he wasn't in trouble for digging.

'I'm pretty sure that whoever levelled off this area removed most of the evidence from the layers above where the body was buried,' Colin said. 'Not necessarily deliberately – if nothing archaeological came up at the planning stage of the renovations, they wouldn't expect anything here.'

'Is there something I can do to help?' she asked.

'If you could take some photographs of the bone in situ, please, that would be helpful,' he said.

'Take Bert again for a minute, and tell me exactly the shots you want,' she said, handing the lead back. She took the photographs as he directed, then let her camera hang from the strap again before taking Bert's lead back. 'I'll forward the pictures to you when I've downloaded them to my computer,' she said. 'The signal here isn't great and it won't cope with a big file.'

'All right. Thank you,' he said.

'I'll give you some space to think and make your calls. Yell if you need anything – if I don't hear you, Bert will and he'll nudge me to come over to you,' she said.

Once she was out of Colin's earshot, she asked quietly, 'Doris?'

'I'm here. Happy birthday for Wednesday.'

'Thank you,' Georgina said. 'It was an anniversary for you, too, but I can hardly wish you "happy death day".'

'It doesn't matter. Did you have a good day?'

Georgina smiled. 'A very good one, thanks. Video calls from Will and Bea, cake and coffee at the farm shop with Sybbie, Cesca and Jodie, and a day at the snowdrops and the beach with Colin and Bert.'

'I love snowdrops. And I saw what you did at the grave. Thank you for the flowers,' Doris said. 'Pink carnations are my favourite. I'm really touched you remembered.'

'Of course I remembered.' Georgina paused. 'With you being silent for months, I didn't think we'd talk again.'

'I'm sorry about that,' Doris said. 'Time moves... I don't really know how to put it... *differently*, for me, I think,' she said eventually. 'I didn't go silent on you to hurt you.'

'I know,' Georgina said. 'I guess I made an assumption that Harrison was the reason you were still around, but once you were reunited...'

'Don't ask me,' Doris said. 'I don't get how it works, either.'

'It's good to talk to you again. How are you?' Georgina paused before asking tentatively, 'And how's Harrison?'

There was a sigh. 'We're getting there. I was so angry with him for what he did, Georgie. I don't know about sending him away with a flea in his ear – I think I gave him a whole circus, I yelled at him so much,' Doris said. 'But we've been talking it over, and I... Well, I'd waited half a century for him. I *missed* him.'

'I know,' Georgina said. 'And he missed you.'

'It's good to be with him again. I just wish the circumstances had been a bit different and we'd come back together at the right time,' Doris said. 'He's playing music again now. Connecting with old friends who were musicians. Which is good.' There was a dry laugh. 'I guess it's like when you're used to having the place to yourself, but then your partner retires and is suddenly under your feet all the time, and you really, *really* want them to take up a hobby. Preferably one that takes him out of the house for a few hours each day.'

Georgina couldn't help smiling. 'You sound like Sybbie. She's petrified that Bernard's going to make her cut back on the time she spends in the garden, when he retires.'

'More like she's worried he'll find out just how many of those Staffordshire china dogs she buys,' Doris said. 'And wouldn't Stephen have got under your feet, too?'

'I don't think he would've retired. Not completely,' Georgina said. 'Actors and directors don't really, do they?'

'That's probably true of all creative types – artists and writers and musicians, too. Their job's who they are,' Doris said. 'Actually, I'm discovering that I don't want to retire, either. I miss being an amateur detective with you and helping someone tell the truth about what happened to them. And I miss *you*.'

'Right back atcha,' Georgina said.

Doris groaned. 'If Bea heard you, she'd tell you off for trying to be down with the kids, or whatever the phrase is nowadays.'

'So would Will,' Georgina said. 'But I'm so glad you haven't disappeared completely.' She paused. 'Does this mean you're the main person in a kind of ghost detective agency now?'

'No. I don't do it all the time, I don't go around telling people here what I do, and you're the only person in your world that I have a connection with,' Doris said. 'When you're near someone who went before their time and needs help telling their story, if I'm around then they kind of materialise in front of me.'

'A ghost, haunted by a ghost,' Georgina said thoughtfully.

'It's more like I'm walking in a beautiful garden, and a stranger comes over and starts chatting to me,' Doris said. 'There's still none of this woo-woo stuff, you know. No rattling of chains or walking through walls.'

'Got it. So what can you tell me about the body by the lighthouse?'

'His name's Ryan Everett,' Doris said. 'He was staying with his great-aunt Joan in the village.'

'When?'

'From what he's told me, it was after the Beatles became famous, but before the moon landing.'

'Mid to late 1960s, then,' Georgina said. 'Could Ryan tell you what happened to him?'

'He remembers lying in the dunes, looking up at the stars. Kissing someone. Suddenly there was a lot of shouting and hitting and kicking – and then he couldn't breathe.'

Bert gave a soft wuff and nudged Georgina's knee.

She looked round, and Colin waved at her.

'I need to go,' Georgina said softly. 'Find out what you can, and we'll talk later. And, Doris – welcome back.'

FOUR

'I've called it in. Mo's going to talk to the finds liaison officer,' Colin said. 'I think our bones are human, so he'll ask her to get permission to exhume and bring a kit with her to record and bag any bones that are found. This isn't a known cemetery or burial site, so a phone call will be enough for her to get permission,' Colin said.

'Good.' Georgina glanced at her watch. 'You don't happen to carry a set of lockpicks on you, by any chance?'

'No,' Colin said. 'And if you're suggesting that I could pick the lock in the lighthouse cottage door if I did, that's a *definite* no. We don't have enough of a reason for breaking and entering.'

'It's not as if we're planning to burgle the place,' Georgina said. 'We're supposed to be here.'

'Breaking into someone's property without that person's permission – even if you're not planning to steal things – is still a criminal offence,' Colin said. 'OK, so Manson had arranged to meet you here, and you're supposed to be taking photographs of the building, but he's obviously not here, is he?'

'But his car is, and he's not answering his phone. Which is odd. Aren't you concerned about him?'

'He's a grown man and not vulnerable, to my knowledge. There might be a very plausible explanation. Maybe he went for a walk and lost track of time. And you know there are still dead areas for mobile phone reception in Norfolk. This might be one of them and that's why the call went straight to voice-mail.' He looked at Georgina. 'When he gets here, he's not going to be very happy to find out there's a skeleton underneath the area where he's planning to build an extension, especially as what's in that skip suggests he intended to start work on the building any day now. We need to get those remains exhumed and checked to see if they're of forensic interest – and, if they are, that'll mean more delays.'

'Meanwhile, we wait.' Georgina rolled her eyes. 'Hopefully his PA won't be too long.'

Twenty minutes later, a car drove slowly up the sandy track. A young woman parked next to the other two cars and climbed out. Her business suit marked her out as an office worker rather than a building site worker; her dark hair was neatly pulled back in a ponytail and her make-up was minimal. 'Mrs Drake?' she asked.

'Yes. I assume you're Phoebe?' At the younger woman's nod, Georgina said, 'Thank you for coming.'

'Mr Manson still isn't here, then?' Phoebe bit her lip. 'I tried calling him from the car, but it went straight to voicemail. I have no idea where he's got to.'

She took a set of keys from her handbag and slid one into the wrought-iron lock. The key squeaked slightly as she turned it and twisted the old-fashioned ball handle, while pushing on the heavy wooden door.

'Mr Ma—' Halfway through calling her boss's name, still holding on to the door, Phoebe screamed in shock. 'Oh, my God! What's happened to him?'

Georgina held Bert back while Colin gently moved Phoebe away from the door. Through the open doorway, Georgina could see the body of a red-faced man slumped at the table, facing them, with a nearly empty bottle of what looked like whisky and another of cola beside him. There was an unpleasant smell seeping through the open door, along with a blast of heat.

Oh, dear God. Was he unconscious... or dead?

From Phoebe's reaction as well as the description Jodie had given them – shorter than Tara, bald, with designer stubble – this had to be Eliot Manson.

'I'm a policeman,' Colin said quietly. 'Can I ask you to stay outside the cottage for the moment, please, Phoebe, and stand over there with Georgie while I take a look at the situation?'

At her silent nod, he went over to the body and checked for signs of life, then turned back to face Georgina and Phoebe. He shook his head very slightly to tell Georgina that Manson was beyond a doctor's help.

Georgina put her arm round the young woman's shoulders and moved her so she couldn't see the dead man at the table. 'I'm sorry. This must be a horrible shock for you.'

'He's dead? How can he be *dead*?' Phoebe asked, shaking her head. 'I only talked to him last night. He hadn't answered his emails today, but I just assumed he was too busy. I never thought he might be...' She choked and clapped a hand to her mouth.

'I'm sorry. There's no pulse and he's cold,' Colin said, 'so it looks as if he's been dead for a few hours. Though it's strange that his face is red instead of pale.' He looked at Georgina. 'I apologise, Georgie. You were right when you said we needed to check the inside of the cottage.'

She shrugged off his apology. 'That's not important.' Though she was glad he'd had the humility to acknowledge her instincts had been right.

'I'll call it in,' Colin said. 'And hopefully we can get a doctor out here quickly to confirm the death and give us some idea of the cause.'

Accident, murder or suicide? Georgina wondered. That wouldn't be known for a while. But what was clear was that they'd need to wait around.

'I'm sorry to ask you this, Phoebe, but do you know if Mr Manson had any health problems?' Colin asked gently.

'I know he was on some tablets,' Phoebe said, 'because he used to get me to pick up his prescription. But I never asked what they were for.' Her face flushed. 'I mean, it's none of my business. I'm only his PA.'

'That's fair enough. Had he said anything about not feeling himself, or a bit under the weather lately?' Colin persisted.

'No.' Phoebe's eyes widened with worry. 'What happens now? Do I have to go back to the office and tell everyone the boss is dead?' Suddenly, she looked very young indeed. It was obvious to Georgina that this was the first time Phoebe had ever had to deal with death.

'Who runs the firm when Manson's away on holiday?' Georgina asked.

'Nobody. He works late before he goes away and then long hours when he gets back, to catch up,' Phoebe said. 'He doesn't really take much holiday, either.'

'Does he have a manager at any of the sites?' Colin asked.

'There's Steve Carey – he's the site manager at the development just outside Norwich,' Phoebe said. 'I think he's meant to start at Summerstrand, too, next month.'

'What about the architect who did the plans for the lighthouse renovation?' Georgina asked.

'Mike Butler,' Phoebe said. 'He does all the plans for Mr Manson. He's freelance, though.'

Because it was cheaper than employing him full-time? Georgina wondered.

'I'll start with them,' Colin said. 'Don't worry. I'll help you sort it out.'

Georgina blew out a breath. 'I think we could all do with some coffee. But obviously we can't go into the lighthouse and make some because—' She broke off. Telling Phoebe that this might end up being classed as a crime scene and they couldn't risk contaminating it would do nothing to settle the younger woman's nerves. 'It's disrespectful,' she said in the end, and ushered Phoebe towards her car. 'Let's see if we can find somewhere that will sell us a hot drink while Colin makes his calls' – and made notes for an initial report – 'and then we'll call Manson Developments and get you some help. Are you all right with dogs?'

Phoebe nodded. 'Sorry. I'm a bit all over the place. It's the first...' She glanced back at the lighthouse cottage, clearly upset at seeing her first dead body.

'Finding a dead body can be very unsettling,' Georgina said, opening the back door of her car and clipping Bert's harness into the seatbelt. 'Sit in the back with Bert. He's very friendly – and making a fuss of him might help you feel a bit less wobbly.'

The petrol station, which seemed to double as the village shop, was only a couple of minutes' drive away in the centre of the village. Luckily it had a vending machine which claimed to deliver barista-standard hot drinks. Georgina asked Phoebe what she drank, then bought three coffees, adding sugar to Phoebe's for the shock. Bert was already provided for; whenever she took him out for the day, she always put his bowl, a couple of stainless-steel bottles of water and a tub of dog kibble in her backpack.

When they got back to the lighthouse, there was an unfamiliar car parked next to Manson's.

'Stay here in the car with Bert and drink your coffee,' Georgie said to Phoebe, 'and I'll find out what's happening.'

She went over to Colin with his paper cup of coffee.

He accepted it gratefully. 'Thanks. Georgie, this is Dr Wilson from the practice in the village. Dr Wilson, this is my partner, Georgina. She's the one who had the meeting arranged with Mr Manson today to interview him and take his photograph. Obviously, that's not going to happen now.'

The doctor, a slight, sandy-haired man in his late twenties with a worried expression, exchanged pleasantries with Georgina.

'What happened to him?' she asked.

'The coroner will need to confirm it, and you'll probably need a chat with his own GP to find out if he was being treated for anything,' he said, 'but to me this looks like a case of carbon monoxide poisoning. See all that redness in his face? That's caused by high levels of carboxyhaemoglobin in the blood.'

'What does that do?' Georgina asked.

'It stops the body being able to transport and use oxygen, especially in the brain,' Dr Wilson said.

'I assumed the red face was the effect of the whisky,' Georgina said, indicating the bottle on the table.

'No. But, depending on how much he drank, the alcohol probably added to any wooziness he might've felt,' Dr Wilson said.

'Though there's no way of knowing how much was in the bottle before he started drinking,' Colin pointed out.

'Get the pathologist to check his blood alcohol levels,' Dr Wilson advised.

'What if he was on blood pressure tablets?' Georgina asked, remembering Sally's comments.

'If his GP put him on beta-blockers but he hadn't followed advice to cut down on his drinking, it might've lowered his blood pressure to the point where he felt dizzy or even passed out. Again, it'll show in the blood tests.' He indicated the room. 'There doesn't seem to be any ventilation in here, so it looks to me as if the fumes from the paraffin heater he was using simply built up and overpowered him.'

The room appeared to be a sitting room, although the only furniture in it was the table and a couple of mismatched chairs. The carpet had already been pulled up and the radiator looked as if it had a rust stain running down one end. A panelled door with peeling cream paint led to the rest of the cottage on the right; a similar door on the left led to the lighthouse tower.

Georgina shivered as Sally's words came back to her again: *nobody finds him until it's too late.*

Just like Stephen. He'd died alone, too. Though she pushed the thought away. Her late husband had been dearly loved by a lot of people; Manson was his complete opposite.

'The room was stiflingly hot. I've turned the heater off now and left the door open to ventilate the room, so it'll be safe for people to enter. When do you think he died?' Colin asked.

'My best guess is somewhere between midnight and two,' Dr Wilson said. 'If he'd been sitting here all evening with the heater on, he might've had a bit of a headache from the fumes and assumed it was the whisky. He might've felt a bit sick, or tired, or maybe even a bit short of breath, and blamed that on any blood pressure tablets. And then he would've just fallen asleep.'

And he hadn't woken up again, Georgina thought. 'So it's an accidental death?'

'That's one for the coroner to decide,' Dr Wilson said. 'But I think it's the most likely explanation.'

'Thank you for your help,' Colin said. 'I'll get the body taken to the pathologist, with a note of the things you've suggested to check.'

'What do you need me to do?' Georgina asked, when Dr Wilson had left.

'If you can get the number for the surgery at Great Wenborough, that would be helpful,' Colin said. 'I'll need to talk to his

GP, and his next of kin – I assume Jodie's friend Tara is most likely to know who that is and how to get hold of them. Could you ask Jodie for Tara's number, without telling her what's going on here?'

'Sure,' Georgina said.

'I'll ask Phoebe to set up a meeting with the site manager and the architect,' Colin said thoughtfully. 'I'll need to tell them about Manson's death and then I can ask them for information. Sorry, I know we were going to spend the day together, but it'll need to be this afternoon.'

'You don't think Manson's death was an accident, do you?' Georgina asked.

'It feels like too much of a coincidence. Manson seems to have upset a lot of people; and he died alone, in a cottage that's attached to a lighthouse. The main door of the cottage is locked, and it's not the kind of automatic latch that locks itself behind you. Someone had to physically lock that door. And the back door is bolted from the inside, so it couldn't have been the exit,' Colin said.

'Dr Wilson said the cause of death was probably carbon monoxide poisoning from the heater,' she reminded him. 'If Manson had locked himself in...'

'That's what's making me twitchy,' Colin said. 'It's understandable that Manson might not want to trust the wiring of a place that had been empty for twenty years, so he used a paraffin heater instead of an electric fan heater. But the guy made his money from the building trade, Georgie. He'd be well aware of the safety issues around combustible fuel. The boarded-up windows meant he couldn't have one open for ventilation, so why didn't he use a portable carbon monoxide alarm?'

'Maybe he didn't intend to be here for very long, so he didn't think he needed one,' Georgina said.

'What about the bottle of whisky and the cola? That

suggests to me that he was planning to stay over. Unless, of course, he was stupid enough to consider driving back to Great Wenborough after he'd had a few drinks and was over the limit,' Colin said.

'From what we've heard about him, maybe he was arrogant enough to think that way,' Georgina said. 'But if he stayed here last night, where's his bedding?'

'Presumably in his car – which the forensic team will check – or in one of the other rooms in the cottage,' Colin said. 'Actually, could I use a couple of Bert's poo bags? They're the next best thing to proper shoe coverings, and I really want to check the rest of the cottage.'

Georgina knew that the team always wore suits and shoe coverings to avoid contaminating a crime scene. 'Of course.' She took some bags from her pocket and handed them to him. 'I have spares in the car, if you need them. You really think it's a suspicious death?'

'That depends on what Sammy says when she's done the postmortem,' Colin said. 'Right now, it's an unexplained death, so I'm being cautious. There's no sign of forced entry or any kind of disturbance in the sitting room.'

'I'll ask Phoebe to set up those meetings for you and get Tara's number, while you do what you need to do,' she said.

While Colin and Phoebe were busy making calls, Georgina rang Jodie and got Tara's number. She messaged it to Colin, and checked that Phoebe was doing OK.

'Thank you both for helping out,' Colin said, coming over to them.

'You're welcome,' Georgina said. 'I told Jodie that you wanted some information from Tara to help with a case. Jodie says Tara's been on a shoot in London – she's a model – but she's due back this afternoon. I've messaged you the number.'

Colin nodded. 'Were you able to arrange for Steve Carey

and Mike Butler to see me this afternoon?' he checked with Phoebe.

'Yes, at three,' Phoebe confirmed. 'I didn't tell them Mr Manson was dead. I just said you were from the police and you needed some information. They're coming to the office to meet you.'

'That's perfect. Thank you,' Colin said. 'The finds liaison officer will be here at half past one; the mortuary team will be collecting Manson's body to take him to the pathologist around the same time, and the forensics team should be here in a few minutes.' He glanced at his watch. 'So either we get some sandwiches and more coffee from the petrol station you went to and wait in your car until they turn up, or we ask if Claire at the George and Dragon can do us a sandwich or something to take away.' He looked at Georgina, an apology in his eyes. 'Sorry. A proper lunch is off. I need to stay here until the team gets here.'

To maintain the integrity of the scene, she knew. 'I'll drive over to the pub and see what Claire can offer us. Phoebe, would you like to join us?'

The young woman shook her head. 'I'd better get back to the office.'

'I know this morning's been very upsetting, but please keep what you know about Mr Manson confidential for now,' Colin said. 'I'll see you later this afternoon and I'll break the news to the team for you then. I'll hang on to the spare cottage keys for now and bring them back this afternoon.' He paused. 'Are you sure you're OK to drive back?'

'I think so. Thanks, though,' Phoebe said.

'If you're sure. Drive safely,' Georgina said. Once Phoebe had left, she turned to Colin. 'Did you find the bedding?'

'No. The place is pretty much gutted. There's a roll of toilet paper, some soap and a grubby towel in the bathroom, and that's it. I presume the bathroom and kitchen were going to be ripped out next.' Colin shrugged. 'Maybe there's something in his car.'

'I'll go and get us some food while you have a look,' Georgina said.

'Thanks. Leave Bert with me.'

'All right,' Georgina said. But she was thoughtful as she climbed behind the wheel of her car. The doctor's conclusion was that Manson had died from accidental carbon monoxide poisoning. Was it really an accident, or was it something more sinister than that? Colin obviously couldn't discuss the case properly with her, but he'd given her the impression he didn't think this was straightforward. But if someone had murdered Manson... who? And how had they managed it, with Manson being in a room locked from the inside?

And what of the human remains that Bert had started to dig up? Was there any connection to Manson? Or was it something else entirely?

FIVE

Five minutes later, Georgina parked behind a pretty flint-faced building with dormer windows, a red-tiled roof and an enormous chimney. The pub sign showed a knight in gleaming silver armour on a white horse, bearing a shield with the cross of St George on it, and a fearsome-looking dragon.

The car park was full enough to tell her that the pub was popular. As soon as she walked into the bar, she could see a proper fire crackling in the hearth, and the food smelled delicious. Several people were sitting at the bar, and several dogs were sitting nicely under tables. A glance at the specials board told her this was just the sort of place Colin would love. Maybe they could come back together, another time.

Behind the bar, a woman was serving drinks; she looked like a young, female and slender version of Ben, with the same wavy dark hair and soulful brown eyes. When she'd finished with her customer and came over to Georgina, Georgina smiled. 'Hello. Would you be Claire?'

'Yes. And you are?'

'Georgina Drake. I know your dad a little. Sally told me to come here because your food's good.'

'Nice to meet you,' Claire said. 'That's right, they told me you might be coming – though I was expecting to see a spaniel and a bloke who looks a bit like Mr Darcy with you.'

Georgina chuckled. 'His name is Colin and yes, he does. He makes a bit of a fuss when someone teases him about that, but he enjoys it really. I've left him and Bert, my spaniel, at...' She winced, aware that this was likely to be an awkward subject for Claire, too. 'The lighthouse.'

'Sally told me you were doing the photo session. But the village has been abuzz with gossip. Kitty from the doctor's surgery said a policeman with a London accent asked if Dr Wilson could go to the lighthouse,' Claire said. 'If Manson was ill, you'd either have taken him to the doctor, or called an ambulance. A policeman asking for a doctor to attend usually means someone's dead. So is he...?'

'Sorry. I can't really talk about it,' Georgina said. 'Let's just say Colin and I would've preferred to both be here with Bert, as planned. I was wondering, could I buy a couple of sandwiches or something to take away, please, and some coffee? Or, if not, could you tell me where I can get something?'

'Of course I can do you something. How about some toasties? If I wrap them in foil, they'll still be hot when you get back to the lighthouse,' Claire suggested. 'I can do you cheese on its own, with ham, or with bacon.'

'Cheese on its own would be perfect, thanks,' Georgina said gratefully.

'White or granary bread?'

'Granary, please,' Georgina said.

'Just as well you came this week,' Claire said as she rang up the order and Georgina paid by card. 'Next week, we'll be in the middle of redecorating the pub.'

'During half term?' Georgina asked, surprised. Surely school holidays were when people took a quick break and a seaside resort was going to be busy?

'It's not great timing, because my son's going to be bored stuck at home,' Claire said. 'But at least we had Valentine's Day without interruption, and we'll be done before Mother's Day. It was supposed to be done last month, but the plasterer and the decorator went down with Covid, so they're running a bit behind.'

'So Kitty's right, then? Manson's dead and he's not going to build those overpriced eyesores after all?' one of the elderly men sitting at the bar with a pint of bitter asked when Claire had left for the kitchen.

'I'm afraid I really can't comment,' Georgina said politely, trying to keep a poker face so she didn't damage Colin's investigation.

'Nobody round here wanted those houses built, you know.'

His friends at the bar nodded their agreement.

Clearly, he was the leader, Georgina thought; he was dressed ever so slightly more smartly than the other two and very clean-shaven, though his shock of white hair was unruly.

'The way he behaved towards people, I'm not surprised someone bumped him off.' He raised an eyebrow. 'And it wouldn't be the first murder around here.'

Could he be referring to the skeleton next to the lighthouse? Georgina wondered, her pulse quickening. 'Have there been many murders locally, then?' she asked, trying to keep her tone as casual as possible.

'Plenty of captains over the years, thinking they could outrun a storm instead of dropping anchor in the Yarmouth Roads and keeping the crew safe – when the ships were wrecked and all the sailors drowned, I'd say that was akin to murder,' he said, looking stern.

Not the body by the lighthouse, then, Georgina thought.

'And then there were the skirmishes between the revenue men and the smugglers in the eighteenth and nineteenth centuries,' he continued. 'There were deaths on both sides.'

'Didn't smugglers mainly operate in Cornwall?' Georgina asked.

'No. They were all round the coast. The local squires and vicars would turn a blind eye when people brought in tea, gin and brandy. Parson Woodforde used to get gin smuggled from Bacton, just down the road from here, and he wrote about some of the smugglers in his diary,' the elderly man said.

'Parson Woodforde? I've heard of him,' Georgina said. 'Are you a historian?'

'Retired history teacher, for my sins,' he said. 'Frank Burton.' He held his hand out to her.

'Georgina Drake,' Georgie said.

'I still keep my hand in, a bit. I run the Summerstrand local history website and I was going to help Sally set up the museum in the lighthouse, before that arrogant b—' Frank paused. 'Sorry. Before *that man* stole it from under her nose.'

Again, his friends nodded, but made no attempt to join the conversation. Either they were more wary of strangers, Georgina thought, or they were used to Frank taking the lead.

'That's a shame,' she said sympathetically. Maybe if she chatted to Frank while she waited for the food, she might be able to nudge the conversation round to the right area – and he might know something about Ryan. 'Can I get you all a top-up?' she asked as Claire came back to the bar to say that the toasties were being made.

Frank looked pleased. 'That's kind. Thank you.'

Claire rolled her eyes, but pulled three more pints; Frank's friends gave her a silent nod of gratitude.

'And one for yourself, Claire,' Georgina added.

'Thanks,' Claire said.

'How did the smuggling business actually work?' Georgina asked.

Frank's face lit up at her interest. 'Well, it was a very clever operation. The smugglers would sink the tubs of contraband in the Yarmouth Roads and signal to the shore; quite a few houses on the coast have hidden squints where they'd see the signals out at sea. At low tide, the local fishermen would go and retrieve the goods. Or the smugglers would let their ships be beached on a sandbank at low tide and just throw parcels of tea and kegs of gin overboard. They'd be scooped up by the locals and hidden in a cartload of kelp,' he explained. 'There aren't any caves around here, because the sandstone's too fragile to support them, but parcels could be dropped down a well outside a house and picked up later.'

'And nobody ever caught them?' Georgina asked.

'As I said, there were skirmishes. Sometimes the smugglers were caught, and sometimes they got away. But local folk knew better than to interfere. Either they bought the smuggled goods and knew they'd get in trouble with the Revenue men if they were caught, or they didn't buy anything but they were scared of crossing the gangs,' Frank said. 'I reckon that's what's behind the legend of Black Shuck on the coast.'

'Who's Black Shuck?' Georgina asked.

'Not who, *what*,' Frank corrected. 'He's a huge black dog with one eye. The legend is, if you see him, you'll die within the week. He haunts the coast as far down as Suffolk. Back in the sixteenth century, it was said he burst through the doors of Holy Trinity church in Blythburgh in a clap of thunder, killing a man and boy and making the steeple collapse – and the scorch marks are still visible on the door even now.'

'Sounds more like a lightning strike, to me,' Claire said dryly.

'Ahh, but the same day, something similar was reported at St Mary's church in Bungay, just down the road from Blyth-burgh,' Frank said with a grin. 'You're right, though. It probably was a storm that killed people, and the pamphlet was printed by a Londoner who exaggerated the story quite a bit. But there are tales of other ghostly black dogs along the East Coast – like the barghest in Yorkshire, which probably came from the Viking raiders telling tales of Odin's dog. If you want to frighten people and keep them away from places where you don't want them poking their noses in, a good story's the way to do it.'

'And the smugglers here said this Black Shuck was around?' Georgina asked.

'People claimed they'd seen a huge black dog. Some say the smugglers hung a lantern round a ram's neck and trotted him out, but people around here aren't so daft as to confuse a dog and a sheep,' Frank said. 'My theory is the gang had an Irish wolfhound – back in the day, they were even bigger than they are now – and trained it to prowl around at night.'

'That makes sense. If people were scared of seeing the legendary dog, they wouldn't go poking around where they'd heard it had been seen,' Georgina said thoughtfully.

Frank nodded. 'Apparently there are old smugglers' tunnels beneath the pub which lead to the local manor house and the church. Though I've never been able to verify exactly where they went,' he admitted with a mournful glance at Claire.

'That's because there *aren't* any tunnels – anyway, it's against my health and safety licence to let you go poking around in the cellars,' Claire said. 'I grew up in this pub, remember. Apart from you, I've never heard anyone talk about smugglers' tunnels.'

'You obviously never listened to your granddad. "Watch the wall, my darling, while the Gentlemen go by",' Frank quoted, tapping the side of his nose. 'That's exactly how it used to be around here, years ago. It was a hard life, fishing. On the coast, they supplemented their income with a bit of smuggling and a bit of wrecking.'

'They actually *caused* the shipwrecks?' Georgina asked, shocked.

'No, no. When you knew what it was like to worry about your family being out on a boat in a storm, you'd never risk another sailor's life,' Frank said hastily. 'When a ship was in trouble, people on the shore would always try to save the sailors. But they also picked up whatever was washed up on the beach. It was known as wrecking rights.'

'Wrecking, for short?' Georgina guessed.

Frank nodded. 'I remember my granddad telling me about his great-granddad; he was one of the fishermen who picked up the odd keg of gin and left it by the squire's door.' He smiled. 'I've actually got a photograph of him, where he's holding my granddad. It's one of the things we were going to put in the museum.'

'How amazing. I'm a photographer, and when I use film instead of a digital camera I develop my own negatives,' Georgina said. 'I love looking at old photos.'

'Here.' Frank took out his phone, turned the screen on and navigated through his photo app. 'That's them.'

She looked at the photo of an old man holding a baby.

'He's my three-times great-granddad. That was taken in 1880 – and he's the same age there in 1880 as I am today,' Frank said, his face filled with pride.

'A photograph of a man born more than two hundred years ago – that's really special,' Georgina said. 'Your family's lived in Summerstrand for hundreds of years, then?'

'And they were all fishermen, until me,' Frank said. 'Always had my head in a book, and my dad despaired until the headmaster told him I could be a teacher and make a good living. My children found it too quiet around here, though, and left for the city as soon as they could. They live in Norwich now, and my grandchildren are in London.' He smiled. 'But they all still come back to see me from time to time.'

'Have you lived in Summerstrand all your life?' Georgina asked.

'Apart from my three years at teacher training college in Keswick Hall, just outside Norwich, yes. Luckily, when I finished the course, I got a post at the high school in Martham and it only took twenty minutes to cycle there from Summerstrand. Kept me fit.' Frank smiled. 'Since I retired, I've kept my hand in by researching local history. The smugglers are fascinating.'

'As long as you don't go thinking you can hunt through my cellars and find tunnels that don't exist,' Claire said, but there was warmth beneath the sternness of her words.

'Obviously you know a lot about the history of Summerstrand,' Georgina said. 'Are there any stories about the lighthouse?'

Frank looked slightly uneasy. 'Nothing much out of the ordinary.'

Georgina wondered what he was hiding.

When Claire was called away to serve another customer, Frank lowered his voice. 'I didn't like to say anything in front of Claire, seeing as Sally ended up marrying Claire's dad, but Sally's father, Dennis Armitage, used to be the lighthouse keeper back in the sixties and seventies. Sally's ten years or so younger than me, and I don't think she had a very happy childhood.' He winced. 'Let's just say her dad had a bit of a temper.'

Sally's family had lived at the lighthouse when Ryan had been in the village. Sally would've been a child at the time, but would she know anything about what had happened to Ryan and why he was buried next to the lighthouse? Georgina couldn't think of a tactful way to ask.

'I won't mention it in front of Claire, Sally or Ben,' she said. Back in the 1960s, Frank would've been in his late teens or early twenties. Had he known Ryan? 'Frank, this is a weird question, but did anyone in the village ever go missing?'

'Not really,' Frank said. 'Why?'

'Idle curiosity,' Georgina said.

Frank gave her a disbelieving stare.

'If you can keep this to yourself for now,' she said, lowering her voice. 'We found a skeleton. Rather, my dog dug up a bone that was obviously human.'

'Got you,' Frank said. 'Mum's the word.'

'If you do think of anyone who left the village in the last, say, fifty or sixty years, and something felt a bit odd about it, I'd appreciate it if you could let me know.' She fished in her handbag for one of her business cards.

'Will do,' Frank said, with a gleam in his eye.

Given what he'd told her about Black Shuck and the smugglers' tunnels, it was clear to Georgina that he loved a good story – and a mystery. Hopefully he might remember something that would help her find out more about Ryan.

Claire came over then with a brown paper bag and a cardboard holder with two paper cups. 'Here you go. Toasties and coffee. And there's a cold sausage in there for Bert – bring him in, next time you come. We like well-behaved dogs.'

'Thank you.' Georgina smiled at Frank. 'Nice to meet you, Frank,' she said.

'And you.' He sketched a salute. 'Thanks for the pint.'

'Don't take too much notice of Frank,' Claire said quietly. 'He likes a bit of a mardle, as they say around here. He loves all the myths and legends. It's all a load of nonsense about Black Shuck, though. And there really aren't any smugglers' tunnels under the pub.'

'Got it,' Georgina said, equally quietly. 'Though, Claire, I'd appreciate it if you didn't say anything to your dad, Sally or Vicky about something going on at the lighthouse. Colin will need to talk to them first.'

'It's serious, then?' At Georgina's nod, Claire said, 'Of course. Though I don't think many people will be sorry he's gone,' she added. 'He was barred from here because of the way he treated Vicky, and everyone in the village sent in an objection to the development. Not that it made any difference, because the council still gave him the green light.' She sighed.

'I'm not saying anyone around here would go so far as to murder him, but none of the local businesses would serve him or work with him, and he certainly won't be missed.'

'I'll give Colin the heads-up,' Georgina said.

'Give me a shout if you think of anything you want to ask. If I don't know, I'll probably know someone who does,' Claire said.

'Thank you. I will,' Georgina said with a smile.

Georgina drove back to the lighthouse with their lunch. She and Colin sat in the car to eat, with Bert curled on the back seat, and she filled Colin in on what Frank and Claire had told her.

Colin sipped his coffee. 'He sounds quite a character, this Frank.'

'He was really interesting,' Georgina agreed. 'He knows a lot about the area, so he might be able to help with information about our skeleton.'

'If that body was buried when Sally's family lived at the lighthouse,' Colin said thoughtfully – and Georgina had to stop herself blurting out that it was, because how could she possibly know that? – 'and Sally's dad was known to have a quick temper, he might have been involved in the death or the burial. Then again, he might not. It'd be so helpful to know when that aggregate was laid.' He frowned. 'The Manson case needs handling with kid gloves, and until we know a bit more I think our skeleton under the patio will need the same kind of careful treatment.'

'I asked Claire not to say anything to Ben, Sally or Vicky about Manson until you'd had a chance to talk to them, but I don't know what good it'll do, because the gossip seems to have spread already,' Georgina said. 'And Frank said he'd keep every-thing to himself, too. He'll get in touch if he remembers anything that might be helpful. I gave him my card, as I didn't have one of yours.'

'Thank you,' Colin said. 'That's exactly what I would've asked for.' He smiled at her. 'Are you sure you don't want to join my team as a cold case expert?'

'Not officially.' She smiled back at him. 'But otherwise I'm Team Colin. As are the rest of the Musketeers.'

'Sybbie, Cesca and Jodie. Remind me again, which one of you is d'Artagnan?' he teased.

'All of us,' Georgina teased back. 'And don't say that to Sybbie or she'll start singing Bryan Adams at you. Much as I love our Sybbie, her singing voice is decidedly flat.' She reached over into the back of the car and fed Bert a couple of slices of the sausage Claire had sent for him.

'Two bodies: one inside the lighthouse and one buried outside. Could there be a connection between them?' Colin asked.

'Other than the fact that you found both of them, at the same time?' She wrinkled her nose. 'Sorry. That's in poor taste. But considering you told me in October, before I went to photograph Bea's company in London, not to find any more dead bodies or let Bert dig up a skeleton, and...' She spread her hands. 'Here we are, with one of each.'

'You're right. And I have a nasty feeling that neither of them was an accident.' Colin sighed. 'We'll have to wait for the findings of the forensics team, the pathologist and the finds liaison officer.'

SIX

There wasn't long to wait until Mo, Colin's detective sergeant, arrived with the finds liaison officer, Rowena Langham.

It was the first time Colin had met her in person. Rowena looked like an academic, and he guessed her age at around mid-forties. Her long mid-brown hair was liberally streaked with grey and held back in a ponytail; she was clearly dressed for fieldwork, in jeans, trainers and a padded rainproof jacket. 'Nice to meet you in person at last, DI Bradshaw,' she said.

He remembered that awkward phone conversation, a few months ago, and felt the colour steal into his cheeks. Please don't let her – or Georgina – notice, he thought. 'Call me Colin,' he said, shaking her outstretched hand and hoping that he came across as brisk and professional. 'Nice to meet you, too, Dr Langham.'

'Do call me Rowena,' she said.

He couldn't quite meet her eyes.

'You'll be pleased to know I have permission to exhume the body.'

'Yes. Thank you for arranging that,' he said, feeling awkward. He really needed all the lines drawn very clearly, right now. 'This is my partner, Georgina Drake,' he said. 'Georgie, this is Rowena Langham, the finds liaison officer. She analysed the skeleton at Hartington Hall, too.'

'Lovely to meet you,' Georgina said, shaking the other woman's hand. 'Your job is fascinating. My daughter works as a genealogist, when she isn't acting, so she knows the documentation side of things. She helped me research Anne's story.'

'It was terribly sad, but it was also fascinating,' Rowena said. 'I assume you're the one who sent that file to me via DI Br— Colin,' she corrected herself.

'Yes,' Georgina said, smiling. 'As you gave us some key information about the jewellery, I thought you might like to know what happened.'

'I appreciated that. It's not always that you get to hear the outcome of a case,' Rowena said.

'That's what I guessed,' Georgina said. 'I would offer to make you some coffee, Rowena, but there aren't any facilities here.'

'Plus there's a dead body in the lighthouse and the forensic team won't want us trampling about in there, destroying evidence,' Rowena said.

'I can go to the petrol station and get you some coffee, if you like,' Georgina offered.

'Thanks for the offer, but no. I'll just get on with the body,' Rowena said. 'Though I'm happy for you to come and have a look while I'm working, if you want.'

'I might just do that.' Georgina smiled. 'I promise Bert here won't do any more digging.'

'You're a lovely, clever boy, aren't you, Bert?' Rowena crooned, bending down to make a fuss of the dog. 'And this is the second skeleton you've found.'

'Third. There was one in London at the end of last year, too,' Georgina said. 'Colin says it's getting to be a habit.'

'It sounds as if Bert needs a secondment to my department,' Rowena said. 'Fancy being an archaeology dog, boy?'

Bert licked her, and Georgina laughed.

Colin was left speechless. Shouldn't things have been a bit awkward, given that Rowena had practically asked him on a date and he'd just introduced Georgina to her as his partner? But there the two women were, chatting happily as if they'd known each other for decades, and it looked as if he was the only one who felt embarrassed and out of place.

Another vehicle pulled onto the gravel, interrupting the conversation.

'That looks like the team who's collecting the body,' Colin said, relieved. 'Sorry. I need to have a word with them.'

'I'll show Rowena where the skeleton is while you and Mo brief the team,' Georgina said.

'Thank you,' Colin said, and escaped gratefully.

Colin had definitely seemed ill-at-ease with Rowena Langham. Why? Georgina wondered. Was there history between them? Not that it was any of her business. She concentrated on the here-and-now. 'I know from talking to the forensic team in London that you can tell whether a skeleton's male or female, and how old they are,' she said. 'They told me that any remnants of clothes can help with dating, too.'

'Which is why I need to exhume the skeleton very gently, quite apart from being respectful, in case there's any evidence underneath it,' Rowena said. She glanced up at the sky. 'I'm just hoping the rain holds off. I don't care about getting wet, but it does make my job harder if I'm floundering about in sticky mud.' She smiled at Georgina. 'Do I assume you'll be involved with finding out who the body is for this case, too?'

'Yes. I was supposed to be taking photographs of the lighthouse and interviewing the guy who's renovating it,' Georgina said. 'But, as he died before we got here, obviously I can't do that anymore.' She wrinkled her nose. 'Technically, I suppose, in researching the cold case I'm interfering – though Colin's team don't have time to do the kind of genealogy research that my daughter's teaching me to do. And I don't meddle with the investigation; I just tell them what I've found.'

'Where do you start?' Rowena asked.

By talking to the ghost who'd once lived in her farmhouse; not that Georgina could explain that.

Instead, she said, 'If you can tell us roughly how old the body was, and when you think he or she was buried, I can start with newspaper reports to see if anyone who fits the profile was reported missing around that time, or talk to local historians – they might be able to point me in the direction of someone who has more background information. Once I've got a likely name for the skeleton, I can look up other records and start to piece the story together.'

'So it all starts as an educated guess, then,' Rowena said.

'And then I see if the evidence fits the theory – or changes it,' Georgina said. She watched Rowena gently uncover the bones, every so often asking questions about how the archaeologist worked. 'You know, you'd make a fabulous subject for an article,' she said.

Rowena blushed. 'I just do my job. Sometimes I talk about it to schools, if my boss asks. But I'm not sure people are that interested. Not unless it involves finding buried treasure.'

'Not all treasures are precious metals or gems, though,' Georgina said. 'Imagine what it must've been like to find that ship burial at Sutton Hoo. Not the helmet, even though it's gorgeous, but all the little everyday things that tell us more about how people lived.'

'You're telling me. I'd give my eye teeth to work on the Redenhall project, because I think they're going to discover something even more amazing,' Rowena said.

'And I'd offer to be their official photographer for nothing,' Georgina said.

When the forensics team arrived to look at the scene in the lighthouse cottage, Georgina knew that Colin would want to leave for his interviews soon. She said goodbye to Rowena and took the opportunity to walk Bert.

'Are you there, Doris? Did you manage to get any more information from Ryan?' she asked quietly, as soon as she was out of earshot of everyone at the lighthouse.

'He can't remember anything more, right now,' Doris said. 'Though Harrison sends his best. He was asking me why I looked so happy today, so I told him about helping Ryan and you.'

'Give him my best wishes, too,' Georgina said. In the short time she'd known Harrison Taylor, she'd grown fond of him. 'Until Ryan can tell you something new, I'll work with the paper records. And I need to drop Colin back at Norwich to do his interviews.'

'I'll catch up with you back at the farmhouse,' Doris said.

Back at the lighthouse, Georgina discovered that Mo was staying to liaise with the forensic team and Rowena.

Once Colin was ready to go, they settled Bert in his harness in the back of the car and headed off. 'As your car's parked in my driveway, give me a ring when you want picking up and I'll come and get you,' Georgina said.

He reached over to squeeze her hand briefly. 'Thanks, but I'll get a taxi. You have stuff to do.'

'Hardly, now my subject's turned up dead,' she said dryly. 'Speaking of which, should I let the magazine know what's happened and that they'll have to replace the feature?'

'I'd prefer you to leave it until tomorrow,' Colin said. 'Or even Monday, because they won't be working over the weekend, will they?'

'True. Well, I meant it about picking you up. I'll only be sitting in front of the wood-burner with a book and Bert snoring next to me, so I really don't mind if you call me.'

'All right. Thank you,' he said.

'Things seemed a bit awkward between you and Rowena,' she said. 'Have you had some kind of run-in with her?'

'Not really,' Colin muttered.

'She seems really nice,' Georgina said.

Colin groaned. 'I was hoping you wouldn't notice the awkwardness. All right. Remember when Bert found the skeleton at Hartington Hall?'

'Yes.'

'When we were on the phone, discussing the bones, she asked me out for dinner. I wasn't sure if it was in a professional capacity or, um, social. I kind of said I was having dinner with you that night.' He coughed. 'I, um, asked if she'd like to join us and we could talk about history.'

Georgina couldn't help smiling. 'You're squirming, Colin.' A quick sideways glance showed her he was blushing.

'OK, so I'm rubbish at reading signals and my social skills outside work are terrible,' he said. 'I panicked. She probably meant it as a professional thing and I got the wrong end of the stick. Telling her that I wasn't interested because I'd just met someone seemed a bit too in-your-face, and I thought dropping a hint might be kinder. That's why I said I was seeing my girl-friend for dinner and that she was welcome to eat with us.'

'But she didn't want to join us, did she?'

'No.' He winced. 'Mo and Larissa overheard the call. They've already said just about everything there is to say on the matter. And I know I said the wrong thing. I'm the one who's made it awkward. You and I were still getting to know each other, and we hadn't officially said we were together at that point, but I didn't want to see another woman when I wanted to see you.'

'It sounds to me as if you turned her down in a nice way, actually,' Georgina said. She reached over to squeeze his hand briefly. 'She probably feels more embarrassed than you do, so just be an Englishman and pretend it never happened. She'll follow your lead, and your professional relationship will be just fine. And you'll probably end up being friends – I liked her very much, and I have a feeling she and I will end up having lunch together and talking about our favourite museums.'

'This stuff is easier for you,' Colin muttered.

Realising that he really did feel awkward, she refrained from teasing him about having Darcy's proud manner as well as his looks. 'Maybe.'

When they were halfway back to Norwich, his phone rang.

'What have you got for me, Mo?' he asked. A couple of moments later, he said, 'Hang on. I'm going to put you on speaker so Georgie can hear. Can you repeat that, please?'

'Rowena says that there are some clothing remnants beneath the skeleton, and she thinks it's 1960s clothing,' Mo said. 'Our skeleton's male; there's a narrow pelvis and some growth plate still evident on the bones, which she says indicates he was in his early twenties. Some of his ribs are broken; there's no sign of healing so the fractures must have happened around the time of his death. And the hyoid bone's snapped.'

'Strangled, then,' Colin said with a sigh.

'Guv, if he was in his early twenties say, in the middle of the 1960s, he'd be around eighty now,' Mo continued. 'Whoever strangled him would have to be at least in their mid-seventies, to be strong enough to kill him in the first place. Even if that person's still alive, and we managed to track them down – and we have absolutely no evidence as to who they might be – there's no guarantee they'd be fit enough to stand trial.'

Georgina knew that argument well. It was why Harrison's mother had got away with her crime.

'Thanks, Mo. That's all useful,' Colin said. 'Can you ask Larissa to check the missing persons files to see if there's anyone from Summerstrand on the list? Check between 1960 and 1970.'

'Will do, guv,' Mo said.

'Please thank Rowena for me,' Colin added before ending the call.

'You need to tell her that yourself. Email or text her if you can't face calling her,' Georgina said gently. 'If you keep talking to her through someone else, the awkwardness will get worse, not better.'

He sighed. 'You're right. I'll text her now.' He busied himself with his phone for a few moments. 'If you wanted to work on this cold case,' he said, 'I'd appreciate your help. What do you make of what Mo said?'

'Male, early twenties, broken ribs and hyoid bone.' Georgina remembered what Doris had told her. *He remembers lying in the dunes, looking up at the stars. Kissing someone. Then there was a lot of shouting and hitting and kicking – and then he couldn't breathe.* 'It sounds as if he came in for a bit of a beating before he was strangled. A jealous boyfriend, perhaps?'

'But why was he buried by the lighthouse?'

'Either it happened there,' Georgina said, knowing that it hadn't, 'or maybe it was the nearest place to the dunes.'

'Why the dunes?' Colin asked.

'I was thinking about it. Courting couples,' Georgina said, 'like the privacy of the dunes. Perhaps he'd been caught making out with someone else's girlfriend.'

'That's a plausible theory,' Colin said. 'It would explain the broken ribs as well as the strangulation. But who killed him?' He paused. 'Frank in the pub told you that Sally's dad had a temper. Maybe he caught our skeleton with Sally's mum.' He blew out a breath. 'Or with Sally?'

'No. Surely not. Sally's, what, in her mid-sixties now?' Georgina asked. 'She'd have been a *child* back then, Colin.'

'But if Sally's dad had caught our John Doe interfering with his young daughter, wouldn't he have reacted by giving our John Doe a good kicking and then strangling him?' Colin asked dryly.

'Probably.' But Georgina didn't think that Ryan was that kind of predator. In the previous two cases that she'd helped Doris solve, the victims had been very much blameless. Admittedly, they knew very little about Ryan Everett right now, but the way things seemed to work with Doris was that she helped someone who'd been wronged in the same way that she'd been wronged, not someone who committed atrocities.

'It's early days,' she said. 'I'll have a word with Bea and see if she has any idea how we might be able to trace him. Male, in his early twenties, went missing somewhere in the 1960s.' The mid to late 1960s, from what Doris had told her. Which would make Ryan around the same age as Frank Burton; but Frank had said he didn't remember anyone going missing. Did that mean their John Doe wasn't local? 'What can you tell me about missing people?'

'Most people turn up again within a year,' Colin said. 'Less than one per cent of people are missing for longer than that.'

'Do people go missing more than once?' Georgina asked.

'If whatever caused them to disappear the first time isn't resolved, then they often go missing again,' Colin said.

'So it's possible he was reported missing more than once.'

'Good point. I'll text Larissa,' he said. 'I'll ask her to let you know if she finds anything.'

'Thank you. And I'll share anything I find,' Georgina promised.

'Dead? But – he *can't* be.' Steve Carey, the site manager, looked stunned. 'What – how?'

'At the moment, I can't tell you because I'm waiting on the pathologist's report,' Colin said. 'But I could do with some background, which is why I wanted to talk to you. I'll write up your statement after our conversation, then ask you to read it and sign it.'

'I... yeah, sure.' Steve was in his late thirties, broad-shouldered and with cropped mid-brown hair that had the odd streak of grey.

'How long had you worked for Eliot Manson?' Colin asked.

'Five years,' Steve said.

'How did you get on with him?' Colin asked.

'All right.'

The other man sounded guarded. Perhaps he was worried that, if he admitted he didn't like his boss, it might make him a suspect. Colin tried a slightly different tack. 'Did he get on well with the rest of your team?'

'He was the boss,' Steve said.

Which, in a way, answered his question; Steve clearly

wasn't going to speak ill of the dead, but at the same time he wasn't going to lie and say that things were perfectly friendly between Manson and his employees.

'We're aware that his development in Summerstrand was unpopular with the local community,' Colin said. 'What about the other sites?'

'People always kick up about new houses, until they're built,' Steve said. 'They moan about doctors, dentists, schools and traffic.'

'Mr Carey,' Colin said carefully, 'I need to build up an honest picture of the deceased. Do you know of anyone who might have wished him ill?'

Steve winced. 'It was just a lot of hot air, that's all. The sort of thing people say when their temper's up and they don't really mean it.'

'So he was threatened?'

Steve sighed. 'It was something and nothing. Mr Manson is – *was* – a bit of a micromanager. He came on our current site a couple of weeks back and accused some of the plasterers of leaving early. Wanted them to stay late to make up for it.' He shrugged. 'But everyone on the crew leaves half an hour early on a Friday. They take a shorter lunch to make up the time. The plasterers were self-employed, not part of the crew, and they were all up to date with their work.'

'What happened?'

'Their team leader called me on the Monday morning to say they weren't coming back because they'd got another job. Self-employed people don't have to give notice,' Steve explained. 'You don't threaten to sack your plasterers. It's supply and demand – and they're always in demand.'

'Doesn't that make it hard for you to make sure a house is finished on time, if they can leave with no notice?'

'As the site manager, yes, it's my responsibility.' Steve looked miserable. 'I tried to smooth things over with them.

Everyone goes for a pint after work on a Friday. I bought a round, and I told the plasterers not to take any notice of Mr Manson because he'd probably had another fight with his missus and he was taking it out on them. We all knew it wasn't fair of him, and it wasn't an excuse exactly – but it explained why he was like he was.'

'And did they listen to you?'

'No,' Steve admitted. 'And the general labourers didn't like him, either. They're employed by Manson Developments, though, rather than freelancers.' He blew out a breath. 'They complain to me all the time, but I can't do anything. Whenever I've brought things up with Mr Manson, he always says – *said*,' he corrected himself, 'if the crew didn't like something, they knew where the door was.'

'Are you self-employed?' Colin asked.

'No. I'm on salary,' Steve said.

'Paid by Manson Developments?' Colin checked.

'Yes. Though when the plasterers walked off site Mr Manson threatened to sack me for being useless,' he said with a grimace.

From what Colin had already heard about Manson's behaviour, the bullying didn't surprise him. 'Did you think about leaving?'

'This is confidential?' Steve checked, looking worried. 'It's not going in the statement? Because I really don't want anyone seeing it.'

'Your statement will be for police use only,' Colin said. 'If it's not relevant to the case, then it can be ignored.'

'Between you and me, then, I've been looking for another job. I even had an interview the other week. But I can't afford to leave Manson's until I've got something else to bring the money in. You know what the mortgage rates have been like recently, going up every time the wind blows. I've got a wife and kids. We haven't got enough savings for me to risk leaving without another job lined up.' He paused. 'What happens to the business now?'

'The only person who could tell you that is his solicitor – assuming he made a will,' Colin said. Divorce cancelled a will, Colin knew; so, even if Manson hadn't made a new will, Vicky Evans wouldn't have inherited the business. He'd need to find out who Manson had left the business to. 'You mentioned earlier that Manson had been fighting with his "missus". Was that something you said to placate the plasterers, or do you know of an actual fight?'

'It was just to calm them down,' Steve said. 'And they're not married yet. Well, I guess they're never going to be married now,' he added, wincing.

'Girlfriend?' Colin checked.

'Fiancée,' Steve said.

'What can you tell me about her?' Colin asked.

'Her name's Tara Cox,' Steve said. 'She's a model, though the only reason I can think of for her being with him is...' He held his hand palm up and rubbed the pad of his thumb against his first and middle fingers in the age-old 'money' gesture. 'She moved in with him about six months ago, when they got engaged.'

'And they got on well?'

'No idea,' Steve said. 'I don't get involved. I just keep my nose clean and keep the site running.'

'Thank you, Mr Carey. I think that's all for now, but I might have more questions for you, depending on the pathology report.'

'I'm not sure what help I can be, but I'll try,' Steve said.

Mike Butler, the architect, was in his late fifties; he had a shock of grey-blond hair, wore small round gold-rimmed glasses, and had an artist's hands. Like Steve Carey, he agreed to make a statement, check what Colin had written and sign it. He confirmed that the plasterers had walked out, leaving the site struggling to make its deadlines. 'Manson was always a bit abrasive with the men on site,' he said. 'He liked to throw his weight about and remind them who was boss. I've heard him yell at them before now, saying if they didn't like how he did things or what he paid, then they knew where the door was.'

Confirming what Steve Carey had said.

'It isn't exactly the way to get the best out of your team,' Mike said, 'whether they're freelance or you pay their salary.'

Colin agreed. 'So Manson had quite a high turnover with his staff?'

'He fell out with a lot of them,' Mike said. 'The self-employed ones didn't often make it to the end of a development before walking out: the plasterers, electricians and plumbers. The brickies and the chippies would leave before he sacked them, so the site manager spent half his time interviewing for replacements. The general labourers hated Manson. The times I've heard people say they were going to sort him out...' He shook his head. 'But nobody ever did.'

'Are you freelance or do you work solely for Manson?' Colin asked. He already knew the answer, but it was worth checking.

'I work for myself,' Mike confirmed.

'Was Manson a difficult client?'

'He tinkers – tinkered,' Mike corrected himself, 'with the plans, and then I tell him why whatever he's done won't work, and we go back to the original and pretend it's his idea.'

'Why did you keep working with him and doing the plans for his houses, if he was difficult?' Colin asked.

'Because he paid well. Plus I knew he was after the lighthouse,' Mike said, 'and I really wanted to work on that. It's an unusual building, and I'm proud of the plans I drew up. Actually, it was the only set of plans Manson didn't alter.' He paused. 'How did he die? Did someone kill him?'

'I can't answer that until the pathology results are back,' Colin told him. 'Do you know of anyone in particular who wished him harm?'

Mike shook his head. 'Like I said, he rubbed a lot of his team up the wrong way. But a lot of people rub others up the wrong way. I don't think anyone would kill him for that – would they?'

'If they did,' Colin said, 'it's my job to find out who. I might have further questions for you later, if you wouldn't mind. In the meantime, if you could stay in the area, I'd appreciate it.'

'Sure,' Mike said.

Georgina sat at the kitchen table with her laptop open, Bert by her feet and a mug of tea next to her.

How did you find a missing person?

She sent a quick text to her daughter.

> Where's the best place to find details of a
> missing person, please? Love you xx

While she waited for Bea to reply, she started an internet search with 'missing persons UK'.

There was a website for the National Crime Agency; when she tried putting in the details she already knew, she discovered that it only went back as far as 1970. It was unlikely that Ryan would be there, but she tried the earliest possible date, just in case. None of the locations, names or ages matched.

Her phone rang; she glanced at the screen to see it was Bea and picked up. 'Hello, sweetheart. How are you?'

'I'm fine, but what's happened, Mum? Who's gone missing?'

'Bert dug up a body at the lighthouse today, and I've got a feeling we're looking at a missing person,' Georgina said.

'*Another* body? Mum, Colin's going to get Bert seconded to the police if he keeps this up!'

'Colin was holding Bert's lead when he started digging,' Georgina said. 'So technically I didn't find either body.'

'*Either?*'

Georgina winced. 'The guy I was scheduled to interview at the lighthouse was also found dead. Probably carbon monoxide poisoning, from the paraffin heater.'

'Oh, Mum. That's grim. But as long as you, Colin and Bert are all right.'

'We're fine, and we're really looking forward to seeing you and Will on Sunday,' Georgina said.

'We can't wait, either,' Bea said. 'Right. Missing persons. Start with the National Crime Agency.'

'I tried that. It doesn't go back far enough.'

'There's a national charity working with missing persons. I'll find the website and send you the link,' Bea said. 'Other than that, social media?'

'The finds liaison officer says there were clothing remnants around the body from the 1960s.'

'Silver surfers enjoy reminiscing on social media,' Bea said. 'And the local newspaper archive could have something – though you might need to access that through the library. I'll send you links. Let me know how you get on, and I'll see if I can help tomorrow before rehearsals.'

'Will do. Thank you, love.'

A couple of minutes later, Georgina's phone beeped with messages from Bea containing links.

She tried the national charity website first, and typed in Ryan's name. A page came up with an 'age-progressed' portrait, showing how the artist thought he might have looked ten years ago, at the age of sixty-nine, and brief details: Ryan Everett, aged twenty, last seen in Summerstrand in 1965. She clicked on the photograph in case there were more details, and there was a photograph of Ryan from when he'd gone missing. In his youth, Ryan had looked like a cross between Marlon Brando and James

Dean, Georgina thought. And the 'aged' sketch was bittersweet, because she knew for a fact he'd died at the age of twenty.

'Who did you meet in the dunes that night, Ryan?' she asked. 'And who was so angry about it that they killed you?'

'He still can't remember,' Doris said. 'Have you found anything?'

'I've only just started looking, so there isn't much,' Georgina said. 'Only what we already know, really. Plus the photo from 1965 and the age-progressed portrait.'

'I would've been eleven, when that photo was taken,' Doris said. 'I think I would've had a huge crush on him, back then, if he'd come to stay in Little Wenborough – and so would all my friends. He looks like Marlon Brando, all dark and brooding. I wonder if he was an actor?'

'Right now, your guess is as good as mine. But he reminded me of Brando – and a bit like James Dean, too.' Georgina took a screenshot of the page and a note of the website's URL, then flicked back to the previous page and screenshotted that, too. 'I'll send these to Colin.'

'I know there wasn't any internet, back then, let alone social media,' Doris said. 'But people love sharing memories. Maybe there's a website sharing memories of Summerstrand back in the fifties and sixties. It would still have been a fishing village, rather than a resort like Cromer or Great Yarmouth – no pier, no holiday camps, no fairground rides and not even donkey rides – but people would still have gone for the sea and stayed in a B&B. There would've been weekly dances in the village hall. And a shop selling buckets and spades, windmills and fishing nets. Ice cream, too – in those rectangular blocks, and they'd cut a slice and stick it between two wafers, or in a rectangular wafer cone. Sometimes it'd be a Neapolitan – a third strawberry, a third vanilla and a third chocolate. If you were really lucky, you'd get a chocolate flake in it.'

'Is that the sort of holiday you had?' Georgina asked.

'Dad didn't really do holidays,' Doris said. 'He couldn't really go away, not with the cows needing milking every day. But I did go on holiday with my best friend's family, just once. When I was eleven. And we had a week at the seaside, in the holiday camp at Mundesley. Three meals a day – they were like school dinners, and not as good as my mum's cooking, but they kept us filled. We spent our days making sandcastles, finding shells, paddling in the sea and playing with an inflatable stripy beach ball. Oh, and trying to get a kite to fly. And they had dances in the ballroom so we could dress up and sing along with the Beatles songs, and giggle over boys we were too shy and too young to dance with.'

'Sounds like the perfect holiday for an eleven-year-old,' Georgina said. 'And that's a good point you made about people reminiscing on websites. Maybe someone's written something about Summerstrand in the 1960s, and mentioned Ryan in passing. Plus I was wondering if his family might've put something on social media.'

A search on Ryan's name and 'missing' came up with a website that had clearly been made by Ryan's family.

'We should've done that first,' Georgina said, rolling her eyes. 'Why on earth didn't we? It seems so obvious.'

'What *are* we like?' Doris agreed, sounding amused. 'Though I suppose it makes sense to look at the official missing persons stuff first.'

On the family website, there were several photos of Ryan, including one where he looked relaxed and happy rather than brooding.

'He was staying with his great-aunt, Joan, when he went missing,' Doris read. 'And look – the contact details are for a woman at a gallery at Holt. Webster's Fine Art. You could always pop in to see her.'

'I could,' Georgina agreed. 'This sounds like a road trip with Sybbie.'

'Doesn't it just?' Doris asked, a teasing note in her voice. 'Holt. Antique shops. Staffordshire dogs.'

Georgina laughed and picked up her phone. When Sybbie answered, she said, 'How do you fancy lunch in Holt on Monday?'

'With you? Definitely,' Sybbie said.

'No Staffordshire dogs,' Georgina said, 'or Bernard will have my guts for garters. But there's a little gallery I'd like to go to.'

'A gallery,' Sybbie said, 'sounds delightful, dear girl. Shall I drive? I'll pick you up at ten.'

'Perfect,' Georgina said. And, even though she had a feeling that Ryan's story would turn out to be as sad as the others she'd investigated, part of her was excited to be back on the trail again, helping to discover the truth...

EIGHT

Colin picked his phone up from his desk. 'Bradshaw.'

'Hi, Colin. It's Sammy Granger,' she said. 'Obviously I'll send you the official report through later, but as I've managed to fit the post-mortem in this afternoon I thought you'd be interested in the preliminary findings.'

'Definitely,' he said. 'What have you got?'

'The time of death was around midnight,' she said. 'From the notes you sent, the room wasn't ventilated properly, and there are definite signs of carbon monoxide poisoning.'

'Is that what killed him?' Colin asked. 'Carbon monoxide?'

'It's a contributory factor,' Sammy said. 'His blood alcohol level was high enough for him to feel woozy from that, so he might not have been aware of the fumes. But there's something else.'

Colin felt his antennae twitch. 'What?'

'According to his medical records, he was on beta-blockers for high blood pressure.'

Sally had told them that. But Colin also remembered what Sally had said afterwards. 'Go on,' he said, having a nasty feeling what was coming.

'The levels in his bloodstream were higher than they should be.'

'You think he might have forgotten that he'd already taken them that day and took another dose?' he asked.

'I'm not sure. If people aren't meticulous about taking their medication, they're more likely to forget to take them at all than to take them twice,' Sammy said.

'Could someone have forced him to take the extra ones?'

'Maybe, but there's no sign of bruising around his face or jaw to suggest it,' Sammy said.

'Which pretty much wipes out that theory,' he said.

'You found him slumped at a table with a glass and a bottle in front of him,' Sammy said. 'Was there any liquid left in the bottle?'

'You're thinking the alcohol might have contained the extra beta-blockers?'

'It's a possibility,' Sammy said.

'Forensics should have the bottle and the glass,' he said. 'I'll get someone to bring them over to you, if you wouldn't mind testing them.'

'Sure,' Sammy said. 'I'll keep you posted.'

He called the forensics team, firstly to ask if they could get the bottle and glass over to Sammy Granger's lab, and secondly to find out what they knew so far. He learned that there were footprints and fingerprints in the lighthouse cottage, most of which belonged to Manson, but there was only one set of fingerprints on the bottle and glass. It was a fair presumption that Manson had been drinking alone.

But could anyone else have had access to the cottage?

The door had been locked when he and Georgina had arrived. There were only two sets of keys for the building: the ones that Phoebe had brought out to Summerstrand, which Colin had returned to the office later that afternoon, and Manson's own set.

What was he missing?

He tapped his biro against the jotter on his desk, thinking, but nothing came to mind.

He also needed to see Manson's next of kin to break the news of the death, then make a courtesy call to Vicky, Sally and Ben to tell them the news. Maybe Sally could shed some light on the beta-blocker issue.

He called Tara next. 'Miss Cox? I'm Detective Inspector Colin Bradshaw. I'm aware that you're travelling back from London, but would it be possible to come and see you for a quick chat, this evening? I'm based in Norwich, so I can meet you at your house.'

'What's it about?'

This wasn't news he could break over the phone. 'It's something I need to talk about in person, I'm afraid, in connection with a case,' he said as neutrally as he could.

'I'll be back in about an hour,' she said. 'Do you know my address?'

He double-checked his notes, and she confirmed it. 'Thank you. I'll see you then.' He turned to Larissa. 'I need you and a family liaison officer with me to break the news to Tara Cox about Manson's death, please.'

'Sure, guv,' Larissa said.

'Did you get anywhere with missing persons?'

'Yes and no,' she said, referring to her notes. 'There's a Ryan Everett, aged twenty, who was last seen at Summerstrand in 1965. He was reported missing by his great-aunt, Joan Riggs. The file suggests that maybe he ran away to London, but nobody found him. There hasn't been any new information on the case for decades.'

'If he was twenty in 1965, that'd make him seventy-nine now,' Colin said thoughtfully. 'So either he really didn't want to be found, and he stayed well hidden, or he's our skeleton.'

'If he changed his name so he couldn't be traced easily, he

might have died some time ago. And we've got no way of knowing if he changed his name, or what he changed it to,' Larissa said.

'Maybe Georgina can come up with something in the records,' he said. He remembered that the case of the body found under the stage in the Islington theatre, where Bea was currently working, had involved a change of name, and Georgina and Bea had managed to trace the victim's relatives.

Half an hour later, Larissa had arranged for a pool car and for a family liaison officer to join her and Colin, and they drove out to Great Wenborough.

There was just enough room to pull off the road in front of the gates leading to Manson's enormous house. Colin wasn't sure whether the centre stuccoed block was the original house that had been extended each side with yellow brick and glass, or whether the whole thing had been built from new, but to him the three slightly angled roofs and the building itself looked boxy and out of place. It certainly had none of the charm of the pretty flint-and-brick cottages in the village, and he'd guess that Georgina's gardener, Young Tom, hadn't been commissioned to work here, because there wasn't a single flower in sight either.

Though it wasn't his place to judge Manson's home. He was here to do one of the harder parts of his job.

The gold-painted gates were closed, but Colin couldn't see the intercom button he'd half-expected on the yellow brick pillars. Fortunately, the gates weren't locked and he was able to open them. In case she had a dog who might escape onto the road, he stopped to close the gates behind them, then parked beside the small red sporty car on the gravel in front of the house. The three police officers climbed out of the car.

Colin rang the doorbell. It took a while, but eventually a tall, slender woman with long, dark shiny hair and delicate features opened the door, and her blue eyes widened.

'May we come in, Miss Cox?' Colin asked. 'This is DC Larissa Foulkes and PC Helen Robinson.'

'Three of you?' She bit her lip. 'This must be something bad, then.' She stepped back from the door and let them in, then ushered them through into the large kitchen, dining and living-room area. As Colin had suspected from the outside of the house, the combined area was ultra-modern and glossy, lacking the warmth and colour of Rookery Farm.

'Best sit down, love,' Colin said gently.

'What's happened?'

'It's Eliot Manson,' Colin said. 'I'm afraid he was found dead earlier today.'

'Dead? But – he can't be.' Tara stared at him. 'He was here yesterday morning when I left for London. He can't be dead.'

This was the bit Colin really loathed about his job: the moment when he took away all hope. 'I'm sorry. I was there when he was found.'

Tara's face was white with shock. 'What happened?'

'We're not sure at the moment,' he said. 'We need to check a few things, but the doctor who confirmed the death thinks it was carbon monoxide poisoning.'

She shook her head and started twisting the diamond engagement ring round her finger. 'How? How does something like that happen?'

'He was in the lighthouse cottage,' Colin said. 'It looks as if he'd turned the paraffin heater on without making sure the room was properly ventilated.'

'Did he... do it on purpose?' Tara continued turning her ring round and round, and he noticed that her hands were trembling. 'I mean, is this the same sort of thing as him sitting in a car with a pipe running from the exhaust through the window?'

'We still need to work out exactly what happened,' Colin said. 'The pathologist is doing some tests, and the coroner will reach a conclusion. But you live with him, so we needed to let you know that he'd died. I'm sorry to ask this, but do you know who his next of kin is?'

She bit her lip. 'Would that be Vicky?'

'His ex-wife? No,' Colin said. 'When someone's not married, it's usually a parent, a sibling or a child.'

'He's – *was*,' she corrected herself, 'an only child, his mum and dad died years ago, and Vicky's son wasn't his. We weren't married, but we were engaged,' Tara added.

'I'm sorry for your loss,' Colin said. 'Is there anyone I can ring to come and be with you?'

'My mum, or my sister,' Tara said. She bit her lip. 'Though they never liked Eliot. A lot of people didn't like him, but he was different with me. He wasn't all mouthy and difficult. He treated me like a princess.'

'I'm sorry,' Colin said gently. 'It's a shock when someone dies unexpectedly. Come on. I'll make you a cup of tea and call your mum.'

'I'll sort the tea,' Helen said.

'Helen's our family liaison officer,' Colin said. 'She'll be the point of contact between you and my team, so we can keep you up to date with progress, and she can help you get the right support.'

'I just...' Tara shook her head. 'I don't know what to think.'

'And that's OK, too,' Colin said. 'You don't have to make any decisions or do anything straight away.'

'I'm here for you. I'll answer any questions as far as I can. If I don't know the answer, I'll do my best to find out,' Helen said.

'I'll call your mum,' Colin said. 'If you wouldn't mind giving me her number.'

Barbara Cox turned out to be sensible and no-nonsense, and she was at her daughter's house in ten minutes flat, wrapping her arms round Tara and letting her cry herself out.

'I'm sorry, love. I didn't like him,' she admitted, 'but I wouldn't have wished this on him.' She looked at Colin. 'What happens now?'

'The pathologist will finish doing tests, and the coroner will look at all the information and come to a conclusion. Then they'll release the body to you,' Colin said. 'I can arrange for you to go and see him, when the pathologist has finished, but there's no pressure because we've already had a positive ID. Whenever you feel ready. Just talk to Helen, and she'll make sure we get it sorted for you.'

When they left Tara and Barbara with Helen, Colin looked wearily at Larissa. 'I really hate this bit of our job.'

'Me, too,' Larissa said. 'Carbon monoxide poisoning is usually accidental. But there's more to this case than that, isn't there?'

'Sammy's looking at a possible overdose of beta-blockers,' Colin said. 'Combined with whisky and the carbon monoxide – it does make me wonder if someone else was involved. And he's made a lot of enemies.'

'Or, like Tara suggested, did he kill himself?' Larissa asked. 'As a builder, surely he'd know the risks of using a paraffin heater?'

'Especially in a room without proper ventilation,' Colin said. 'Unless his judgement was impaired, either by the alcohol or by the beta-blockers.' He sighed. 'I need to break the news to his ex-wife, her mum and her stepdad.'

'A divorce suggests potential tension,' Larissa said.

'Put it this way, I don't think any of them will be grieving for him,' Colin agreed, remembering his conversation with Sally.

'Are any of them potential suspects?' Larissa asked.

'We will need to rule them out,' Colin said. 'Sammy puts the time of death at midnight. Eliot would have needed to have drunk enough alcohol and/or taken enough beta-blockers to make him woozy enough to impair his judgement about the heater. Say that takes a couple of hours, so that would be ten. It's a forty-minute drive from here to the lighthouse. We need to add in time for whoever it was to persuade Manson to let them into the lighthouse cottage, and he would've had to be out of the room while they dissolved the beta-blockers in his whisky.'

'That's quite a complicated set-up,' Larissa said. 'Surely it's more likely that whoever spiked the whisky did it at some time during the day?'

'Until Sammy's tested the remaining contents of the bottle, we can't be sure that was how the extra beta-blockers got into his system,' Colin said. 'He might have taken a second lot after forgetting he'd already taken them for the day. But let's assume someone did spike the bottle. If your theory's right and it happened during the day, then firstly they had to know the bottle of whisky was there, secondly, they had to know he'd be there that evening and would drink the whisky, and thirdly they'd need access to the lighthouse. There are only two sets of keys; Manson had one set with him, and the other set was kept at his office.'

'Could someone have borrowed the keys and cut a third set?' Larissa asked.

'Maybe – but, if so, who? And which set did they borrow?' Colin frowned. 'There are a lot of unanswered questions. Ben and Sally Forrester couldn't have spiked the bottle last night – Georgie and I had her birthday dinner at the Feathers, and when we left at about half past nine Sally and Ben were both there.' He sighed. 'Though Sally did say something that I'm going to have to ask her about formally.' He filled Larissa in on the conversation he'd had with Sally, and the background.

Larissa looked thoughtful. 'The divorce wasn't recent, was it?'

'No. Years ago. Apparently Vicky's son – who isn't

Manson's – is friends with Jodie's son Harry, so that would make him about eight,' Colin said.

'So, even if the divorce was really acrimonious, it was long enough ago for things to have settled down,' Larissa said.

'Or maybe it's a mum thing, with Sally not being able to forgive him for hurting her daughter?' Colin suggested. 'And all the bad feelings were raked up again after he gazumped her to buy the lighthouse.'

'Enough to kill him?' Larissa asked.

'That's what I need to find out,' Colin said.

'Supposing the combination of how he treated her daughter and buying the lighthouse is her motive for wanting him dead,' Larissa said. 'Then there's the means. Manson was once her son-in-law so she'd know he drank whisky. Ben's a publican, so he'd have easy access to whatever brand of whisky it is. And Sally's a GP. Even though it's against regulations, she could have accessed his record to find out what medication he was on.'

'She told me he was on beta-blockers,' Colin said.

'Yeah, but there are different sorts of beta-blockers,' Larissa said. Colin remembered that Larissa's wife, Alison, was a nurse; Larissa had obviously picked up bits of medical knowledge from her. 'Sally would've needed to know which ones he was on. Supposing she found that out; could she then have taken some from the pharmacy?'

'It's unlikely,' Colin said. 'Pharmacies are inspected regularly, and they have to account for all their stock, not just the controlled medication. If anything was missing, they'd have to report it. We need to check if the pharmacy has reported anything missing.'

'What if the beta-blockers had been prescribed for someone else?' Larissa asked.

'So whoever tampered with the whisky either used their own medication, or they had access to someone else's? Good point. We'll need to check whether any of our potential suspects have been prescribed whatever Sammy finds in that bottle.' He blew out a breath. 'Let's go to the Feathers. And then, afterwards, can you drop me at Georgie's, please? She's probably been talking to Bea about our skeleton and she might have found out something useful.' He wrinkled his nose. 'Plus I left my car there.'

Larissa grinned. 'Right, guv.'

NINE

Colin was relieved to discover that Vicky, Sally and Ben were all at the pub. He introduced Larissa to them. 'I know you're gearing up for dinner, and I'm sorry to interrupt,' he said, 'but we need a quick word in private, please?'

'That sounds serious,' Sally said.

'It is,' Colin said quietly.

Sally led them through to the living room of the flat above the pub.

'It's about Eliot Manson,' he said. 'I know you used to be married to him, Vicky, and things were difficult between you. But I need to tell you that he died in the early hours of this morning.'

'*Died?*' Vicky's eyes widened. 'Oh, my God. What happened?'

'We're waiting for the pathologist's report to tell us that,' Colin said, glancing at Sally and Ben.

'He's dead?' Sally went pale. Because the news was unexpected, Colin wondered, or was there a more sinister reason? She rubbed a hand over her face. 'Oh, God. And I said to you last night, I hope he dies alone. Colin, I freely admit loathed the man, but I didn't kill him.'

'I'm afraid I do have to ask you some questions,' Colin said gently. 'All of you, and I'll need to interview each of you separately. Is there another room we can use?'

'The kitchen,' Sally said. 'Or if you want to do the interviewing here, we'll wait there until you're ready to see us.' She looked at Larissa. 'Can I make you a cup of tea?'

'That would be lovely. Thank you,' Larissa said. 'I'll be in the kitchen with you and Mr Forrester, while DI Bradshaw interviews Ms Evans.'

Vicky was sitting on the edge of one of the armchairs, her hands twisted together.

'May I sit down?' Colin asked when the room had emptied.

'Yes – yes, of course.' She shook her head. 'Sorry. I... I guess the news has knocked me for six. I wasn't expecting...'

He sat on the sofa, facing her, his notebook open and resting on the arm of the sofa.

She bit her lip. 'I can't believe he's dead.'

'I'm sorry. I know this must be a shock to you,' Colin said. 'When was the last time you saw Mr Manson?'

Vicky frowned, concentrating. 'I'm not sure. Months ago. He's got no reason to visit Little Wenborough Primary, so I haven't seen him around where I work, and he doesn't drink here because Ben refuses to serve him. I usually avoid going anywhere he's likely to be.' She gave a grim smile. 'I had thought about moving to the other side of the country to get away from him, but Robbie needs stability and it'd be unfair to take him away from both sets of grandparents.' She blew out a breath. 'This is going to sound horrible, but now it's sinking in I'm relieved Eliot's gone. Though I didn't kill him,' she added swiftly, clearly realising how bad her words sounded.

'I'm sorry for dredging up bad memories of the past, but can you tell me what happened between yourself and Manson?'

'From the start?' At his nod, she blew out a breath. 'I met him at a party. Friend of a friend kind of thing. I was living in London at the time – it was the year I was doing my teacher training. Anyway, we danced together a bit, drank too much... You know how student parties are.'

'I do,' Colin said.

'We spent the night together. The next day, I was going to make my excuses and leave – but he brought me breakfast in bed. He'd gone out to get these fabulous pastries and coffee from the deli round the corner. And it was kind of *nice* being cherished. When he asked me out properly, I agreed. Mum was a bit iffy about him, but I thought it was just her being a bit overprotective. We got married.' She sighed. 'And then he changed. He didn't like my friends, he didn't like my job, and I couldn't do anything right. And then there were all the little clues that he was cheating on me. Restaurant receipts in his pockets – left for me to find when I did the laundry, because in his view all housework was women's work and it was just easier to do it than keep rowing over it. He'd come home late and refuse to say where he'd been. He was funny about his phone; half the time, he smelled of someone else's perfume. Eventually I'd had enough of him and I left.'

Colin could understand that. 'And that's when you met Robert's dad?'

'Actually, I met him before that. At work,' Vicky explained. 'Dan and I were just friends, but the way he treated me was so different to Eliot. He *listened* to me. We were interested in the same things. I told him I'd had enough of Eliot cheating on me, and he asked me to leave Eliot for him. I didn't think Eliot cared about me anymore, and I thought he'd be happy to be free to do whatever he wanted. But he was really, really angry when I left him. Vindictive. I don't know how the hell he managed it, but his lawyer made the split appear to be all my fault, and the judge took his part – he completely ignored all Eliot's affairs. I walked away from my marriage with nothing.' She shrugged. 'Not that I cared about money. I wanted to be with someone who loved me for who I was. Dan and I moved to Norwich so I could be a bit closer to Mum. Eliot moved to Norwich, too, to a house not far from us, but we just tried to ignore him and got on with things.'

Manson had followed his ex? Interesting, Colin thought.

'Dan and I were so happy when we found out I was pregnant.' She closed her eyes. 'And then one night he was knocked off his bike on his way home from work. There wasn't any CCTV. The witnesses thought it was a white van. It all happened so fast – whoever did it just scarpered. They didn't wait to see if Dan was OK. He hit his head in the wrong place... and he died before the ambulance arrived.' She blew out a breath. 'I've always thought Eliot had something to do with it, because I knew how much he hated that I was happy with Dan, but I couldn't prove it was him. And I was so lost without Dan. Mum and Ben were still at the George and Dragon in Summerstrand, and they took me in. As soon as I moved in with them, Eliot bought a house in the next village. When they bought the Feathers, I moved here with them and got a job at the primary school – and Eliot bought that house in the village and did it up.'

Following her twice more, Colin thought. Rubbing her face in his business success, maybe? Or had he not been able to handle her rejecting him?

'But you try to avoid him?'

'As much as I could,' Vicky said. 'Though I'm always careful with Robbie. Just in case Eliot...' She stopped.

'In case what?' Colin asked.

'He's vindictive. And Robbie's the only thing I have left of Dan. I worry,' Vicky said, biting her lip. 'Though I've got no proof, so I couldn't go to the police or try to get an injunction against Eliot. Whatever I say just makes me look paranoid.'

'Did he threaten Robbie?'

Vicky winced. 'I told you, it makes me look paranoid. He's never said anything explicitly to threaten Robbie. But the way he's in my face all the time...'

And if Sally was protective of both her daughter and her grandson, that would give her a motive to get rid of Eliot Manson.

'Thank you for telling me,' he said. 'Can I ask what you did yesterday after work?'

'I came home with Robbie. I normally leave school at about quarter to four, so we would've been here by four. I supervised his homework and cooked dinner for us and Mum,' she said. 'Ben was busy in the bar, and he was going to grab something from the pub kitchen when he had a moment. After we ate, I played games with Robbie and got his things ready for this morning while he had a bath. Then I read him a bedtime story. When he was in bed, I did some lesson plans – I can show you them, if you like. I watched a documentary about Roman emperors. I went to bed about ten and read for a bit.'

'Was anyone with you during the evening?' he asked.

'Only Robbie. Mum was working in the bar after we ate,' she said.

Colin asked a few more questions and made notes. 'I'll write up your statement before I go and ask you to check it and sign it, please,' he said. 'I'm sorry I've brought up bad memories.' He gave her an awkward smile. 'Could you ask your mum to come in next, please?'

Sally came in with a cup of tea. 'Larissa said you have just a dash of milk and no sugar.'

'Thank you. That's kind,' he said gratefully, accepting the hot drink.

'Am I in trouble, because of what I said to you last night?' she asked.

'You're not the only people I'm talking to about the situation,' Colin said. 'But, yes, I'm aware you have a motive for wishing him ill.'

'He treated Vicky appallingly,' Sally said. 'The divorce is all a matter of record, and he seemed to follow her wherever she went – he was in her face the whole time. It's almost as if he couldn't forgive her for being the one who got away. Ben and I have both said before, we'd like to rearrange his face for him. But that's not the way to deal with things, is it? So we avoided him as much as we could. We refused to serve him here and, as I've told you before, I didn't treat him at the surgery.'

'When did you last see him?' Colin asked.

'I've no idea,' Sally said. 'Sometimes I've passed his car on the road; obviously we have to drive past his house if we want to go to Norwich. But I couldn't tell you when I last saw him or spoke to him.'

'Can I ask if you, Ben or Vicky take any medication?' Colin asked.

'I take thyroxine for an underactive thyroid. Vicky's on anti-depressants, though she's coming off them. Ben takes medication for diabetes and blood pressure, which is why I nag him about what he eats and to watch his sugar intake.' Sally looked at him sharply. 'Was medication involved in Manson's death?'

'I'm still waiting on the pathology results, so I couldn't say,' Colin reminded her. 'It's a possible line of enquiry at the moment. Can you tell me what you did after, say, four p.m. yesterday?'

'I was doing a stock check in the bar yesterday. I started about half past three; Vicky and Robbie came home at four, and I finished the stock check about half an hour later. I spent a bit of time with them, and then Vicky cooked dinner for us. After that I was working with Ben in the bar – but you know that because you were here and you saw us,' she said.

'What time did you go to bed?'

'On a Thursday, we normally close about ten – most people

are at work, the next day, so there are only a couple of stragglers left in the bar by then. We stop serving food at nine. Hannah sorts out a list of anything she wants us to pick up from the wholesaler, while Jenny deals with the dishwasher and cleans the kitchen. Jenny's our pot washer, though Hannah's teaching her a few things and giving her a bit of experience because she wants to go to catering college. Then Ben and I collect any stray glasses, stack the glass dishwasher, clean the tables and mop the floor before we have a shower and fall into bed. That's usually about eleven,' she said.

'And last night was a usual night?'

'Yes,' Sally said.

He asked a few more questions, and told her he'd write up her statement and ask her to sign it. 'One last thing,' he said. 'Do you remember anyone going missing from Summerstrand, when you were a child?'

'Missing?' She flinched; it was only the tiniest of movements, but Colin noticed.

'It's not necessarily connected,' he said. 'But we're looking at a cold case. Something that happened in the 1960s.'

'You're right, I was a child, back then,' she said. 'I wouldn't really have known about anything that went on with adults.'

But he'd seen that flinch. And her words were equivocating; he was pretty sure she knew something. 'You're not in any trouble,' he said gently. 'We're trying to piece something together, that's all.'

Sally's eyes filmed with tears. 'My brother didn't exactly go *missing*, but he left home at eighteen – and back then you were still a minor until you were twenty-one,' she said. 'Martin was ten years older than me. He wanted to be a footballer. He was really good; he could've made it as a professional. Except Dad said Martin had to follow in his footsteps and be a lighthouse keeper. Looking back, Martin was exactly the same age as George Best. He could've done just as well as Bestie.' She smiled sadly. 'Though it wasn't about the money and the fame. Martin just really, really loved football. He didn't want to be a lighthouse keeper.'

The only missing persons report had been about Ryan Everett; Larissa hadn't mentioned anyone called Martin. Maybe Sally's family hadn't reported him missing, despite the fact that he'd left home underage.

'What was his full name?' he asked gently.

'Martin Armitage.' She swallowed hard. 'He played football in the local league. A spotter saw him play and offered him a trial at Arsenal. Because he wasn't twenty-one, he had to have Dad's permission before he could go to London, and Dad wouldn't give it. They had this huge fight. A few days later, he wasn't there when I got up in the morning. Mum said she thought Martin had run off to London. Dad wouldn't even let us mention his name. Martin never made it as a footballer – but he didn't come home, either.' A tear leaked down her cheek, and she brushed it away. 'I did try to find him. It's one of the reasons I studied medicine at London, so I'd be able to look for him, but those were the days before the internet made it easier to find people. I asked around, but nobody knew anything – or, if they did, they weren't saying.'

'Did you ever find him?' Colin asked.

'That's the bit that really upsets me,' Sally said. 'I finally tracked him down, four years after Dad died. But Martin had already died. And it's my biggest regret that I didn't find him earlier. That I didn't get to tell him we missed him. That I wasn't there when he needed me.'

So it was unlikely that the body buried next to the lighthouse was Sally's brother. At least that was one bit of bad news he wouldn't have to break.

'I'm sorry,' he said.

'So am I,' she said quietly. 'I wish Dad would've let him be who he wanted to be.' She swallowed hard. 'Dad was old school.

Even though lighthouse keepers were in a reserved occupation, he joined up in the Second World War because he wanted to do his bit, and he didn't want people to think he was a coward. Mum said he'd changed a lot when he came back from the war. He never talked about what he saw, what he did. In hindsight, I think he probably had PTSD, and if he'd had treatment for it maybe he wouldn't have been so hard on Martin. Maybe he wouldn't have...' She stopped and shook her head. 'He wasn't great to my mum, either. And he was a drinker. Ironic that I ended up married to a publican, second time round. But Ben's a gentle giant. He's nothing like my dad. And, even though he's as angry as I am about the way Manson treated our Vicky, Ben wouldn't have killed him.'

'I'm sorry I've brought back bad memories,' Colin said.

Sally gave a rueful shrug. 'It is what it is.'

'May I ask about your first husband?' Colin asked.

'Vicky's dad? Robert Evans.' Sally looked sad. 'She named Robbie after him. We met as students. He became a doctor, too. He used to work in A&E, and spent a week every year helping Doctors Without Borders. When Vicky was ten, he went to help out after an earthquake. Only there was a landslide, and he was killed.'

'I'm sorry,' Colin said.

'So am I. He was a good man. But so's Ben. When I came back to Summerstrand, he'd split up with his wife the year before. Nobody was to blame; they just drifted apart. They shared Claire's care. Ben was running the George and Dragon there, and trying to figure out how to parent Claire on his days alone. We exchanged some parenting woes, he asked me out, and we ended up together.' Sally bit her lip. 'Vicky doesn't know about my dad and Martin. She thinks I was an only child. And I'd prefer her not to know.'

'Noted,' Colin said. But all the same something niggled. Frank at the George and Dragon had said that Sally's father had a temper. It sounded as if Sally's childhood had been seriously unhappy. Surely she was more likely to have wanted to stay away from the lighthouse and never have to see it again, rather than buying it and turning it into a museum? Or maybe she'd wanted the lighthouse to represent the good it had done over the years, the people that it had saved, to help take away her own bad memories.

Ben was next. Colin went through similar questions, and Ben's answers were very similar to Sally's. But he knew they couldn't have collaborated, not with Larissa present in the kitchen.

'We all loathed Manson, so I suppose that makes us potential suspects,' Ben said.

Though the divorce had happened years ago. If that was the reason Ben or Sally had killed Manson, why now? Unless it was linked to the sale of the lighthouse, and Colin wasn't sure that was enough of a motive, either. After all, Sally hadn't lived there for years. Yet again, he found himself circling back to Sally's childhood. Had Sally confided in Ben how difficult her father was?

A killer would have a motive, means and opportunity. Colin had worked out some possible motives for Ben and Sally, but they were all related to things that had happened a while back and he couldn't see what might have triggered either of them to act now. Given that Sally was a GP and Ben was a publican, they definitely had links to the probable means of Manson's death. That left the opportunity. Had either of them gone to the lighthouse last night? And, if so, why?

What was he missing?

As if Ben was reading Colin's mind, he said, 'We have CCTV covering the front and back doors and the car park. If you want to see it, to prove that none of us left the Feathers last night, you're very welcome.'

'Thank you. Yes, I would like to see it,' Colin said. 'I'll write up your statement and ask you to check it and sign it. But one last thing – you ran the George and Dragon in Summerstrand before you bought the Feathers, didn't you?'

Ben nodded. 'My daughter runs it now. But my parents had the pub before me. It was pretty much expected that I'd take over from Dad when I was old enough.'

'So you grew up in Summerstrand in the 1960s?' Colin double-checked.

'Yes,' Ben said. 'Why?'

'Do you remember anyone going missing in 1965?'

Ben winced. 'Did you ask Sally that question?'

Colin nodded. That answered one of his questions, then: if Ben knew about Martin, he'd also have an idea of how difficult Sally's father was. 'She told me about her brother.'

'She never got over Martin leaving. She looked for him, for years and years and years. And it almost broke her when she finally got a lead and then found out she was too late – he'd already died,' Ben said. 'I wish you'd asked me first. I would've told you what happened and asked you not to bring back bad memories for her.' He paused. 'Her dad – Dennis – let's just say he wasn't an easy man.'

'So I gathered. Though it's part of my job to ask difficult questions, Ben,' Colin said quietly. 'I don't do it to upset people. Asking questions is part of how I find the truth and see that justice is done. And I did apologise for upsetting her.'

'Hmm,' Ben said.

Colin wrote up the statements from his notes while Ben sorted out the CCTV and photographs of himself, Vicky and Sally. Once they'd checked and signed their statements, Colin organised for someone back at the station to review the CCTV, and Larissa dropped him at Georgina's.

'See you tomorrow, guv,' she said. 'I'll get the CCTV and photos through to the team.'

'Thanks,' he said. 'See you tomorrow.'

. . .

There was a rap on the kitchen door, and Bert started leaping about and wagging his tail joyfully as Colin walked in.

Georgina greeted him with a kiss. 'How did your interviews go?'

'I'm pretty much at a brick wall, at the moment,' he said with a grimace. 'I have suspects who loathed Manson, but at the moment nobody seems to have a strong enough motive to kill him, let alone the means or the opportunity,' he said. 'I felt sorry for Tara Cox, though. Manson seems to have behaved differently towards her than he did to everyone else – maybe he really did love her. She seemed devastated by his loss.'

'Poor girl,' Georgina said. She knew what it felt like to get the news you'd never see the love of your life again.

Colin clearly realised what she was thinking, because he held her close. 'She's got her family with her, and the family liaison officer.'

'But once they've gone, then she has to deal with things on her own. I'll drop some flowers round to her, next week,' Georgina said.

'That's kind,' Colin said. 'Oh, I have some information that might be helpful for you. Larissa's been doing some work on the skeleton and found a missing persons case that might fit.'

'Would that be Ryan Everett, who went missing in Summerstrand in 1965, aged twenty?' Georgina asked.

'Yes.' He gave her a wry smile. 'I thought you'd probably find him, too.'

Plus she'd had the extra information from Doris. Not that she could explain that to him. 'Bea told me about some sites. One didn't go back far enough, but he appeared on the second one I tried, and then I did a general search and found the page his family had put up. They had a photo of how he looked in 1965 and there's an artist's impression – how the artist thinks he would've looked ten years ago.' She brought the pictures up on her laptop and Colin looked at them.

'Ryan would be seventy-nine, now. If he isn't our skeleton, that is, and if he hadn't died in the meantime,' Colin said. He winced.

'I couldn't find a death record for him. It's possible that Ryan changed his name, but I couldn't find any evidence. So either he's still alive, or he's your skeleton.' She looked thoughtfully at him. 'How often are those kinds of cases reviewed?'

'Annually,' Colin said. 'But apparently it's a lot of years since there was any new information on Ryan's file.'

'It's starting to sound more like he's our skeleton,' Georgina said. 'Actually, you know I said his family had put something up on the internet? It turns out his niece is a sculptor, and she has a gallery in Holt. Sybbie and I are going for lunch in Holt on Monday, and I thought we could pop in and have a chat.'

'We don't have proof that our skeleton's definitely him,' Colin warned.

'No. But I could tell her that my dog found human remains in Summerstrand. And I could tell her about what happened with Friedrich Schmidt's family, when we found the skeleton at the theatre last year.'

'You know, that probably counts as interfering with an investigation,' Colin said.

She folded her arms. 'Then you could always come with us to Holt. Except I rather think you'll be busy interviewing people, looking at forensic reports and trying to work out whether Eliot Manson's death was an accident or not.'

He sighed. 'Yes. You're right.'

'And your cold case is on the edge of being historical,' she said. 'Which means I'm not interfering.'

'It isn't historical, yet – so, technically, you are interfering,' he said.

She spread her hands. 'You don't have the manpower to

investigate a cold case from nearly sixty years ago. It's not going to be a high priority, is it?'

'No,' he admitted. 'OK. We haven't had this conversation. But just keep me in the loop, please.'

'And I won't make any promises you can't deliver,' she said.

'Thank you.' He wrapped his arms around her. 'I appreciate you. And I appreciate your help. I'm just at the—'

'—grumpy stage of investigation,' she finished. 'Sit down and let me feed you. I have gnocchi, though I admit I bought both the gnocchi and the sauce from Cesca's.'

'I've never had anything from the farm shop that I haven't enjoyed,' he said. 'Gnocchi and sauce sounds perfect.'

TEN

Saturday was a day of frustration for Colin. The CCTV from the Feathers showed that neither Vicky, Sally nor Ben left the building from 5pm until midnight. Tara, too, had a firm alibi: she was doing a shoot in London and had stayed in the city on Thursday night. It was possible that she could have driven the three hours each way from the centre of London to Summer-strand, but she would have had to leave early enough to tamper with the medication well before eight p.m., and the photoshoot ruled that out. Manson's site manager and architect had alibis for their whereabouts on Thursday night, as did the leaders of the village pressure group against the development.

Had it not been for the presence of the beta-blockers, Colin would've agreed that Manson's death had been from carbon monoxide poisoning – that Manson had drunk enough whisky and cola to forget about sensible safety precautions, and it was an accidental death.

But.

Sammy Granger had tested the contents of the whisky bottle and emailed him her findings. There were definitely beta-blockers mixed in with the alcohol. Forensics hadn't found Manson's prescription drugs, but if the guy had planned to take an overdose, surely it was more likely that he would have swallowed the tablets straight from the packet? Why would he have gone to the trouble of grinding up the tablets and mixing them with the whisky? It pointed towards someone tampering with the bottle.

The question was, who? And why now?

Eliot Manson had been generally disliked by a lot of people, but Colin hadn't found anyone who'd seemed to be driven to the point of murdering him. Whoever was responsible for Manson's death would have needed access to the medication as well as to the lighthouse cottage – and also would have needed to know that he was going to drink the whisky alone.

The dilemma occupied Colin to the point where he really had to make an effort with Georgina's son and daughter on Sunday – even though he'd got on well with them in the past and liked them enormously. They were meant to be celebrating Georgina's birthday; Will had driven Bea down to Norfolk from London and he was cooking them all a late lunch, something with chicken that smelled delicious.

Although Colin was sitting with the three of them at the ancient table in Georgina's kitchen, sipping coffee from one of her collection of ladybird mugs, he was aware that his thoughts weren't wholly concentrated on the conversation. He just hoped he was nodding and smiling in the right places as Bea regaled them with anecdotes about the Regency Theatre and Will teased his mother about poetry.

Then he realised that everyone was staring at him.

Clearly someone had asked him a direct question and he'd failed to answer. A nod and a vague smile hadn't been enough to bluff his way through it. And they all deserved better from him, anyway.

'Sorry,' he said, feeling his face flood with colour. 'I know I'm being rude. It isn't you, it's me. I'm a bit preoccupied with a tricky case at the moment.'

'Dad used to be like that,' Bea said, patting his shoulder. 'We could always tell if he was working through a directorial issue in his head. He looked as if he was on another planet. You've got that look about you, too.'

'I'll try harder,' Colin promised. 'Can I ask you something as a chemist, Will?'

'Sure,' Will said, taking the chicken saltimbocca tray bake from the oven and adding fine beans and a few more sage leaves. 'Fifteen minutes until lunch, by the way.'

'If someone crushed some tablets and put them in alcohol, would it be easy for someone else to tell they'd done it? I mean, would there be a film on the alcohol, or a colour change, or any other sign?'

'If you had tablets with, say, an orange dyed coating and dissolved it in vodka, you'd end up with something that looked like flat orangeade – so, yes, it would be noticeable,' Will said. 'But if you dissolved white tablets in something like rum or whisky, you might not notice the liquid was a bit paler than usual or a little bit cloudy, especially if you'd already been drinking. Why?'

'I'm not planning to do that to anyone,' Colin said. 'I'm just thinking about how someone might take an overdose of medication without knowing it.'

'Usually tablets have a coating to hide the taste. If you crush them, it'll release all the bitterness,' Will said.

'Supposing I added cola to the whisky-and-ground-pills mix – would that hide the bitterness?' Colin asked.

'Pretty much,' Will said.

'Is that what the pathologist said happened?' Georgina asked.

'Yes.' Colin sighed. 'But now I need to work out who would have access to the medication and the victim's whisky, and who had the opportunity to do it.'

'You'll figure it out,' Bea said confidently. 'You worked it out when Mum was poisoned.'

'I can assure you I'm not going to let her be in that kind of situation with this case,' Colin said.

'And I can look after myself,' Georgina said. 'I don't take stupid risks.'

Colin looked at her. 'You took a huge risk at the theatre, last year.'

'A calculated one,' Georgina corrected.

'Knowing everyone at the theatre as I did, I would've done the same, in Mum's shoes,' Bea added.

Georgina raised her mug of coffee. 'Thank you for the vote of confidence.'

'Seconded,' Will said.

Colin sighed. 'OK. I'm outvoted. And I probably worry too much.'

'It's your age,' Bea said with a grin. 'So are you any further forward in finding out the identity of the skeleton?'

'I'm going to visit a sculptor at a gallery tomorrow,' Georgina said. 'It's possible that he was her uncle.'

'Are you going to do DNA testing?' Will asked.

'Potentially,' Colin said. 'Now, we're meant to be celebrating your mum's birthday, not letting my work get in the way. Plus I'm not—'

'—allowed to discuss cases with people who aren't colleagues,' Georgina, Will and Bea said in a chorus.

He gave them a wry smile. It wasn't the first time they'd all said it to him. They knew the situation – particularly Will, who as a government scientist had signed the Official Secrets Act – and he trusted them to keep the little he'd already said confidential. 'Thank you. So shall we change the subject?'

. . .

Later that evening, Georgina lay curled up in bed beside him. 'You know, Colin, I'm not like a character in a terrible horror movie who decides to go and investigate a strange noise or situation on my own. Or who underestimates a threat.'

'I know. I'm just grumpy and out of sorts,' Colin said. 'I'm stuck with this one.' He was missing something important, and he couldn't for the life of him work out what it was. 'I've been through the usual structure: who had the motive, who had the means, and who had the opportunity. I can't see a link. Or maybe I'm getting too caught up with the beta-blockers in the whisky. I don't know.'

'Just go to sleep and let it tick over in the back of your head,' Georgina said. 'And maybe something will come up from Ryan Everett's case to help unlock the Manson case.'

'Maybe,' Colin said. But it made him antsy. Although Georgina fell asleep, he couldn't switch off. He listened to her quiet, regular breathing and almost wished he'd gone back to his poky little flat in Norwich instead of staying over. At least then he could've gone out and paced along the river while he thought things through. It wouldn't be fair to Georgina to get up now and prowl around her garden, particularly as it would also disturb Bert.

In the meantime, the thoughts spun round and round his head. Was there a link between Eliot Manson and the young man who'd been beaten, strangled and buried next to the lighthouse? And, if so, what?

On Monday morning, Colin left early and Georgina was getting her bag ready for her trip with Sybbie when Doris said, 'Ryan's remembered something. He sketches. *Sketched*,' she corrected herself.

'Thank you – that's really useful,' Georgina said. 'I'm going to visit his niece's gallery this morning, with Sybbie. She's a sculptor.'

'Sounds as if the artistic gene runs in the family, then,' Doris said. 'Hopefully she can tell you something about him that will help us jog memories for him.'

'Are you coming to Holt with us?' Georgina asked.

'I'm tempted,' Doris said. 'But I don't think I'll be much help.'

'And you want to spend your time with Harrison,' Georgina said gently.

'He's being a bit quiet today. A touch of the black dog. He's full of regrets,' Doris said. 'So, yes.'

'Give him my love,' Georgina said.

'I will,' Doris agreed.

Bert wuffed softly, and Georgina glanced out of the side window. 'Sybbie's here,' she said. 'And not in the MGA.' Sybbie's turquoise 1961-vintage MGA was her pride and joy.

'Hmm. I've never trusted that car, not since Hartington Hall,' Doris muttered.

'That's not fair. It wasn't the car's fault,' Georgina reminded her.

'Even so. Your car's a lot safer. And so is Bernard's. We'll talk later,' Doris said.

Georgina settled Bert on his bed, set the house alarm, and locked the back door.

'Morning,' she said, opening the door and getting into the car. Sybbie was wearing one of her trademark silk scarves and slightly tinted driving glasses. 'You're using Bernard's car today, then?'

'It's not really the weather to take the MGA out,' Sybbie said.

'A few spots of rain won't do any harm,' Georgina teased.

'I'm not taking her out to get wet and miserable. She's

staying dry, in the garage, where she belongs,' Sybbie said. 'Hurry up and fasten your seat belt. I'm looking forward to seeing this gallery.'

On the way to the pretty Georgian market town, Georgina filled Sybbie in on the discovery of what they thought were the remains of Ryan Everett.

'Buried under the patio?' Sybbie asked. 'That doesn't sound like an accident. Poor boy.'

'We don't know it's *definitely* him,' Georgina cautioned.

'And the last thing we want is to raise his family's hopes and dash them again. We'll tread carefully,' Sybbie said. 'You know, Bert's making a bit of a habit of this. First the bones at Hartington, then at the theatre, and now the lighthouse.'

With a little help from Doris. But Georgina knew that Sybbie also didn't believe in ghosts, despite the stories linked to Little Wenborough Manor. 'I think Bert has a secret ambition to be a police dog,' she joked. 'The finds liaison officer said he could have a job with her, too.'

'Well, that'd keep him in dog treats for a bit.' Sybbie laughed, and they kept the conversation light until they arrived in Holt. They left the car in the town centre car park and walked to the gallery; on the way, Georgina just about managed to nudge Sybbie past her favourite antique shop.

Webster's Fine Art was gorgeous from the outside, taking up the ground floor of a Georgian red-brick building. It had the original Georgian double shopfront with wide bow windows, painted grey, and the glazing bars were painted white.

Some stunning framed prints were displayed in the window, along with glazed bowls that seemed to shimmer, and various sculptures of dogs. Sybbie sighed over a pair of Labradors, one sitting and one standing; both were a little smaller than the size of her palm.

'That one's so like Max,' Sybbie said, pointing at the standing dog.

'We're not here for shopping,' Georgina reminded her.

'*You* might not be, dear girl,' Sybbie teased.

Georgina groaned. 'I told Bernard I'd be your responsible adult today and keep you out of the antique shops.'

'Dear girl, this isn't an antique shop. So you're keeping your promise.' Sybbie raised a mischievous eyebrow.

The double door between the bow windows was half-glazed, painted the same glossy mid-grey as the windows but with white-painted glazing bars. Sybbie pulled the brass handle down and pushed the door open; an old-fashioned bell at the top of the door clanged to signal that a customer had arrived.

The woman at the far end of the shop looked to be in her late forties, tall and loose-limbed, with a mass of fair hair pulled back in a ponytail by a multi-coloured silk scarf. 'Good morning,' she said. 'Please feel free to browse without any pressure. I'll be here if you need any help.' There was a tiny wuff, and she smiled. 'Oh, and of course Poppy, as my shop assistant.'

'And a lovely assistant she is, too,' Sybbie said, looking at the elderly Westie curled in her basket. 'I'd like a closer look at the two Labrador bronzes, please.'

'They're both in a limited edition of one hundred,' the gallery owner told her, and opened the door of an antique glass-fronted china cabinet. 'I'm Niamh Webster, by the way.'

'Nice to meet you, Niamh,' Georgina said.

Niamh took the two bronze labradors from the cabinet; she handed Sybbie the standing dog, then placed the sitting dog on top of the cabinet.

'Just feel the weight.' Sybbie held the bronze sculpture. 'And it feels beautiful in the hand.'

A glance at the price tag told Georgina that Sybbie was about to spend far more than she would've done if she'd simply added another pair of antique Staffordshire china dogs to her collection.

'It's proper cast bronze, not resin or cold cast,' Sybbie said.

'You know your stuff,' Niamh said.

'I know what I like,' Sybbie said.

'Usually Staffordshire dogs. I'm not supposed to let her add to the collection, or her husband will have my guts for garters,' Georgina said with a sigh.

'Yes, but this isn't a Staffordshire dog, dear girl. It's just one little – oh, actually, I *do* want both of them. Max and Jet, don't you think?' Sybbie asked, tipping her head on one side as she looked at the second bronze. 'I'll buy them for Bernard's desk.'

'And we all know they'll end up on yours,' Georgina said.

Sybbie looked completely unrepentant and peered into the cabinet. 'Ooh. I've just spotted a springer – it's the spit of your Bert,' she said.

'No,' Georgina said.

'Now, look, should I wish to buy you a late birthday present...' Sybbie slow-blinked at her.

'No,' Georgina said, though she couldn't help picking up the bronze spaniel. Sybbie was right; it did look like Bert, with that wonderful plumy tail and noble face. 'You're such a bad influence,' she said with a sigh. 'It's lovely, but I wasn't looking to buy sculpture today.'

'I'll have both Labradors, please,' Sybbie said.

'They come with a certificate of authenticity, signed by the artist,' the woman said. 'That is, by me.'

'Oh, that's wonderful,' Sybbie said. 'I'm sorry – we haven't introduced ourselves. I'm Sybbie Walters.' She shook Niamh's hand, then made a fuss of Poppy.

'Georgina Drake,' Georgina said, smiling and echoing Sybbie's handshake, then bending down to stroke the little Westie.

'Are you local?' Niamh asked.

'Ish. We're from Little Wenborough, just outside Norwich,' Sybbie said. 'We've escaped to Holt for the day. The plan is lunch and a spot of shopping.'

While Sybbie was chatting to Niamh, Georgina browsed the mounted print section, and her attention was grabbed by a watercolour of a beach in wintertime. The foreground was windswept marram grass on the dunes; the sky was full of ominous clouds. In the distance, a pewter sea capped with foam surged up on the dark, flat sands, and further back still a ray of sunshine illuminated a strip of sand, turning it to pure gold.

It would look perfect in her dining room.

'This is gorgeous,' she said, taking the print from the box and bringing it over to the counter. 'I'd like to buy it. Did you paint the original?'

'No. My aunt Joan did, years ago – well, she was actually my great-great aunt,' Niamh said. She smiled. 'She would've been a hundred and twenty-four, this year. She used to have a cottage on the coast, at Summerstrand; she moved there to have a studio by the sea. That's the view from her cottage. I remember her as a very old lady – though, thinking about it, at eighty she would've been a couple of years younger than my mum is now, and nobody would ever call my mum old. Joan used to let me play with her paints. Mum inherited her paint-box, though she uses acrylics and oils rather than watercolours like Joan did.' She gestured to the print. 'Joan's watercolours are in a class of their own. It's the way she uses light. I've made a limited-edition print run of my favourite ones, because I think they deserve to be seen and loved by other people, not just me.'

'I agree with you,' Georgina said. 'I'm a photographer. Mainly portrait, but I take landscapes for fun. And I have very a soft spot for seascapes like this one.' She paused. 'Actually, I should be honest with you. I'm doing some research into Summerstrand and I came across the name of your aunt. When I looked her up on the internet, I found your gallery. I was hoping you might be able to help me.'

'What sort of research?' Niamh asked, her eyes widening

with obvious surprise. 'Are you doing something on local artists?'

'It's a bit complicated,' Georgina said. 'Would you have time to join us for lunch so I could explain it to you?'

'Not today, I'm afraid. It's half term, so my daughter Faye's home with the children instead of here with me.' Niamh glanced at her watch. 'Tell you what – I'll make us a coffee and we can have a chat in the kitchen, if you like? Though, if a customer comes in, I'll need to see to them.'

'Of course,' Georgina said. 'I appreciate your time.'

'Come through,' Niamh said, leading them into the back of the gallery. Poppy followed sedately, and curled up in her basket as Niamh made coffee and the three of them sat at the small table. 'So what's your research about?' Niamh asked.

'Summerstrand in the 1960s,' Georgina said. 'I was commissioned to do a piece on the old lighthouse, and Joan's name came up.'

'She did paint a couple of watercolours of the lighthouse. Though I didn't make a print of them, because... I don't know.' Niamh wrinkled her nose. 'There's just something I don't like about the building. I preferred her seascapes.'

'So your family are all artists?' Sybbie asked.

'Pretty much,' Niamh said. 'Joan made her living from painting; so did Mum. I sculpt, and Faye, my daughter, does ceramics. From what Mum says, my gran had the same artsy gene. Mum reckons Gran did some incredible embroidery and she would've been amazing at needlepoint, but she was from the war generation – there wasn't the time or money to do fancy stitching, just mend and make do.' She rolled her eyes. 'By the time Gran was free to sew whatever she fancied and had the time to do complicated needlework, she had arthritis and couldn't hold a needle easily.' She bit her lip. 'It wasn't just the women in the family. My brother's a cartoonist, and Mum's brother, my uncle Ryan, used to sketch. He could've been an amazing artist.'

'Could've been?' Sybbie asked.

'Except he disappeared,' Niamh said. 'It's so sad. We never found out what happened to him. Mum's looked for him for years and years and years, but she's never had any luck. My brother set up a web page, but nobody's ever come forward with any useful information.'

Georgina and Sybbie exchanged a glance.

'I came across that web page when I was looking into Summerstrand and the 1960s,' Georgina said gently.

'Is *that* what you're looking into?' Niamh asked. 'Why you wanted to see me in particular?'

'Yes,' Georgina said.

For a moment, Niamh's face was flooded with hope. 'Have you found him?'

Yes, but there wasn't a way to explain that wouldn't hurt Niamh. 'I... I'm not sure,' Georgina said. It wasn't a total fib. She didn't have physical evidence to back up what Doris had told her. 'I'm a photographer. I was commissioned to do an interview with a local builder who was doing up the lighthouse. That's kind of fallen through, but while I was there...' She blew out a breath. 'My dog started digging in an area that had been cleared. There were human remains.'

'And you think they were Ryan's?'

'We don't know for sure, right now,' Georgina said. 'I don't want to cause your family any more hurt. And I can't make any promises. But knowing Ryan's story might help the police to work out whether it's him or not. My partner's involved in the case.'

'But it could be Ryan,' Niamh insisted.

'Or it might not be,' Georgina said. 'I'm so sorry if I sound harsh. I just don't want to give you hope of – well, closure, and then snatch it away from you again.' She paused. 'Ryan disappeared in 1965, didn't he?'

Niamh nodded. 'Ten years before I was born. He was twenty, and Mum was twenty-two. My grandfather... well, let's just say he was a product of his time.' Her mouth thinned. 'He threw Ryan out when he found out Ryan was gay.'

'I'm sorry,' Georgina said. 'That's hard.'

'Joan took him in. Joan was lovely – kind, tolerant and she let Ryan be himself, knowing he was safe with her. And Ryan used to write to Mum. He sent the letters to her best friend's house so their dad didn't recognise his handwriting and destroy the letters.' She blew out a breath. 'From what Mum says, Ryan met someone special when he stayed with Joan. He never told her the guy's name, just his initial – "M". There were a few sketches in Ryan's portfolio, and I always wondered if that was him, but Mum said he was probably just a life class model.'

'Could he have gone abroad with "M"?' Sybbie asked.

'It's possible,' Niamh said thoughtfully. 'Joan thought Ryan was going on a day trip to Norwich – he had to get the bus, because the railway had closed three years before. Ryan had been out late somewhere the night before, so she didn't see him before she went to bed. She didn't check on him before she took her dog out that morning, and when she came back Ryan wasn't in the kitchen having his breakfast. She assumed he'd already gone to get the bus and she'd missed him. But when he didn't come back that night, or the night after, she was worried. She checked his room – and he'd packed all his things. Everything was still there, but it was in a suitcase and holdalls. And he'd stripped the bed.'

'That sounds as if he was planning to go away for more than a day trip,' Georgina said gently.

'But Mum says her brother was *nice*. He wouldn't have left without saying goodbye to Joan, not if it was going to be for good.

If it was a case of him being hounded out of the community by a few neanderthals, at the very least he would've left Joan a letter telling her why he'd gone, so she didn't worry. And he would've called her, to let her know he was OK. Then again, if he was going for good, why would he have left all his stuff behind? There's no way he would've left his portfolio.' She sighed. 'I know at the time it was really difficult for gay men, but things were starting to change. And Ryan knew he had Joan on his side, even if some of the locals in Summerstrand had worked out that he was gay and were giving him a hard time about it. Mum was on his side, too.'

'I'm sorry,' Georgina said. 'I didn't mean to open old wounds.'

'I know you didn't,' Niamh said. 'And they're not really my wounds, because I never actually met my uncle. But my mum loved him very much. I wish I could find out what really happened, for her sake.' She looked sad. 'If he was still alive, he'd be nearly eighty now. He's been missing for nearly three times longer than he was with the family. But if those remains you found were his, and you can prove it, I think that would help, because at least then Mum would have closure. Being in limbo, not knowing – that's always upset her.'

Mindful of the fact that she'd assured Colin she wouldn't make any promises, Georgina sighed inwardly. 'Can I tell Colin – my partner – what you've told me?' And then maybe he could talk to Niamh about DNA sampling.

'Yes. Can I tell Mum?'

'Maybe it'd be better to wait. I don't want to get her hopes up, or yours, in case nothing comes of it,' Georgina warned.

'I suppose you're right,' Niamh said. 'I'll tell you what I know. Ryan really was a talented artist. His sketches were gorgeous. There's a few he did of a dog, and I'm tempted to make prints from them.'

'If it's a Labrador or a springer, you have a definite customer sitting right in front of you,' Sybbie said, and took out her phone to show the lock screen photo. 'My Max and Jet.'

'They're gorgeous,' Niamh said, smiling. 'I can see exactly why you bought my bronzes.'

'This is Bert,' Georgina said, proffering her own phone.

'The digger?'

The one who found the bones,' Georgina confirmed wryly.

'He's a beauty. Very like my best friend's, who modelled for me,' Niamh said. She stood up and took a laptop from a drawer, then found a file of photographs. 'These are Ryan's sketches.'

'A border collie,' Sybbie said immediately. 'You're right. He's got a good eye for movement. They're lovely.'

As they browsed through the gallery of pictures on the laptop, a sketch of a man appeared. It was clearly drawn with affection, and something about him looked familiar, though Georgina couldn't put her finger on it.

'Sorry. That's in the wrong file. I still think that's the mysterious "M",' Niamh said. 'Look at the way he's drawn. I don't think that's a life model. That's someone Ryan knew. Someone he loved.'

'Did your mum give the picture to the police, or tell them about "M"?' Georgina asked.

'No.' Niamh winced. 'I know it would've been the obvious thing to do – at least, it would now. But the thing is, being identified as gay could've got him and Ryan into serious trouble, back in 1965. Even in this century, there's still a fair bit of prejudice. Back then, it was a lot worse.'

'Again, I can't promise anything,' Georgina said, 'but I could ask my partner to check the file. If this is new information, maybe the police can work on it. Maybe they can find out who "M" is and see if he knows anything about what happened to Ryan.'

Hope flared in Niamh's face. 'I could email you the JPEGs.'

'Please do. The dog would be helpful as well, I think.

People often remember animals more than they remember people. As I said, I can't promise anything, but I'll talk to my partner.' Georgina took a card from her handbag and gave it to Niamh. 'My details are here.'

'Thank you,' Niamh said. 'I'll email them to you and send you my private mobile, if he needs it. I know it's probably going to come to nothing – if "M" is still alive, he'd be of a similar age to Ryan, and he might not be able to tell us anything. But it's a chance.'

ELEVEN

'"M"? That sounds a bit James Bond,' Doris said drily, later that afternoon, when Georgina was sitting at her kitchen table with her laptop. 'But OK. I'll ask Ryan if that means anything to him.'

'This is what he looks like,' Georgina said, opening the email to reveal the photographs Niamh had sent her. 'Niamh – his niece – thinks this is the special person he told his sister he'd met.'

'Ryan being gay – that could be why he was murdered,' Doris said. 'Maybe the killer didn't intend to actually take his life, just rough him up a bit, and it went too far. But even if it had stopped at a beating, which would've been bad enough, Ryan wouldn't have been able to tell the police about it and get justice. If someone saw him even kissing another man back then he would've been up in court on a charge of gross indecency.'

'Which is utterly wrong,' Georgina said. 'And sadly there's still a lot of prejudice.'

Bert bounded over to the kitchen door, wagging his tail.

'That's probably Colin,' Doris said. 'I'll go now. I'll talk to Ryan and let you know what he says.'

'How was your day?' Georgina asked when Colin came into the kitchen.

'Frustratingly slow,' he said. 'How was yours?'

'Sybbie bought a couple of bronzes at the gallery,' Georgina said. 'And I bought a print of a gorgeous watercolour by Niamh's great-aunt. But we also got some more information on Ryan Everett.' She showed him the photos of Ryan's sketches. 'Apparently Ryan wrote to his sister that he'd met someone special, but he wouldn't give her a name, just an initial – "M". Then there are these sketches he did. Niamh's mum thinks this might have been a life model from a class, but Niamh thinks the model could be "M".'

'If Ryan was gay,' Colin said slowly, 'given the attitudes of the time, that would explain the broken ribs; someone had beaten him up shortly before he died. That doesn't excuse it,' he added firmly, 'because someone's sexuality is in no way a valid reason for beating them up. But a certain element in the population will hit out at anyone who's different from them – whether it's their sexuality, the colour of their skin, or their religion.'

'Ryan was definitely gay,' Georgina said. 'According to Niamh, her grandfather threw him out when he found out about Ryan's sexuality. His great-aunt Joan Riggs, a painter who lived in Summerstrand, took him in.' Her eyes narrowed. 'You've got that look on your face. You've just made a connection, haven't you?'

He nodded. 'Obviously this is strictly between us.'

'And even that's a lot more than you should be saying,' Georgina finished. 'I know. Just as you know it's going nowhere other than me.'

Colin nodded. 'You were there when Bert found the skeleton, so you know the remains were buried under what was the patio next to the lighthouse. There are some photographs with dates on the Summerstrand local history website, and it looks as if the aggregate – the patio – was laid at some point between

1959 and 1969,' he said. 'Sally's family lived at the lighthouse in 1965. And she had an older brother called Martin.'

'Who shares an initial with the mysterious "M". And might even *be* "M".' She looked at the sketch again. 'Earlier, I thought there was something familiar about his face. Now, I think I can see a likeness to Sally. Unless I'm reacting to what you just said and over-reading it.'

'I'm not sure. Can I have a copy of that?' Colin asked.

'I was planning to send you the files anyway, for Ryan's missing persons case. I didn't promise anything to Niamh, but she thinks her mum wouldn't have given these to the police or told them about "M". At least, not back in 1965.'

'When, if they'd identified him and worked out his relationship to Ryan he could've been jailed; and if Ryan had still been alive he would also have ended up in court,' Colin agreed. 'It's understandable Niamh's mum would want to protect her brother and didn't give them the information – even though it probably would have helped to find him, at the time. I'll get these added to the file, and I'll have a quiet word with Sally. Tomorrow morning, I think, before I go into the office.'

'Niamh asked me why I was interested in Ryan, so I had to tell her about Bert finding the skeleton,' Georgina said. 'I didn't want to lie to her. But I did say I couldn't make any promises, and the remains might not be Ryan's.'

'But with what she told you there's enough evidence now to justify DNA sampling,' Colin said. 'If she'll agree to that.'

'I'm pretty sure she will. She wants closure for her mum,' Georgina said.

'I'll do what I can,' Colin said. 'Closure's important.'

'Supposing Sally's brother was Ryan's "M",' Georgina said. 'We know Ryan's dad threw him out for being gay. Frank, the history teacher I met in the George and Dragon, said that Sally's dad had a bit of a temper, and I'm guessing Dennis Armitage shared the same views as Ryan's dad. If he'd found

Ryan and Martin together, he might have reacted badly.' She frowned. 'But Frank also said he couldn't remember anyone going missing. And he told me he's eighty, so he was around the same age as Ryan and Martin. He must've known them.'

'Frank might have assumed that Ryan was only staying at his aunt's for a holiday, and had simply gone back to where he came from,' Colin said. 'According to Sally, her brother wanted to be a footballer, but her dad wanted him to be a lighthouse keeper and refused to let him go to London. Martin had a fight with him and left home, even though at eighteen years old he was still a minor, and he never came back.'

'That's the sort of argument that would've been common knowledge in the village,' Georgina said. 'Half the village would've been on Martin's side, wanting him to have his chance to follow his dream; and the other half would've expected him to keep a stiff upper lip, do his duty and stay in the family business.'

'Maybe I need a chat with Frank, too,' Colin said. He blew out a breath. 'It'd be good to make progress in *one* of the cases. Right now, it feels as if I'm going nowhere.'

On Tuesday morning, Georgina took Bert for his usual morning walk, leaving Colin in peace to catch up with paperwork at her kitchen table. Colin emailed the sketches to his team and asked them to add them to Ryan Everett's file as a possible likeness of someone who might have known where he was.

Georgina wasn't back by the time he left to see Sally at the Feathers, so he left her a note propped against the kettle, set the alarm and locked the back door.

Sally answered his knock at the back door of the pub. 'Hello, Colin. I wasn't expecting to see you. Is something wrong?'

'Can we have a quick word, please?' he asked.

'Of course,' she said. 'Come in. Can I get you a cup of tea or anything?'

He smiled. 'Thanks for the offer, but I'm fine.'

'Vicky's not here – she's taken Robbie to see his other grandparents, and Ben's at the wholesalers,' she said.

If his theory about the sketch being Sally's brother was right, Ben – who'd also grown up in Summerstrand – would have recognised him, too. But Colin would work with what he had. 'You're the one I was looking to talk to, actually,' he said with a smile.

'Is it to do with Manson?' she asked.

'No. It's about a cold case,' he said. There wasn't a way of preparing her for this. 'Do you recognise this man?' He showed her the sketch Georgina had printed out for him.

'No,' she said.

She said it a little too quickly for Colin's liking, and he noticed that she wouldn't meet his eyes.

'Sorry I can't be of any help,' she said brightly.

It was pointless leaving a copy of the picture with her and asking if Ben would mind taking a look when he came home. Ben, wanting to look out for his wife and worried about the significance of the sketch, would no doubt claim he had no idea who the likeness was, either. No. Colin needed to find someone else who might recognise Martin. Maybe Frank, the history teacher Georgina had talked to at the George and Dragon, would be able to confirm the identity of the man in the sketch.

'Thanks for your time,' he said, and climbed back in his car, ready to drive to Norwich.

Georgina read the note and smiled ruefully. She'd only just missed Colin, then. Still. They were going to the cinema this evening, and that would be fun.

The kitchen was spotless, so clearly he'd not only washed up the mug from his coffee, he'd dried it and put it away, too.

She made a fuss of Bert. 'I'm not sure if Tara likes dogs, so I'm leaving you here. But I'll be back soon.' Even though Georgina only knew Tara through Jodie, she did know what bereavement felt like, and maybe a sympathetic ear and some flowers would help brighten her day just a little.

She drove to Great Wenborough, opened the gate to Tara's house and parked in the large driveway next to Tara's car. When she pressed the doorbell, there was no answer. Maybe Tara's mum had picked her up? Georgina didn't want to leave the pale pink tulips by the front door with a note. She tried a second time; again, there was no answer. She climbed into her car and was just about to put it into reverse when a white van pulled up behind her and the horn pipped.

She glanced in her rear-view mirror, recognised Jodie getting out of the van, and wound down her window.

'Morning,' Jodie said. 'What are you doing here?'

'I thought I'd bring Tara some flowers,' Georgina said. 'I know I'm just an acquaintance, through you, but...' She wrinkled her nose.

'... you've been through it, so you know what it feels like,' Jodie finished, and reached into the car to give her a hug. 'That's so kind of you. She'll appreciate that. Hasn't she let you in?'

'I did try the doorbell. Twice,' Georgina said. 'There's no answer. I was just about to go home.'

'She might've gone to her mum's,' Jodie said. 'I'm doing her ironing, so I can let you in and find a vase for your flowers.'

'Where's Harry?' Georgina asked as they stood outside the front door and Jodie rummaged in her bag for the door keys.

'He's helping his Uncle Mike polish the tables and put the beer mats out,' Jodie said cheerfully. Mike, Jodie's brother, was the landlord of the Red Lion in Little Wenborough. Jodie unlocked the door and pushed it open.

'That's weird,' she said. 'Normally the alarm starts beeping and I've got ten seconds to put the code in. Tara always sets the alarm if she's out.' She dragged in a breath. 'Oh, God. You don't think she's done something...?'

'I hope not,' Georgina said grimly.

'Her car's outside, so maybe her mum picked her up,' Jodie said, though there was a note of doubt in her voice. 'It's still weird that the alarm's not set.'

'Jodie – can you smell that?' Georgina asked, wrinkling her nose. There was a coppery scent in the air.

'Yes, I can. What is it?' Jodie asked.

'You need to make a phone call,' Doris said quietly, and Georgina gave a single nod of acknowledgement.

'I think something's wrong,' Georgina said.

'Tara? Tara?' Jodie called.

There was no answer.

Before Georgina could warn her that they needed to be careful where they trod, Jodie marched through the lobby and pushed the door on the right open. Jodie gave a sharp intake of breath before shrieking, 'Oh, my God! Tara!'

'What's happened?' Georgina called, running in after her.

Tara was lying in the middle of the living room. A pool of blood had formed round her head, soaking into the carpet – and the scarlet looked even more horrifying against the whiteness of the carpet. Even though Georgina had expected it, having been warned by Doris, the sight made her shiver.

'We need an ambulance.' Jodie's face was pale. 'I'll find a blanket to keep her warm while you call nine-nine-nine.'

'Wait a second. I'll check her pulse,' Georgina said. 'That's the first thing they'll ask me.'

But, as Georgina had suspected, Tara's skin felt cold, she wasn't breathing, and there wasn't a pulse.

'You won't need a blanket, Jodie,' she said gently.

'No. *No*,' Jodie said, a hand covering her mouth and her eyes wide with shock. 'She can't be dead.'

'It looks as if she fell and hit her head on the corner of the coffee table,' Georgina said.

'Or someone pushed her. Look at the state of the place,' Jodie said, gesturing to the jumble on the floor and the opened drawers of the cabinet in the living-room section. 'Tara's really neat. You'd think a model would just drop stuff everywhere and expect someone else to clear up after her, but she didn't. She was incredibly tidy. She even had a compartment in her pouffe where she put her throw when she'd finished watching telly on the sofa. What if she found a burglar going through her things and they bashed her on the head?' Jodie was spiralling, her words coming out in a tangled heap.

'We can't do anything to help Tara now. But, in case this *is* a crime scene,' Georgina said, 'let's get out of this room and I'll call nine-nine-nine.'

The phone was answered within seconds. 'Which service do you require?'

'Police, please.' Georgina knew the routine, now. 'My name's Georgina Drake.' She gave her phone number and Tara's address. 'I'm with Jodie Fulcher. We've found Tara...'

'...Cox,' Jodie supplied.

'Cox,' Georgina repeated. 'It looks as if she's either fallen and hit her head, or someone hit her over the head, because there's blood seeping into the carpet around her head. She's not breathing or conscious – she's cold and there's no pulse, so I don't think putting me through to the paramedics will help. We need the police, and an ambulance to collect the body.'

The call handler took a few more details. 'I'll get someone despatched,' she promised.

Georgina ended the call and blew out a breath. 'Hopefully they'll send Col—' She stopped abruptly. Colin had been planning to talk to Sally this morning. There was a chance he might still be in the village. 'Hang on,' she said to Jodie, and called Colin's work number.

He answered swiftly, clearly using the hands-free system on his car because it sounded as if he was driving. 'Georgie? What's wrong?'

'I need your help,' she said. 'Where are you?'

'Halfway to Norwich,' he said.

'I'm at Manson's house, with Jodie,' she said. 'Tara's dead. And we're not sure it was an accident.'

TWELVE

Even though Georgina sounded her usual calm, unflappable
self, Colin knew that finding a dead body would be a shock for
anyone. 'I'm on my way,' he said. 'I take it you've already called
nine-nine-nine?'

'Yes,' she said.

'And I also assume you've checked Tara's pulse?'

'She doesn't have a pulse, and she's cold. It looks as if it's a
head injury, because there's blood on the carpet around her
head. Jodie and I are standing in the hallway, by the front door,
and we haven't touched anything other than Tara's forehead
and pulse point,' Georgina confirmed.

'Good. I'll be with you in a few minutes,' he said. He ended
the call, and rang the office. 'Larissa? A shout's probably already
come through from the call centre about an unexpected death,
but I need you and Mo with me to help sort the witness statements.' He paused. 'Remember when we visited Tara Cox to let
her know Manson had died?'

'Yes.'

'She's the victim.' He paused. 'And Georgie is one of our
witnesses.'

'We're on our way,' Larissa said.

'Cheers.' He ended the call. This was a turn he hadn't expected. If Tara's death wasn't an accident or suicide, then who had killed her? And was it linked to Manson's death?

Questions swirled in his head as he drove back to Great Wenborough. He parked on the other side of Tara's car and went to join Georgina and Jodie by the front door. Jodie's face was blotchy from crying, and Georgina had her arms round the younger woman, comforting her. She gave Colin a meaningful look that said, *be gentle with her*.

'Are you both all right?' he asked.

Georgina gave him a brief nod, to let him know he didn't need to worry about her.

'Not really,' Jodie admitted, shivering. 'This the first time I've seen a d...' Her teeth chattered. 'A dead body,' she managed eventually.

Poor kid, Colin thought. She was in bits. No wonder Georgina was being protective. 'Where's the kitchen? I'll make you some hot, sweet tea,' he said.

'You can't.' Jodie shook her head. 'It's in there,' she said, pointing to the door on the right. 'It's one of those huge open-plan living rooms with a kitchen and dining space at one end.'

In other words, the same room as the crime scene.

'OK. You're right – I can't make you tea,' he admitted. 'I'll just have a very quick look through the door, and then I'll come back to talk to you and take some notes.'

The room was enormous, one of the trendy spaces that included a kitchen, a dining room and a living room area. The kitchen was at the front of the house, all white and chrome; the appliances were expensive brands. The dining table was big enough to seat ten, the light wood French-polished and gleaming. There was an enormous skeleton clock on the wall, easily a metre wide, with bronze Roman numerals set into the black rim; it was flanked by large abstract canvases that were clearly expensive originals.

The wall at the end of the room leading to the garden was completely glass. There were a couple of antique walnut display cabinets set against one wall. The drawers were open and the contents spilled out as if someone had been rummaging through them. Had Tara perhaps disturbed a burglar?

Between the white leather sofas was a large coffee table. Tara was lying next to it; the pure white carpet was stained with blood around her head. He could see a stripe of dried blood on the corner of the coffee table, hinting that Tara had hit her head there. The pathology team would note any defence wounds from a struggle, and might be able to give more detail about whether Tara had been hit by a blunt instrument or had hit her head as she'd fallen. With any luck, the forensics team would also find some DNA to lead them to whoever had killed Tara.

But he'd also noticed the diamond bracelet still fastened around Tara's wrist and the engagement ring on her finger. An opportunist thief would've taken them, which suggested to him that the intruder had been looking for something specific, instead. Was it something to do with Manson's death? And had Tara got in the way of the person who was searching for whatever it was?

It was all too vague, right now. But the scene definitely didn't look right. He went back out to the hallway. 'Firstly, Jodie, I'm sorry about the loss of your friend.'

'She's my best friend's big sister.' Jodie's eyes glittered with tears. 'Tara taught me how to do my make-up properly and everything. And now...' She shook her head. 'It doesn't seem possible she's dead. I know she was a model, and everything, but she was just like a normal person. She was *nice*. And I...' She bit her lip. 'Poor Bethany. And Barbara – Tara's mum. How are they going to...?' Her voice broke.

Georgina put her arms round the younger woman, who was openly sobbing now. 'How are they going to cope? You muddle through it, love. Together. Now, Colin needs to know everything we did when we came in, what we saw and heard. He's going take a statement, then get you to read through it to check he's got it right. That's the best thing you can do to help Tara, now.'

'All right.' Jodie's voice was shaky.

'Jodie, I need to interview you and Georgie separately,' Colin said gently. 'Obviously we don't want to use the living room. Are there any other rooms we can use?'

Jodie nodded. 'On this floor, there's the utility room, the cinema room, the snug, Manson's study and the gym.' She gestured to the other side of the hallway.

'That's great. Thank you. Mo and Larissa – my team – will be here shortly, and one of them will talk to Georgie while I have a chat with you. Are you OK with that, or would you prefer Mo or Larissa to take your statement instead?' Colin asked.

Jodie gave him a watery smile. 'The way you were when I first met you, grumpy and – you're not like that, anymore. I don't mind you doing it. And you've got to take my prints, yeah?'

'Fingerprints and shoes,' he said.

'My fingerprints will be all over the house,' she said. 'I clean for Tara.'

'Noted,' he said. 'Actually – thinking about it, I can sort that tea for you, after all.' He phoned Larissa. 'You're not far from us, are you?' At her confirmation, he said, 'Can I ask a big favour, please? I need some hot sweet tea for Jodie, who found the body. I can't make her a cuppa myself because the deceased is in the same room. But if you can pick up some hot drinks for her and Georgie from Little Wenborough Manor farm shop, I'd really appreciate it. Let me know how much I owe you and I'll ping the money over.'

'All right, guv,' Larissa said, amusement in her voice. 'So that's tea with sugar for Jodie, an Americano for you, and what would Georgie like?'

'Cappuccino, please. Plus whatever you and Mo want,' Colin confirmed. 'Thanks.'

As soon as his team arrived and Larissa had dished out the drinks, he took Jodie into the cinema room.

'OK. Talk me through what happened this morning,' he said. 'As much detail as you can, please.'

Jodie nodded. 'I was coming to do Tara's ironing. I was a bit late; Harry was in a grump because it's half term and he wanted to go and play with Robbie at the Feathers, but Robbie's gone to see his other grandparents today.' She rolled her eyes. 'Kids. I left him with my brother. When I got here, Georgie was in her car, about to leave, and she said Tara hadn't answered the door. I have a set of keys, because sometimes the house is empty when I come here to clean or do Tara's ironing, so I let us in. I thought it was a bit strange, because Tara's car was here, but I reasoned maybe her mum had come and picked her up.' She dragged in a breath. 'I unlocked the door, and the alarm wasn't set. That's when I thought something might be wrong, because Tara's always good about putting the alarm on. She's got some really expensive jewellery. I called her name, but she didn't answer. It crossed my mind that she might have done something stupid – I mean, Manson was a horrible bloke and everyone else hated him, but she loved him. And with him dying only last week, Tara still wasn't thinking straight.' She bit her lip. 'Then Georgie said there was a funny smell. I opened the door to the living room and then I saw Tara on the floor, and all the blood round her on the carpet. That's what the smell was.'

'You're doing really well,' he reassured her. 'What happened then?'

'Georgie checked her pulse, but she said Tara was cold. I...' She shook her head. 'And then I noticed the mess everywhere. Tara's not messy. She's really organised and really tidy. I think maybe she found someone going through her stuff and they hit her.'

'It's a theory,' he said. 'Did you notice anything missing?'

'I didn't look, to be honest,' she said. 'But what would a burglar take? Her handbag and her phone? Her jewellery?'

'What about a laptop or a tablet?' Colin suggested. 'Or would she keep them in the study?'

'The study was only for Eliot's stuff. She never went in there,' Jodie said. 'She had a MacBook. Expensive. Her phone was expensive, too. She always had the newest one the day it came out, and would give Bethany or her mum her old one.'

'That's really helpful,' Colin said. 'Thank you. I know it's a tough thing to ask, but could you come with me into the living room and tell me if anything seems missing?'

'You think it might have been a burglar, too?'

'Right now,' Colin said, 'we're still gathering evidence. I can't speculate.'

Jodie looked at him. 'That's fair. All right.'

Clearly trying not to look at the dead body, she looked at the cabinets. 'Everything's still there on the shelves. I don't know about what was in the drawers – you know, just because I'm a cleaner, it doesn't mean I snoop,' she said, sounding nettled.

'I know, and that wasn't why I asked you,' Colin said. 'You're familiar with the house. You know what Tara normally kept where, so you're the one who's most likely to notice if something's out of place.'

Seemingly slightly mollified, Jodie looked him in the eye. 'All right. Apart from the drawers being tipped out, it looks normal. I don't know if they took any jewellery – she's got a safe in her wardrobe but, before you ask me, I don't have a clue what the combination is.'

'We'll check the rest of the house,' Colin said. 'What about her handbag and her phone? Where would she keep them?'

'Her phone would normally be in her pocket or her handbag. She's got lots of handbags – she has a special wardrobe just for them, and another one for her shoes,' Jodie said. 'But the handbag she's using that day is kept on a hook on the back of the door of the cupboard in the hall, until she goes to bed.'

'Cupboard?' He hadn't noticed one.

'It's like her kitchen cabinets. There isn't a door handle. You just push the door and it opens,' Jodie explained. 'I told you, Tara's really tidy. I'll show you.' She took him back to the hall, where Larissa was waiting. 'Um – have I got to wear gloves or something, so I don't accidentally put fingerprints over someone else's?' Jodie asked.

'I swear that you, Cesca, Sybbie and Georgie watch too many TV cop shows,' Colin said, but he smiled to soften the words and gave her a latex glove from his pocket.

She pushed against what he'd assumed was part of the wall, and a door opened. On the back of the door was a hook, and on the back of that hook was a pink leather shoulder bag.

'Oh, now that's clever,' Larissa said admiringly. 'And *tidy*.'

'Do you want me to take the bag off the hook and give it to you?' Jodie asked.

'Yes, please.' He was careful to use a latex glove, too, when he took the bag. Larissa held out an evidence bag, and he slotted the handbag into it. 'I'm going to write up your statement, now, if you want to wait here with Larissa. And then I'll ask you to check it through, make any changes if I've got it wrong, and sign it.'

She nodded. 'All right. But promise me you'll find whoever did this to Tara and lock them up.'

'I'll do my best,' Colin said.

'Then I know they'll be caught,' Jodie said. 'Because Georgie says you're really good.'

He'd remember that, the next time he had one of those days when everything felt as if it was going wrong. 'Thank you. Last thing – do you know if there's any CCTV in the house?'

'There's a smart doorbell on the front door,' she said. 'I think she's got it set up to record if there's any motion. The video goes to her laptop and her phone. But you're not going to get in to either of them without her password.'

'Would her sister know her password?' Colin asked.

'Maybe,' Jodie said. 'I can give you Bethany's number if you want to ask her yourself.'

'If she doesn't know it, the smart doorbell company will be able to give me access to the footage,' he said, 'provided I get a warrant. Which shouldn't be a problem, in this case. Can I have Tara's mum's address, too, please? And I know Bethany's your best friend, but please don't mention what's happened to them until I've had a chance to speak with them.'

Jodie took her phone from her pocket and found the information he needed. 'When you're all done with the forensics,' she said, 'let me know so I can clean up. I don't want her sister and her mum seeing this place in a mess. It'll upset them even more, because they'll know how much Tara would've hated it.'

'I will,' Colin promised. He didn't want to make her feel even worse by explaining that she'd need a specialist to help her with the bloodstains on that white carpet; he'd give her time to come to terms with her loss, first. 'Once you've signed the statement, you can go home, if you like.'

Georgina came back into the hallway with Mo. 'When you've signed your statement, Jodie, do you want me to come back to the Red Lion with you?' she asked.

'No, thanks. It's all right. I'll be OK,' Jodie said. 'This isn't the best day – but I've known worse.' She looked at Colin. 'Tell Barbara I'm sorry, and tell her if I can do anything to help just get Bethany to call me.'

'I will.' He gave Georgina an awkward smile. 'Sorry. I think I'm going to have to cancel the cinema, tonight.'

'It's fine,' she said. 'We'll go another time.'

He was glad that she understood, but he still felt guilty.

By the time Jodie and Georgina had signed their statements – which Colin could see tallied – and left, the forensic team had arrived. Colin gave them Tara's handbag and asked them to look out for her phone and laptop. He arranged for Helen Robinson, the family liaison officer, to meet him at Tara's mother's house; and he asked Larissa to sort out a warrant and get in touch with the smart doorbell company in case Bethany didn't know the passwords.

Once Tara's body had been taken to the pathology lab, he set out for Barbara Cox's house. This was the really hard part of his job. He was relieved that Helen was already parked outside, waiting for him.

'Thanks,' he said. 'I know it's your job, but I appreciate you being here.'

Tara's mum answered the door at the first ring. Colin showed her his warrant card. 'Can we come in, please, Mrs Cox?' he asked.

'What's happened?' she asked. She looked at Helen. 'Hang on. I remember you, from when you came to tell Tara about Eliot.' Her face paled as she made the connection. 'No. Not my girls. Please don't tell me anything's happened to either of my girls.'

'It might be better if you sat down, Mrs Cox,' he said gently.

Barbara took them into the living room – which he noticed was scrupulously neat, like Jodie had said Tara's house was supposed to be, so clearly Tara took after her mother – and gestured to them to sit down.

'I'm so sorry, Mrs Cox,' he said. 'We were called to Tara's house on an emergency callout, and we found her dead.'

'No. Not my Tara!' Barbara stared blankly at him, as if too shocked to take in what he'd said. 'No. She *can't* be dead.'

'I'm so sorry,' he said gently.

'Oh, my God. Please tell me she didn't do it herself,' Barbara said. 'I couldn't bear it if she did. I wanted her to come home with me yesterday, but Tara said she'd cope better in her own house. Oh, God. If I hadn't left her...'

'We're not entirely clear what happened,' Colin said, 'but I'm pretty sure it wasn't self-inflicted.' He was also pretty sure it wasn't accidental, either, but he'd wait until he had the evidence to back that up before he said so. 'Helen will stay with you and do what she can to support you, and make sure you know what's happening with my team.'

'Is she dead because of Manson? Did whoever bumped him off kill her, too?' Barbara asked.

It was a question he'd been asking himself, but he couldn't yet see a connection. 'It's too early to say at the moment,' he said. 'But if you or Bethany know Tara's password to her phone or laptop, that would be helpful.'

'I don't. It's hard enough to keep track of my own passwords. But Bethany will know – for her phone, at least.' Barbara closed her eyes. 'Oh, God. How am I going to tell Bethany?'

'I'll help you,' Helen said.

Grateful to the family liaison officer and her tact, Colin said goodbye and took his leave.

There was nothing more he could do on Tara's case; he had to wait until Sammy came back with the pathology information. Even if the forensic team found Tara's laptop and phone, he'd have to wait until they had a password so they could access the data. He'd have to wait for the forensic team to finish going over the crime scene before he could take a proper look there, too. And Manson's case was still stuck.

But maybe he could progress Ryan Everett's case.

He called the gallery in Holt; to his relief, Niamh Webster was free to see him in half an hour.

'I'm sorry we haven't been able to progress your uncle's case before now,' he said when he met her at the gallery. 'Thank you for sending the sketches through, via Georgina. We're trying to identify the subject now.'

'I'm glad,' she said. 'But isn't this something you could've told me on the phone?'

'That part of it, yes,' Colin agreed. 'I know Georgina talked to you a little bit about it earlier, but I wanted to let you know in person that we've found a skeleton in Summerstrand and there's a possibility that he might be Ryan. We haven't identified him formally, though we know from the finds liaison officer that the skeleton is male, he was in his early twenties when he died, and the clothes he was wearing date to the 1960s.'

Niamh paled. 'Then it really *could* be Ryan. Do you know what happened to him?'

'Not completely,' Colin said. 'And there's also the possibility that the remains aren't Ryan's.'

'But it probably is him. I mean, what are the chances of there being two men in their twenties who went missing in a little place like Summerstrand in 1965?' Niamh asked.

'We think the body was moved from where he died to the burial site, so he could have been from practically anywhere in Norfolk,' Colin said. 'But I wondered if you'd be willing to give me a DNA sample. We can get it tested against the skeleton to see if you're related.'

'And that would confirm if it's Ryan?' Niamh looked thoughtful. 'Obviously I'd be happy to do that, but would you get a stronger result if you tested my mum?'

'Because she's his sibling, you mean? Possibly,' Colin said.

'Only, I'd prefer not to get her hopes up,' Niamh said. 'Is there another way you could do the test?'

'It's illegal for me to get a biological sample for DNA testing without informed consent,' Colin said gently. 'You need to tell her the truth; or give me the sample yourself.'

Niamh sighed. 'All right. I'll talk to her. Let me know what we need to do, where and when.'

'I will.' He smiled at her. 'I'm not trying to be unhelpful or obstructive, and I apologise if it came across that way.'

'I guess.' Niamh smiled wryly back at him. 'In some ways, sad as it will be, I hope it *is* Ryan. At least it will give Mum closure, and she'll stop wondering if she could've said or done something to make a difference.'

Colin's next stop was to see Frank Burton in Summerstrand. The former history teacher was dapper and sharp as a tack, just as Georgina had described him, and as soon as Colin showed Frank the sketch the older man nodded. 'Yes, I know him. That's Martin Armitage. He was a couple of years below me at school. He was really good at football – the head at school thought Martin stood a good chance of being a professional player.' He smiled sadly. 'Of course, Martin's dad was having none of it. He thought it was the boy's duty to be the lighthouse keeper. And Dennis Armitage was one of those men who thought his word should be the law for his family.'

'So Martin became the lighthouse keeper?' Colin asked.

'No. He left home and went to London. I heard he'd had the chance of a trial at Arsenal.' Frank shook his head. 'I've no idea what happened to him. Dennis wouldn't have his name spoken, and I assume he cut Martin off from his mum and his sister, too. I used to read the sports pages on a Sunday and always wondered if Martin's name would come up, but it never did, so I suppose the Arsenal thing didn't work out.' He frowned. 'That lovely young photographer asked me if I could remember anyone going missing, and I said I didn't. I mean, Martin

Armitage wasn't *missing*. Someone saw him getting the bus to Norwich. He just never came back – and, if Dennis Armitage had been my dad, I wouldn't have come back, either.'

'Thank you,' Colin said. 'That's really helpful.'

Though Sally – Martin's sister – had said she didn't recognise him.

What was she trying to hide?

THIRTEEN

'Ryan remembers sketching,' Doris said. 'Martin's family had a border collie called Cracker. Ryan sketched the dog on the beach – charcoal, he said. And he did some pen-and-ink sketches of Martin.'

'They're the ones Niamh showed me,' Georgina said.

'Martin wanted to be a professional footballer,' Doris continued. 'He'd been spotted, playing for a local team, and he had the chance to join Arsenal – but his dad wouldn't give permission.'

'And they had a huge row about it. Martin left home.' Georgina paused. 'I wonder if that row was the same night that Ryan died? Maybe Martin went to seek comfort from Ryan, and Ryan suggested they left together. But then Sally's dad caught them together and killed Ryan to stop Martin leaving.'

'That's so sad,' Doris said.

'Colin's going to try and get DNA testing done, so at least Ryan's family will get closure and be able to bury him properly,' Georgina said. 'Though this other case is turning really nasty. Well – you know about Tara.'

'First Manson was killed, and then Tara. Is there a connection, apart from them living together?' Doris asked.

'I have no idea. There wasn't much in the room where we found Manson in the lighthouse cottage – just a table and chair. It looked like a temporary office more than anything else,' Georgina said. 'Tara's house looked as if someone had been rummaging through the cabinets to find something. It could've been a burglar, and she came downstairs at the wrong time, they pushed her and she hit her head. I don't know. The pathologist's report will tell Colin more.' She sighed. 'Right now, there's nothing we can do. We're stuck.'

'You need coffee,' Doris said. 'And some music.'

'George?' Georgina suggested.

'Our song,' Doris said.

The song that had been top of the charts on the day Georgina had been born – and the day Doris had died.

'Our song,' Georgina echoed, and switched into her streaming app to play 'My Sweet Lord'.

Colin called Alexsy Nowak, who was in charge of the forensics team, on his way back to the station. 'How's it going?' he asked.

'Slowly,' Alexsy said. 'But I can tell you that the smart doorbell wasn't working. The wire to the plug had been disconnected. Until we see the footage, we won't know when it was last connected.'

'Jodie said Tara was meticulous about setting the house alarm,' Colin said. 'It seems odd she'd disconnect the doorbell. Though I guess she'll have been distracted this week, with losing her partner.' He frowned. 'If she hadn't locked the front door, someone could've walked into the house without her knowing. Or maybe they entered the house by a different route.'

'There's no sign of forced entry through any door or window,' Alexsy said.

'Jodie said the footage went to Tara's phone and her laptop. Have you found either of them, yet?'

'Her phone was in her handbag. I'll bring that back to the station when we're done here,' Alexsy said. 'Her purse, her credit cards and her bank cards were all in her handbag, too. We haven't found the laptop yet. We had a quick look through the rest of the house, but the only room in a mess was the living room.'

'It doesn't sound like a burglary,' Colin said. 'We both know casual thieves go for the things they can grab quickly and sell easily. They check the master bedroom first, for cash in the sock drawer and jewellery in the bedside cabinet.'

'She was still wearing her watch, a diamond bracelet and a huge diamond engagement ring, too,' Alexsy said. 'A burglar would've taken those – even if they'd been panicking that they'd pushed her and accidentally killed her. That makes me think whoever ransacked the living room was looking for something in particular, and wasn't an opportunist thief.'

Exactly what Colin had thought, too. 'Hopefully her sister knows the passcode to the phone; and in the meantime Larissa's organising a warrant to get access to the footage from the smart doorbell company,' Colin said. 'Thanks for your help, Alexsy.'

'We'll catch up later and see what the footage shows,' Alexsy said.

Sammy called Colin later that afternoon when he was at the station. 'I managed to fit in the post-mortem for you, but I'm afraid there's nothing useful,' she said. 'Your victim was healthy, definitely ate her five a day that night with a chicken stir-fry, and had drunk half a glass of rosé wine. It looks to me as if someone caught her by surprise, pushed her to the ground, and she knocked her head on the corner of the coffee table. Time of death around ten p.m., I'd say.'

'No petechiae or anything that puts up a red flag?' he asked.

'No. I did wonder if there was some kind of struggle. There's a little bruising on her wrists, as if someone had caught hold of her and was trying to restrain her, but there aren't any defence wounds. There's nothing under her nails, and the only other significant bruises are on her head where it struck the table. Alexsy's team sent me all the photographs of the body in situ, and it all looks pretty clear-cut,' Sammy said.

'Can I tell the family it was quick and she didn't suffer?'

'That would be kind,' Sammy said. 'And, from the angle of the wound, I'd say someone pushed her, rather than her tripping and falling.'

'Right. Thanks, Sammy.'

'I'll send my official report over when I've finished writing it up,' she said.

'Any pointers on the person who pushed her? Tall, short?' he asked.

'With Tara being tall, it was likely that the perp was, too,' she said. 'Strong enough to push her down – even if they'd had a light altercation first – with one shove, so most likely male. But that's not really narrowing it down for you.'

'No.' Colin finished making notes. 'But it's a start. Thanks.'

He'd just finished scribbling down a list of questions when an email came in: the smart doorbell company was able to give his team access to the footage. He'd checked to see if Bethany had known the passcode to Tara's phone, but it seemed that Tara had used fingerprint recognition to open her phone and Bethany hadn't been able to remember the passcode.

'Would you mind checking the footage, Larissa?' he asked.

'Sure,' she said.

Half an hour later, she caught his attention. 'Guv, you're not going to like this. There's not a lot of footage; it seems the video's only captured by the doorbell camera when something moves.'

'That's a good thing, surely?' he asked. 'It means we're not wasting hours checking when all that's moving is a sparrow in the front garden – unless that's what you're going to tell me.'

Larissa shook her head. 'There's a person, all right. The last person the doorbell recorded going into the house. And it's a clear shot.'

He went round to her desk, and she played the footage for him.

He recognised the person instantly and sighed inwardly. 'Jodie.'

'I said you wouldn't like it,' Larissa said.

Colin frowned. 'OK, so she's the last person on the footage, but I don't think she's the murderer. What's her motive? She was friends with Tara as well as cleaning for her, and she's best friends with Tara's younger sister.'

'What if they fell out?' Larissa asked.

He considered it. 'That's possible. And you're right to remind me that I need to keep an open mind – I shouldn't discount Jodie just because I know her,' Colin said. 'What's the timestamp on the footage?'

'Yesterday morning. Nine o'clock.'

'Sammy estimated the time of death at ten p.m. – and this footage is thirteen hours earlier. That's a big gap,' Colin said. 'Alexsy thinks the doorbell was disconnected before Tara died. We don't see Jodie coming out after she's finished cleaning, so the disconnection probably happened during her shift. We don't know exactly when Jodie left, or if Tara had any other visitors before she died.'

'You need to interview Jodie,' Larissa said.

He glanced at his watch. 'Right now, she's probably giving her son his dinner. I'll call her.'

To his relief, Jodie answered within a couple of rings. 'Jodie, I need a quick chat with you about Tara. Can I come round now, please?' he asked.

'What's happened? Can't we do this on the phone, or a video call?'

'I'd rather talk face to face,' he said. 'Can you get someone to look after Harry?'

'Not at this short notice,' she said. 'Mike'll be busy at work, my mum isn't very well, I can hardly ask Bethany to come and babysit Harry when she's just lost her sister, and anyway...' She sighed.

'How about,' he said, 'I ask Georgie if you can pop over to hers?'

'That's asking a lot,' she said.

But Georgina had a lot of kindness and common sense. He had a feeling that Jodie would take the doorbell business badly, and he could really do with Georgina's help. 'Let me call her,' he said.

As he'd hoped, as soon as he explained his dilemma Georgina offered to help. Half an hour later, he was sitting in her living room with Jodie and a mug of tea; Georgina was with Harry in the kitchen, helping him make a batch of shortbread biscuits while Bert looked on hopefully.

'I was the last person on her doorbell footage?' Jodie shook her head. 'I don't understand. I can't be. I mean, yes. I was at the house yesterday morning. I was cleaning. And I do the ironing on Tuesdays.'

'Can you take me through your movements yesterday?' he asked. 'Just at Tara's.'

'I vacuumed the house, dusted, and cleaned all the bathrooms. Harry stayed with Mike because' – she rolled her eyes – 'well, I can just imagine him spilling a glass of blackcurrant over that white carpet, and I didn't want to risk it. Tara was a bit upset, so I stayed with her a bit to have a cup of coffee, but I left by half eleven because I knew Mike was going to be busy at the pub and I needed to pick Harry up. You can ask Mike what time I turned up.'

'I will,' Colin said. She definitely needed her alibi confirmed.

She frowned. 'You must've seen *someone* on the footage after me. A delivery driver, or the postie. Or even Tara herself, if she went out to her mum's and came back.'

'Here's the thing,' Colin said. 'We only have footage of you going into the house, and not leaving it. The doorbell was disconnected. So that means it must have happened after you went into the house and before you left it.'

'Disconnected?' She stared at him in utter incomprehension. 'Am I being thick? Because I don't get how her doorbell could be disconnected.'

'The wire was pulled out of the plug.'

'But – that's crazy! Why would Tara disconnect her doorbell?' Her forehead wrinkled as she thought about it. 'I don't have a posh doorbell, but if something goes wrong surely it sends a message to your phone, or something? Or the app would show there's a problem?'

'Maybe she didn't pick up the notification,' Colin said.

'Because she was upset about Manson and she wasn't concentrating on anything?' She shook her head. 'You don't know Tara. She's – she *was*,' she corrected herself, 'careful about things.'

'People make mistakes,' he said gently. 'I'm not accusing you, but just asking... is there the tiniest, remotest chance you might have accidentally knocked the plug and disconnected the wire when you were doing the vacuuming?'

She shook her head. 'I would've noticed when I took the pl—' Then her face lost all colour. 'Oh, my God. I'd just finished the vacuuming and pulled the plug out, ready to wind the cord back and put it away, when Tara came into the hall. She was crying. I gave her a hug, made her a cup of coffee and sat talking to her – you know, like you do if your mate's upset. Then I realised I was going to be late picking Harry up. She said she'd put the vacuum cleaner away for me. It never occurred to me to look at the plug. Maybe I *did* knock the wire, and I didn't notice because she was upset and I was focusing on her.' Colin saw the exact moment the penny dropped, because Jodie's face crumpled. 'Oh, God. If her doorbell wasn't working – that means whoever killed her could've walked into the house without leaving a trace.' She rubbed the tears from her face. 'Because I didn't check, she got killed.'

'You didn't kill her,' Colin said.

'But it was my fault the doorbell stopped working,' Jodie said.

'You might not have been the one who knocked the wire,' he said gently.

'But you just said I was the last one seen on the CCTV, instead of whoever killed her.' She put her mug of tea down on the coffee table. 'I didn't kill her, Colin. She was my *friend* as well as my client. I've known her ever since her little sister became my best mate at toddler group. That's, like, as long as I can remember.' Shaking, she wrapped her arms tightly round herself. 'I don't understand why her phone didn't tell her the doorbell wasn't working. And she'd been careful about the doorbell, especially because—' She stopped abruptly.

'Especially because what?' Colin asked.

'It's not my place to tell,' she said.

'Whatever it is,' Colin said, 'it might have a bearing on the case. And you're telling me in my official capacity, not gossiping.'

Jodie looked uncomfortable. 'She'd been getting letters.'

'What sort of letters?' Colin asked.

'Anonymous ones.'

An old-fashioned poison pen letter? he wondered. 'Anonymous, how?'

Jodie rolled her eyes. 'They weren't signed.'

He couldn't help smiling. 'I guessed that. I meant were they printed off a computer, written by hand, or letters cut out and pasted to make words?'

'They only do that last one in Agatha Christie,' Jodie said confidently. 'They were printed off a computer. They said Manson was cheating on her.'

'Was he cheating on her?' Colin asked.

'I don't know. Bethany said Tara confronted him about it, and he said it wasn't true. He reckoned it was Vicky, trying to stir trouble and come between them.' She shook her head. 'I can't see that, myself. Vicky's not a troublemaker. Anyway, it's not like she wanted him back, so what would be the point of splitting them up?'

All the same, Colin made a mental note to have a word with Vicky.

'Did Tara keep any of the letters?' he asked.

'I've got no idea,' Jodie said. 'Bethany told her to throw them away and just ignore them. Maybe she did.'

'It's a pity I didn't know about this earlier. I could've asked the forensic team to look out for them during their search.'

'Sorry,' Jodie said. 'The last one was a couple of weeks back. I didn't think about them.'

Colin raised an eyebrow.

'Well, they didn't *threaten* her,' Jodie said. 'They just upset her. It's not very nice if you move in with someone and then someone else tells you they're cheating on you, and you start wondering if you've made a big mistake.'

'When did she first get the letters?' Colin asked.

Jodie thought about it, drumming her fingers on the back of one hand. 'They started a few weeks ago. I think that's why she got the doorbell, to try and get video footage of whoever was putting the notes through the door so she could see who they were and confront them.'

'OK,' Colin said. 'Thanks for your help, Jodie. I know this can't have been easy.'

'I didn't kill her,' Jodie said, 'but I'll never forgive myself for not doing things properly yesterday. If I hadn't been in a rush and I'd put the vacuum cleaner away myself, I would've noticed the wire had been pulled out.'

'Your friend was upset. Of course you were going to comfort her – the vacuum cleaner could be sorted later,' Colin said. 'I'd think less of you if you'd tidied up first.'

She gave him a watery smile. 'I think that's supposed to be a compliment.'

'You care. And that's important,' Colin said. 'Also, Tara might've been the one who accidentally knocked the wire out. And you couldn't possibly have known that someone would enter the house and hurt her.'

'I suppose,' she said.

'Go and chat to Georgie and Harry and eat shortbread while I write up my notes,' he said gently.

'All right,' she said and left him to write everything up.

FOURTEEN

After Jodie had checked and signed her statement, Colin sampled one of the shortbread biscuits Harry had baked.

'This is really scrumptious,' he said after the first taste. 'Just as good as Georgina makes.'

'Georgie helped me with the oven,' Harry said. 'But I did all the mixing and rolling out and cutting.' He beamed at Colin.

Cathy had done this sort of thing when she'd been eight years old, he thought with a pang. And he'd missed out on it because he'd spent too much of his focus on work; by the time he'd come home each day, she'd been in bed and Marianne had had to mask the disappointment in her eyes when she'd given Colin whatever Cathy had put so much time and love into making for him. And leaving a little thank-you note before you left early for work really wasn't the same as praising a child to their face. Guilt prickled at the back of his neck. 'I'd vote them ten out of ten, Harry,' he said. Then he turned to Georgina. 'Sorry, Georgina. I need to go and see couple of people.'

'It's your job,' she said.

She wasn't judging him, and he knew she really did understand, but he still felt guilty.

He called Helen Robinson, the family liaison officer, to see if Bethany was at home with her mother; at her confirmation, he headed to the Coxes' house.

'How are you doing?' he asked.

Barbara Cox's eyes were reddened and puffy, and her daughter Bethany looked as if she'd been crying for most of the day, too. 'I still can't take it in,' she said. 'Who would've wanted to hurt my Tara? She wasn't stuck-up and she remembered where she came from. Everyone got on with her.'

'I'm doing my best to find out,' he said gently. 'Bethany, can I have a private word, please?'

'You can say whatever you like in front of me,' Barbara said.

He wasn't sure whether Barbara knew about the anonymous letters, and the last thing he wanted to do was to make things more painful for her. 'Sorry if this sounds harsh, but it's a line of investigation,' he said, 'so I'm afraid I can't, at the moment.'

'All right,' Bethany said. 'Let's go in the kitchen. Do you want a cup of tea?'

'That's kind,' Colin said, 'but I'm fine.'

A handsome ginger cat leapt up on Bethany's shoulder as they sat down, and she stroked it absently.

'Lovely cat,' Colin said.

'Yes. Tara really missed him when she moved out,' Bethany said. 'She was going to get a kitten from the cat rescue place. She was going to get the bed and the litter tray and what have you from their shop, and she'd bought a squeaky mouse and one of those feathery things on a string you dangle for a kitten to bat about. And she'd got a pet camera so she could keep an eye on the kitten when she wasn't there.'

A kitten she'd never give a home to, now. Clearly Bethany thought that, too, because she blinked away tears.

'I wanted a chat about the letters Tara had been receiving,'

Colin said quietly. 'I asked to see you on your own because I wasn't sure if your mum knew about them.'

'She doesn't.' Bethany grimaced. 'Thank you for not saying anything in front of her.'

'I'm not in this job to trample over people's feelings,' he said. 'I'm sorry for your loss. And I'm sorry to ask, but can you tell me what you know about the letters?'

'They started a few weeks ago,' Bethany said. 'The first one said that Eliot was cheating on her.'

'How did Tara react?' Colin asked.

'She told him about it when he got home from work that night,' Bethany said. 'He read the letter, said it wasn't true, and got really angry about it. He ripped the letter up and threw it in the bin.' She blew out a breath. 'The next letter came after Tara had been away on a shoot. It said he'd been kissing another woman in his car. No names, no real details she could pin down, but it upset her.'

'Of course it would,' Colin said. 'Did she ask Eliot about that one, too?'

'Yes. He went mad again and said it was obviously Vicky sending the letters. She's his ex, and she teaches at the primary school,' Bethany said. 'He reckoned she was stirring things, because she couldn't bear to see him happy. She had a grudge against him because of the divorce – though the divorce was her fault, and the judge could see that, so that's why she got nothing when he took her to court.'

'What did Tara think about his theory?'

'She didn't know what to think, really. I mean, the divorce and all that happened well before Vicky moved here.' She bit her lip. 'Vicky's friends with Jodie, because their sons are best mates. Jodie says she's really nice. And I've known Jodie since our mums took us to toddler group. She's my best friend. She's got her head screwed on right and she's good judge of character.'

Bethany rolled her eyes. 'Well, apart from Harry's dad, but I guess we all make mistakes.'

'Did you get on with Manson?' Colin asked.

Bethany wrinkled her nose. 'Mum and I didn't like him very much. There's something...' She paused, as if thinking of the right word. 'Something *sly* about him. And we couldn't see what Tara saw in him. I mean, she's – *was*,' she corrected with a wobble, 'a model. She could've snapped her fingers and gone out with any bloke she chose. She's not super-famous like Gigi and Bella Hadid, or anything, but she's doing OK. She should've moved to London and met someone who deserved her, not stayed here in Norfolk and got engaged to a bloke who's nearly old enough to be her dad – and, well, even his gran wouldn't say Manson was anywhere near good-looking. Tara really loved him, though.'

Or maybe she wanted the security, Colin thought. A life in the public eye was a precarious one, and it was all too easy to fall from grace. Someone who was the nation's darling one moment could be vilified the next. 'Did she get many of these anonymous letters?'

'I'm not sure, but they usually arrived just after she'd been away for work,' Bethany said. 'And they always upset her. I told her to throw them away without opening them. If Manson really was cheating on her, he'd slip up soon enough and she'd find out the truth. If he wasn't and someone was just being vile, using her to get at him, then she'd be better off not reading them in the first place, so they didn't mess with her head. But I suppose it's like when newspapers print something about you, or there's something on social media – you can't stop yourself wanting to know what they say.'

'Did you see any of the letters yourself?' Colin asked.

She nodded. 'A couple.'

'Can you describe them for me?'

'They were printed off a computer,' Bethany said. 'No fancy stuff – just normal, like you'd get with any letter.'

'A4 paper?' Colin checked.

She nodded. 'Plain white.'

The kind of paper that could be bought in any supermarket or office supplier, he thought. 'On its own, or in an envelope?'

'Folded in half, and put in a brown envelope,' she said.

Again, the kind of envelope that was readily available. Nothing to help narrow it down. Not like the days when paper and envelopes were watermarked, and typed documents could help determine the make and model of typewriter that had produced them, perhaps down to an individual machine if any of the keys left a particular mark or was slightly out of line.

'Any postmark or stamp?' he asked.

Bethany shook her head. 'They were always delivered by hand. That's why she got the doorbell, to see if she could find out who was sending them. Though nothing ever showed.' She paused. 'I never said it to her, because I didn't want to fall out with her, but I wondered if Manson was sending them. I mean, if he dropped the letter on the doormat from the inside, that'd explain why she never saw anyone on the doorbell camera.'

'Why would he send her anonymous letters accusing himself of cheating on her?' Colin asked.

'He didn't like her being away. If she thought he was cheating on her, then she'd be jealous and stay here so he didn't get the chance to cheat,' Bethany said.

'That's a risky strategy,' Colin said. 'She might've left him, instead.'

'He had a funny way of looking at things, sometimes,' Bethany said. 'I wish she *had* left him. Because maybe then she wouldn't be dead.'

There wasn't much he could say to that. 'Thank you for your help,' he said.

'If it helps you find who killed my sister,' she said, 'you ask me any questions you like. Even if it's six o'clock in the morning, and Jodie'll tell you I'm really not a morning person.'

He gave her a wry smile. 'Thank you. I'll leave you in peace, now. But I promise we're doing everything we can.'

Bethany nodded. 'Jodie says you're all right. Even if you did think she might be a murderer, at one point.'

It was weirdly heartening to find that the more his life seemed to be merging with Georgina's, the more people seemed to be accepting him. 'I'm glad,' he said.

His next stop was Vicky.

'Can we have a chat in private, please?' he asked.

'What's it about?' Vicky asked.

'Eliot Manson,' Colin said. 'I know it's a difficult subject for you, and I'm sorry to bring up any bad feelings. But I need some information to help with the case.'

'I'm not sure I'll be of much help. As I told you before, I've avoided him as much as I can for years,' Vicky said.

'Noted,' Colin said. 'Do you know Tara Cox?'

'Yes,' Vicky said.

'Would you mind explaining how you know her?'

'Well, obviously I know she's engaged to Eliot. But I knew her before she met him. Tara's younger sister Bethany is Jodie Fulcher's best friend, and Jodie's son Harry is my son Robbie's best friend,' Vicky said. 'I taught Harry last year at Wenborough Primary, too, so I know Jodie both as a friend and as a parent.'

'How well do you know Bethany Cox?'

'About as well as I know Tara, really. The two villages aren't that big. Most people know everyone else around here,' Vicky said. She frowned. 'What's this about? Has something happened to Tara?'

'She received some anonymous letters,' Colin said. 'We're investigating who sent them.'

'Well, it wasn't me,' Vicky said, her frown deepening. 'What do I have to do with this?'

'Confidentially, Manson suggested maybe you wrote the letters, to cause trouble between himself and Tara.'

Vicky scoffed. 'That sounds more like *he* was the one trying to cause trouble for *me*! No. I haven't written any letters to Tara, anonymous or otherwise.'

'Have you received any anonymous letters yourself?' Colin asked.

She shook her head. 'What are these letters about? And what – well, apart from Eliot lying – makes her think I sent them?'

'The letters suggested that he was cheating on her. He thought you were trying to come between them.'

Vicky blew out a breath. 'I have no idea whether he was cheating on her or not. He cheated on me, so I wouldn't be surprised if he cheated on her as well. I told you how he lied about it in our divorce – and what happened to Dan.' She sighed. 'I tried to stay out of his way; I just wanted him to leave me alone. I didn't wish Tara any ill, and I didn't send her any poison-pen letters. If anything, I would've advised her not to get engaged to him or move in with him, and to run as far as she could in the other direction, because he's a bastard and he wouldn't make her happy in the long term.'

'Thank you for your frankness,' Colin said. 'And again, I'm sorry for bringing up bad memories.'

'It's not your fault. You have to do your job,' Vicky said, looking resigned and unbearably sad.

'All right. You can have ten minutes of playing a game on my phone,' Jodie said, giving her phone to Harry, who whooped. She waited the few seconds it took him to sit at the other end of Georgina's kitchen table and become absorbed in the game, then looked at Georgina. 'Can I talk to you about something?'

'Of course you can.' Georgina pushed the plate of short-bread towards her.

Jodie smiled her thanks and took one. 'Tara was getting anonymous letters,' she said. 'Bethany told me.'

'Is that what Colin wanted to talk to you about?' Georgina asked.

'It was about her doorbell, and...' Jodie closed her eyes. 'I'm telling this in the wrong order. But it makes sense to tell you about the letters first.'

'Go on,' Georgina encouraged.

'The letters said Manson was having an affair, and it really upset her. She asked him if it was true, and he said it wasn't. He reckoned it was Vicky sending the letters, trying to make trouble between him and Tara, but I can't see that. I mean... Yes, he was Vicky's ex, but she didn't want him back. She hated him. And there was no reason for her to be nasty to Tara.' She shook herself. 'Anyway, that's why Tara bought one of those posh doorbells – the sort that films people who come to your front door. She thought it might show her who was really sending the letters and she could get them to stop.'

Georgina wasn't quite sure where this was heading, but she nodded and kept listening.

'Monday, I did the vacuuming for her. And I must've somehow knocked the wire and disconnected the doorbell.' She dragged in a breath. 'The thing is, when I was just about finishing up, Tara came through and she was crying. I couldn't leave her upset like that, could I? I gave her a hug and made her a coffee and let her talk for a bit. And then I had to pick Harry up from Mike, and I was running late, and...' She wrinkled her nose. 'You know how it is. Colin says Tara might have knocked the wire out, not me. But if I was the one who did it, and she didn't notice – well, it feels like it's my fault she died. If the doorbell had been working, whoever killed her wouldn't have been able to walk in through the front door without her knowing.'

'If someone was that determined to get into the house,' Georgina said gently, 'a smart doorbell or CCTV wouldn't have stopped them. They might've got into the house a different way, or they might've been able to disable the camera. Don't blame yourself.'

'Colin said something like that. But it still feels horrible,' Jodie said.

'It wasn't your fault,' Georgina said. 'Try to put that out of your head. Even if the doorbell had been working properly, whoever killed her might've worn some sort of disguise or somehow avoided their face being recorded.' She paused. 'Did Tara keep any of the letters?'

'I don't think so. Bethany told her to throw them away and ignore them.'

'That's probably easier said than done,' Georgina said.

'It was really funny how they always used to come just after she'd been away on a shoot or something,' Jodie said.

'So if Manson *was* having an affair, that's when he'd have the opportunity to cheat on her?' Georgina asked.

'I guess. And the weird thing was that, even though she'd got that doorbell, she never caught any footage of who shoved it through the letter box. Unless...' Jodie shook her head. 'No. Bethany's probably being paranoid.'

'What?'

'She thought maybe he didn't like Tara going away and he was the one writing the letters?'

'Why would he do that?'

'To make her jealous,' Jodie said. 'So then she'd stay at home instead of going away to work.'

'Well, it's a theory,' Georgina said.

'Probably a stupid one.' Jodie rolled her eyes. 'I'm kind of glad I didn't tell Colin.'

'I'll mention it to him, if you like,' Georgina said.

'Isn't that wasting police time?'

Georgina smiled. 'No. That's suggesting a theory and giving him something to think about. Don't worry.'

'Thanks.' Jodie bit her lip. 'It's so weird, thinking I'll never see her again.' She winced. 'Sorry. I didn't mean to... well, you know.'

'I do,' Georgina said gently. 'And that's the hard thing to come to terms with. There'll be things that'll make you think, oh, I must text her or ring her and tell her, and then you remember you can't do that anymore, and it feels a bit like you've lost them all over again. It hurts. But eventually you get better at handling it and it doesn't feel quite so raw all the time.'

'Thanks, Georgie.' Jodie hugged her. 'I'd better get Harry home to bed. If the police have finished with Tara's house, I'll go and tidy it up tomorrow – so her mum and Bethany don't have to face doing that, too,' she said.

'Let me know when you do, and I'll come and help you,' Georgina offered.

Jodie shook her head. 'I can't ask you to do that.'

'You're not asking. I'm offering. You're my friend, you know – I don't think of you just as the cleaner who sorts out the barn for me,' Georgina reminded her.

'That means a lot,' Jodie said. 'You're my friend, too. Kind of like my favourite auntie, except I don't have to mind my manners in front of you.'

Jodie was the same age as Bea, Georgina's daughter; and Georgina was touched to know that the younger woman thought of her as like an aunt, someone close she could trust. She smiled. 'Absolutely. Go and get some sleep. And let me know when you want a hand with that cleaning.'

When Jodie had gone, Georgina curled up on the sofa with a book, Bert snuggling beside her and resting his head on her knees.

'Anonymous letters, stirring up trouble,' Doris said. 'That's nasty. Though, from the sound of it, Eliot Manson wasn't a very nice guy. I wonder why Tara stuck with him?'

'Who knows?' Georgina asked. 'And we also don't know if the letters were connected with her death.'

'Or if there's a connection between Tara's death and Manson's,' Doris said. 'Obviously they lived in the same house. Was he hiding something, and someone was trying to find it and Tara was simply unlucky because she got in the way?'

'I don't know,' Georgina said. 'It did look a bit like a burglary, the kind where the thief rummages through all your things and grabs whatever's small, easy to transport and easy to sell. But she was still wearing her watch, her engagement ring and a diamond bracelet when we found her.'

'Wouldn't a burglar take that sort of thing?' Doris asked. 'They fit what you describe as their targets.'

'That's what bothers me. Something doesn't quite add up,' Georgina said. 'What's the connection between the lighthouse and Tara?'

'Manson,' Doris said dryly. 'So what was he up to that got him – and Tara – killed?'

'Unless the forensic team found something, Colin's going to have a hard time working that out,' Georgina said. 'Tara was away on a shoot on Thursday, when Manson was at the lighthouse. I wonder why he was there, though, rather than at home?'

'Jodie told you Bethany's theory that he was the one who wrote the letters. But supposing he really *was* having an affair? When she was away, it would give him the opportunity to see his lover,' Doris said. 'Obviously he wouldn't take her to his house, because someone in the village was likely to spot them and tell Tara. Was he meeting his lover at the lighthouse?'

'The windows were boarded up and the place had been mostly stripped,' Georgina said. 'I mean, you were there when

Bert dug up that bone. You saw it yourself: it's not the kind of place you'd take someone for a romantic tryst. There was just a table and chair. It felt more like a temporary site office.'

'Unless he'd only taken everything out downstairs. What about upstairs?' Doris asked.

'I don't know,' Georgina said.'

'Talk to Colin,' Doris advised. 'And I guess we have to wait for the DNA tests to come back before we can do anything else for Ryan?'

'I think so,' Georgina said. 'But tell him that his sister paints gorgeous oils and acrylics, his niece Niamh sculpts amazing bronzes of dogs, and her daughter Faye makes the most beautiful bowls with a shimmery glaze. The artistic gene in the family is still going strong.'

'And you bought a print of his aunt's painting,' Doris said. 'Hmm... you said bronze dogs. Did you buy a springer?'

'Niamh has sculpted one and it was really like Bert. I was really tempted,' Georgina admitted. 'Sybbie bought two Labradors.'

Doris chuckled. 'It sounds to me as if that gallery's going to be as dangerous for your bank balance as the antique shop is for Sybbie's!'

FIFTEEN

When Colin came back to Rookery Farm later that evening, Georgina made him a mug of camomile tea and stirred in a spoonful of honey. 'How did the interviews go?'

'All right, but I'm not much further forward,' he said. 'Did Jodie talk to you?'

She nodded. 'I hope I've helped her see that she wasn't to blame for Tara's death. If someone's determined to get into a house, a smart doorbell isn't going to stop them.'

'Agreed,' he said tiredly, and took a sip of the camomile tea. It didn't help.

Georgina reached over to squeeze his hand. 'What can I do?' she asked.

It amazed him that she could tell something was wrong without him having to say a word. 'Just a bit of a headache. I've taken some paracetamol. It'll go,' he said, but clearly he looked as strained as he felt.

'One of my friends taught me how to massage away a headache, once,' she said. 'Why don't I try that? Come into the living room.'

She led him to the sofa; he lay with his head on Georgina's lap and Bert curled up on his feet. Her gentle fingers stroked away the tight band of his headache.

'Thank you. That's better,' he murmured, his eyes still closed.

'Good,' she said softly.

'Sorry. I'm mumbling at you,' he said, aware that her hearing wasn't great, even with the hearing aids. He was pretty sure that she still lip-read a lot of conversations.

'It's OK. There's just you, me and Bert, with no background noise, so I'm picking you up clearly,' she said. 'This case is really getting to you, isn't it?'

Because it was *stuck*. And he felt a million miles away from finding the clue that would crack it wide open. There were so many unanswered questions. Why had Manson been at the lighthouse on Thursday night? Who had spiked his whisky? Why had he been so careless about the paraffin heater? Who had ransacked his house, and what had they been looking for? Was there a connection to the anonymous letters Tara had received? Had her death been an accident or premeditated? Was there a connection with the skeleton they'd uncovered next to the lighthouse – and, if so, what?

'I'm fine,' he fibbed. 'I've had worse ones.' Though that at least was true.

Georgina said nothing, just letting him be; and because she wasn't pushing him it felt like the right time to tell her. 'Like the one that finished me, in London.'

Still, she didn't interrupt; she simply continued massaging his scalp with her fingertips and let him set the pace.

'It was four years ago,' he said. 'Carly was twelve years old, though she looked sixteen. She'd met someone online who groomed her. Her parents didn't have a clue until she disappeared, leaving them a note saying she'd run away to France with a man who was going to marry her. She was convinced he loved her as much as she loved him, and he was going to treat her like a princess.' He dragged in a breath. 'The poor kid didn't have a clue that he was part of a ring. He knew how young she really was – as did his "clients".' Even now, it made him so angry that his fists automatically clenched. How could anyone treat another human being like that? 'She managed to break out of the room where they kept her. Hid in the attic. Except she knew they'd find her sooner or later and make her do what they wanted, again and again and again.' He swallowed hard. 'She slit her wrists. She'd bled out by the time we found her.'

One of Georgina's hands slid from his head to clasp his, her fingers tightening with sympathy. 'It wasn't your fault, Colin.'

'It felt like it was,' he admitted. 'I went over and over everything, trying to see what we'd missed, how we could've saved her before it got that far. And all I could think of was that little girl, the same age as my daughter – even her name was similar. That little girl could've been my Cathy, targeted and groomed and taken by those bastards.'

'That's every parent's worst nightmare,' Georgina agreed. 'But you found Carly, Colin.'

'Too late.'

'But you *found* her. You didn't miss anything,' she said. 'Were the men caught?'

'Yes. They're in prison now.'

'Then you stopped them doing that to anyone else,' she said.

'It didn't feel like enough,' he said. 'That's when I started drinking. I wanted to blot it out. Stop panicking that anyone would do that to my daughter, too. One glass of vodka turned into two, then two big ones, then...' He sighed. 'I became the oldest cliché in the book. Detective struggles with the case he couldn't fix and tries to drown it out with booze.'

'Don't do yourself down. You had the courage to get help,' she said.

'I was pushed into it, thanks to my Chief Super and my ex-wife,' he admitted.

'If you hadn't wanted to stop, you would've carried on drinking,' she said. 'It's not possible to help someone until they're ready to accept that help.'

'I guess. I had rehab for the drinking, then counselling to get that case out of my head. The first counsellor wasn't much help; he was drippy and vague. It's all very well to say "oh, you must think *this*",' Colin mimicked savagely, 'but he didn't tell me *how* I could change my thinking.'

'A good counsellor will give you the tools to help you change your thinking. Breathing and cues, and homework,' Georgina said.

'That's what the second counsellor was like. She was fantastic. She taught me how to ground myself: something I use even now,' Colin said. 'And I got through it. It was too late for me and Marianne; our marriage had fractured well beyond repair by that point, and I don't blame her at all. I couldn't have lived with someone like me, either. But at least now we're past the really bad stuff. She's happy now. And so's Cathy. Marianne's new partner is good for her, and he treats Cathy as if she was his own. And I know that's a good thing.' He gave a croak of a laugh. 'Even though at the same time bits of me hate it, because *I'm* her dad, not him.'

'She texts you every day. You video call her a couple of times a week and you see her when you can, when you're off duty,' Georgina reminded him. 'She *knows* you're her dad. Having a stepdad doesn't change that. It just means she's got someone else on her side when you can't be there.'

'I guess.' He drew her hand to his face so he could kiss her palm. 'Taking a demotion and moving to Norwich turned out to be the best thing I ever did. I'm not constantly treading old ground and getting moody thinking about what I could have done differently. I miss a few of the characters from my old team, but I like my team here.' He paused. 'And then I met this amazing photographer who makes me see things a different way. You've changed my world, Georgie.'

'You've changed mine, too,' she said. 'Not to mention literally saved it, once.'

'All part of the service,' he deadpanned.

She leaned over and kissed him. 'Thank you for telling me about your nightmare case. That can't have been easy for you.'

'Surprisingly, it was,' he said. 'I think maybe it was time you knew the worst of me, and why sometimes I go a bit quiet and moody.' He paused. 'I don't think I'll ever fully forgive myself for letting Carly down, even though I know my team and I did our best.'

'That's understandable. It was too close to home, and all the might-have-beens will probably always echo in your head,' Georgina said. 'As a parent, you know your job is to protect your child. As a policeman, you must get double that because it's your professional role to protect people, too. And maybe if you and Marianne had been going through a rough patch, as every marriage does, that meant everything happened at the wrong time – which would sideswipe *anyone*. So don't say you've told me the worst of you, Colin Bradshaw. You're a good man. And you're human. I'm pretty sure anyone else in your shoes, with a daughter the same age as yours, would've reacted the same way you did.'

Colin wasn't convinced, and it must have shown on his face because Georgina added, 'When I found out Bea was being blackmailed, I wanted to break every single bone in Neil Faulkner's body – and then break every fractured piece as well. And cut his heart out with a rusty spoon.' She gave a wry smile. 'That's when I learned you were right when you said that everyone's capable of murder, given the right circumstances.'

'I guess you have a point,' he said.

'Don't beat yourself up, because it won't change the past.

All you can do is learn whatever you can from it and move forward.'

'I'm trying,' he said.

'And you'll get there,' she said.

The fact that she believed in him almost convinced him that maybe he could. One day.

SIXTEEN

On Wednesday, Georgina had walked Bert, picked up some groceries and was considering going out with her camera when Jodie called.

'The police say they're done with Tara's house,' she said. 'I've got permission to clean up. I've told Bethany and her mum what I'm doing, but I told them not to come until I'm done tidying the place up.'

'That's kind,' Georgina said. 'I said I'd help you, so I'll come and collect you. What's happening with Harry?'

'They're having a football day at school, so I've just dropped him there. I'm sitting outside the school at the moment. I can pick you up, if you don't mind going in my van.'

'Of course I don't mind,' Georgina said.

A quarter of an hour later, they were standing on Tara's porch. Jodie swallowed hard. 'Poor Tara. I hope it was quick and she didn't know what was happening to her.'

The pathologist could probably answer that, but Georgina didn't want Jodie to dwell on it and upset herself even more. 'I'm sure it was,' she soothed. 'Come on. Let's go and get things tidied up, the way Tara would've wanted it.'

'I don't know what to do about the carpet,' Jodie said. 'I mean, it's a *white* carpet, and there's all the blood. I know I could put salt on it, but it's been there for long enough for the stains to already set.' She grimaced. 'And Tara didn't like using chemicals. All the stuff I use when I clean for her is the posh eco brands that cost an arm and a leg.'

'I used specialist cleaners for Rookery Barn, last year, when everything was over,' Georgina said. 'They're used to dealing with... well, situations like this. Maybe Tara's family could talk to them and see if they can help?'

'Maybe,' Jodie said.

'And, in the meantime, maybe cover the area with a throw or a towel. Just so you don't have to see it and be reminded.'

Jodie unlocked the door, then locked it again behind them. A couple of leaflets that had been shoved through the door lay on the mat; she picked them up and added them to the pile of mail on the narrow table in the hallway.

When she walked into the living room, she winced. 'I don't even know where to start,' she said. 'There's fingerprint dust everywhere, there's all the stuff in the cupboards and the drawers to put back... Where do we start?'

'The dust, I think,' Georgina said. 'Colin's said to me before, it's really fine stuff and it's hard to clean. We'll need to vacuum it first, then use a damp cloth, working inwards. And then we'll tackle the drawers, one by one.'

Jodie unzipped her bag, took out a face mask and a pair of gloves, and handed them to Georgina. 'What you said about the dust being fine – we need face masks so we don't breathe it in. And gloves so it doesn't get under your nails. It's almost impossible to get out again.'

Georgina was touched by the younger woman's concern. 'Thanks, Jodie.'

They worked solidly and managed to deal with the dust

through a combination of scooping, vacuuming and damp cloths.

Then they started sorting out the first drawer.

'All her nice things, left all over the place like it's a jumble sale table when everyone's been through the stuff and discarded it as rubbish,' Jodie said. 'It's just so...' She bit back a sob.

'Would having some music on help?' Georgina asked. When Jodie cleaned the barn Georgina let out as a holiday cottage, she always played music loudly and sang along.

'It probably would,' Jodie said, 'but it feels disrespectful. I mean, Tara's *dead*.'

'If Tara was here,' Georgina said, 'would you have music on?'

'Well, yeah,' Jodie said. 'Tara's only three years older than me. She liked the same music. Her, Bethany and me used to listen to the charts together on a Friday. Sometimes they came round mine, at the Red Lion, and sometimes I went round theirs.'

'Who was her favourite?' Georgina asked.

'Harry Styles.' Jodie gave her a watery smile. 'When she first started modelling, me and Bethany said she had to get famous so she'd get invited to one of his parties, and then she could take us with her as her plus ones.' She shrugged. 'Obviously it never happened – she never met him – but we could dream.'

'Did you name your Harry after Harry Styles?' Georgina asked curiously.

Jodie blushed and mumbled something that Georgina couldn't quite hear. Ordinarily, she might've teased her younger friend about it, but today wasn't the right time for that. Instead, she said, 'Then let's play Harry Styles. For Tara.'

'You might like his music, actually,' Jodie said. 'My mum does. She likes One Direction, too.' She sang a snatch of 'What

Makes You Beautiful' and went a bit red. 'Mum says that could've been written about me.'

'Your mum's a wise woman,' Georgina said gently.

'I dunno about that. Sometimes. Whatevs.' Jodie flicked into her streaming service and set the app to play Harry Styles' last album. Then she and Georgina tackled the first drawer together.

'While we're sorting things out,' Georgina said, 'maybe we should keep an eye out in case Tara kept any of the anonymous letters.'

'I'm pretty sure she would've thrown them out, like Bethany said,' Jodie said.

'She was away last Thursday night,' Georgina said thought-fully. 'If our anonymous scribe was following their usual pattern, they would've sent her a letter, which she would've got on, say, Friday. And if she put it in the bin...'

'It's bin day here today,' Jodie reminded her.

'Yes, but the recycling bin was last week,' Georgina said. 'So if she threw the note away, it might still be in the bin outside.'

'Unless she put it in the black bin,' Jodie pointed out.

'You said Tara was quite eco,' Georgina said. 'I reckon she would've put paper in the recycling bin.'

They looked at each other.

'I told Colin about the notes, last night,' Jodie said. 'He would've passed it on to everyone else in the case. But the forensic team would've been really busy. What if, somehow, they missed a note in the green bin?'

'It won't hurt to check,' Georgina said. She and Jodie were both wearing gloves, after all, so they wouldn't leave fingerprints behind.

'The bins are by the back door – through the gym, not the patio doors,' Jodie said. 'I don't fancy staying out there in the rain to go through it. If we put everything into a bin bag, we could check it indoors.'

'Good idea,' Georgina agreed.

Jodie retrieved a large bin bag from a kitchen drawer; Georgina noted that the packaging said the bag was biodegradable, so her instincts about Tara's green credentials had been right. She followed the younger woman through the house, and Jodie let them both out into the back garden. The bins were neatly hidden behind a trellis fence covered with a climbing plant.

'You hold the bag, and I'll tip the bin,' Jodie said.

Once everything was safely collected, Jodie righted the bin and tucked it back in its place. Then she and Georgina emptied the lot onto the tiled kitchen floor and sorted through it.

Leaflets, inner cardboard tubes from toilet rolls, washed-up pots of yogurt and hummus, a cereal packet, junk mail...

'No brown envelope,' Jodie said when they were nearly at the end. 'So either the person sending the letters didn't send one this time, or our Bethany was right, and Manson was the one sending them – and he couldn't send one last week because he was dead.'

'Hang on,' Georgina said. 'There's *this*.' It was a scrap of lined paper that looked as if it had been torn from a wire-bound reporter's notebook, with perforations along the top. The note on it was handwritten.

Meet me at the lighthouse on Thursday night. We'll sort things out for good.

'The lighthouse was where Manson died, last week,' Jodie said with a shiver. 'And Thursday was the night he died, wasn't it?' Her eyes widened. 'That was obviously sent to *him*, not Tara.'

Georgina nodded. 'I'm going to ring Colin. Can you put the note in a clean plastic bag – a resealable freezer bag or something like that, if Tara has one?' At Jodie's slightly wavery, 'OK,'

Georgina took her phone from her pocket, snapped a photo of the note and messaged it to Colin. Then she called him.

'I'm at Tara's house with Jodie, cleaning up. We found a note. It might be important. I've just photographed it and messaged it to you.'

'Hang on.' There was a pause while he was obviously finding the picture and reading the note. 'Where did you find this?'

'In the recycling bin.'

'I thought the forensic team had bagged everything in the bin.'

'Inside, they might've done,' Georgina said. 'Jodie told you about the anonymous letters that someone sent to Tara when she was away. Given that she was away last Thursday, we wondered if the anonymous letter-writer might have sent something to her. We thought it was worth checking the recycling bin outside, just in case she'd had a letter and thrown it away.'

'Did you find one?' Colin asked.

'Nothing written to her, but we found this note, and to us it looked as if it had been sent to Manson. Maybe that was why he was at the lighthouse on Thursday night. We've put the note in a plastic bag, and we're both wearing gloves to clean up in here, so we've tried not to contaminate the evidence,' she said.

'Thank you for that,' Colin said. 'And you're right. This is something I'd want to see. Strictly speaking, though, you've both interfered in an investigation. You should've spoken to me, first.'

'We had the all-clear to clean the house,' Georgina pointed out. 'It's not as if we went round scrunching everything up and smearing fingerprints everywhere.'

He sighed. 'I know, and I don't mean to sound as grumpy as I probably do. Sorry.'

'Apology accepted,' she said. 'But it looks as if Manson went to the lighthouse last week specifically to meet someone. All we have to do now is find out who wrote the note.'

'All *I* have to do,' Colin corrected. 'Whoever wrote that note might be responsible for Manson's death, and possibly involved with Tara's death, too. Do all the armchair detecting you like – just please don't do anything for real and put yourself at risk.'

'Noted,' Georgina said dryly.

'And I'll send someone to pick that note up from you shortly,' he added.

'OK. See you later,' she said.

Colin looked at the note. Was this what the killer had been looking for when Tara had disturbed them? Would identifying who'd written the note also help him identify the killer?

He could ask his potential suspects to give him to give him informal handwriting samples from their everyday life – letters, a diary or a shopping list – but it would probably be easier to ask for a 'request specimen', where he dictated a paragraph at speed several times and took each sheet of paper when the paragraph was written so it couldn't be used for reference. And then he could give his suspects similar paper to that of his specimen note to make it easier for the experts to analyse. The note appeared to be written in a black ballpoint pen, and they were easy enough to get hold of.

Once he'd written out the plan of who he needed to see to get the writing samples, as well as checking their alibi for Monday night – because he was convinced that Manson's murder was linked to Tara's, even if it had been an accident – he took Mo with him to help conduct the interviews.

By the end of the day, Colin had a file full of handwriting samples, and none of them matched the writing on the note. Everyone in the group in Summerstrand who'd opposed Manson's development had an alibi for both Thursday and Monday, including Ben's daughter, Claire. Even though Colin was Georgina's alibi for both evenings, and he knew the handwriting wasn't hers, he double-checked her, Jodie, Barbara and Bethany, too. Ben, Sally and Vicky gave each other alibis and their handwriting didn't match the sample. And the same was true at Manson Developments, including the office team, the site manager and the site staff who'd been known to openly argue with Manson.

The only useful thing he learned was from the office manager, who'd been on leave the previous week; she admitted that Manson hadn't paid some of his suppliers and they were threatening to take him to court about it.

But Colin was still no nearer to finding out who had told Eliot Manson to meet them at the lighthouse – or why.

Frustrated that everything on the case seemed to be stalled, and knowing that he needed to do something to distract himself before he started to brood about it, he called Georgina. 'Can I cook for us, tonight?'

'Sure. Your place or mine?'

'Yours, if you don't mind,' he said. He wanted to work in a kitchen that felt like the heart of the house, as hers did, rather than the identikit space of his own tiny galley-style kitchen. He wanted to hear her dog pattering about on the pamment tiles, smell the herbs in pots on her windowsill and lose himself in the sheer warmth of Georgina's place.

He called in to the supermarket on the way to Little Wenborough, picking up chicken, vegetables and a pot of crème fraiche, as well as a punnet of out-of-season raspberries and a tub of Greek yogurt.

Bert leaped ecstatically round him in welcome when he arrived, and Georgina made him a mug of coffee before settling down at the kitchen table to do a crossword. There was no pressure to talk, and no awkward silence; it felt as if she was giving him space to process his thoughts but was there if he wanted to talk.

Eventually, chopping onions and garlic, slicing chicken breast and sneaking a couple of bits to Bert, then sizzling the ingredients together in a pan with a little wholegrain mustard, made Colin start to feel better. Once he'd added the stock and the mushrooms and everything was simmering nicely, he turned down the heat, put a lid on the sauté pan, and came to sit at the table with her.

'Thank you,' he said. 'For letting me sulk in your kitchen.'

She smiled. 'Hey. It means I don't have to cook dinner.'

'Everything's stalled,' he said. 'I can't go any further on what we think is Ryan Everett's case, until the DNA results are back. I'm no further working out who wanted to meet Manson at the lighthouse, or who sent Tara the letters, or who killed her and why. I have suspects with motives, at least for Manson; some of them even have the means, but they all have alibis. I'm missing something vital, but what?'

'There was one thing Jodie said to me about the letters.' She winced, looking guilty. 'I meant to tell you earlier, and it slipped my mind. Apparently, Bethany has a theory that Manson—'

'—was the anonymous letter-writer,' Colin finished. At her look of surprise, he explained, 'Bethany told me herself. She thinks he wanted to make Tara jealous so she wouldn't work away from home anymore. And it would also explain why the doorbell never captured footage of anyone putting a letter through the door – well, obviously apart from the postman.'

'It's a weird way to think, though,' Georgina said.

'I agree. There are a lot of weird things about this case,' Colin said.

'Don't think about it anymore tonight,' she said. 'Right now, you're too close to it to see the wood for the trees. Let it percolate in the back of your brain. Finish cooking dinner, do the crossword with me, and make a fuss of Bert.'

Georgina had a kind heart and a lot of common sense, Colin

thought. 'You,' he said, 'are definitely lovelier than a summer's day. More temperate. And more sensible.'

She laughed, clearly enjoying his deliberate misquote of Shakespeare. 'Thank you.'

SEVENTEEN

'Are you horribly busy?' Georgina asked when Sally opened the back door of the Feathers, the next morning.

'Well – I can spare a few minutes,' Sally said. 'What is it?'

'I want some advice. I'm trying to buy Sybbie a sneaky present,' Georgina said, crossing her fingers behind her back.

'I'm not sure I'd be much help,' Sally said doubtfully. 'Wouldn't you be better off asking her daughter-in-law?'

Georgina had to think swiftly. 'Probably, but Cesca's terrible at keeping secrets. I don't want her to accidentally let it slip.'

'Oh. Well, come in and I'll make us a coffee,' Sally said.

'Thanks.' Georgina let Sally usher her into the kitchen in the flat above the pub. 'It's quiet around here this morning.'

'Ben's at the wholesalers and Vicky's taken Robbie over to Summerstrand with Jodie and Harry,' Sally said. 'The boys will play together while Claire, Vicky and Jodie finish sorting out the bar before the painters come this afternoon.'

Perfect, Georgina thought. 'Sorry to have wrecked your quiet morning.'

'That's all right. So what's this present?' Sally asked, putting two mugs of coffee on the table.

Georgina took her phone out. 'We went to Holt on Monday, and we found this beautiful gallery. Webster's. I couldn't resist buying a print.' She showed Sally the painting Joan had made of Summerstrand.

'That looks familiar,' Sally said, frowning slightly.

'It's somewhere on the Norfolk coast. Niamh Webster – the gallery owner – says her whole family are artists,' Georgina said. 'This was painted by Joan Riggs, Niamh's aunt.'

She watched Sally carefully, but maybe Sally had been too young back in 1965 to take an interest in an elderly artist who lived on the other side of the village.

'Niamh's daughter makes these gorgeous bowls.' She showed Sally a shot of the bowl she'd fallen in love with.

'Oh, I like that,' Sally said. 'It's shimmery. All the colours of the sea.'

'Isn't it?' Georgina enthused. 'But I was thinking, Sybbie would probably prefer something more like the colours of her favourite azaleas. And then I saw Niamh's bronzes of dogs.' She flicked to the next picture.

'That's the spit of your Bert,' Sally said.

Georgina chuckled. 'I know. I nearly bought it, but I'd already bought that print and I really couldn't justify buying myself two treats in a week. And then I saw the bronze Labrador.'

Except the next picture wasn't the Labrador. It was the dog Ryan had sketched.

And Georgina could see the film of tears that immediately sprang into Sally's eyes.

'Sally?' she asked softly. 'Sorry, that was the wrong photo. But you look really upset.'

'That picture. It's...' Sally swallowed hard. 'It looks so much like Cracker. He was our collie, when I was a child.' She bit her lip. 'I say "our", but he was absolutely devoted to my brother, Martin.'

'Martin?' Georgina asked gently. Although she knew some of the story, thanks to Doris and Colin, she was hoping to prompt Sally into filling in some gaps.

'He was ten years older than me,' Sally said. 'But he always had time for me. He was really good at football. He could've been as good as George Best.'

'Did he not get the chance to play?'

Sally sighed. 'Back then, there wasn't the freedom kids have now. You were still a minor until you were twenty-one. So, even though he'd been spotted by a scout and offered to try out for Arsenal, he could only do it with Dad's permission.'

'Couldn't your mum have given permission?' Georgina asked.

Sally shook her head. 'Women couldn't even have a bank account without their father or their husband being a guarantor, in those days. It was Dad's permission or nobody's.'

Georgina blinked. 'We are talking about the 1960s here, right?'

'Right,' Sally said, looking disgusted. 'Dad refused. He wanted Martin to be a lighthouse keeper, just like he was.' She closed her eyes. 'I said to him, I could be the one to follow in his footsteps instead, if he let Martin follow his dreams and go to London. He just laughed at me and told me I was a stupid girl, because women couldn't be lighthouse keepers.'

'Couldn't they? I remember learning about Grace Darling, when I was at infant school,' Georgina said. 'She went out with her dad in a rowing boat from their lighthouse to rescue passengers from a shipwreck when the sea was too rough for the lifeboat to come out. And that was in, what, the early nineteenth century?'

'1838,' Sally said. 'I told him that once, actually, and got the back of his hand across my ear for being cheeky.'

Georgina narrowed her eyes. Sally had clearly had a rough childhood. No wonder Frank had been so delicate about Sally's father in the George and Dragon. 'I'm sorry.'

'It's how it was, back then,' Sally said. 'Answer your parents back, and you'd be in for it. I always swore I'd never hit my Vicky, and I never have.'

'I'm with you, there. I never hit either of my two,' Georgina said. 'But tell me about Martin. Did he become a lighthouse keeper, or did he find a way to become a footballer?'

'He just left home without saying a word to any of us,' Sally said. 'Cracker barely ate a thing for a month, even though I tried feeding him out of my hand. He just spent all his time lying outside Martin's room with his head on his paws, moping.' A tear trickled down her cheek. 'Dad said if Cracker didn't buck his ideas up, he'd take the dog to the knacker's yard and they could have him for glue.'

'What a *bastard*.' The words came out before Georgina could stop them, and then she winced. After all, this was Sally's dad. 'Sorry.'

'Don't be. I know exactly what he was,' Sally said. 'He was a bully and a bastard. He drove Martin away. Cracker was quite an old dog, and he died the next year. Dad didn't care. He kept my mum under his thumb. The only reason he let me stay on to do my A-levels and go to university was because the headmaster persuaded him how good he'd look, having a doctor for a daughter.'

Everything Frank had hinted at, and more. Georgina blew out a breath. 'I'm sorry he was such a nightmare.' Guilt flooded through her. 'And I'm sorry – if I'd known this was going to be so painful for you, I would never have brought it up.'

'You weren't to know.' Sally gave a weary shrug. 'So anyway, this bronze you wanted me to look at?'

Georgina skimmed past the next photo to the one of the bronze Labrador, but not quickly enough.

'What was that other sketch?' Sally asked.

'Really, it doesn't matter,' Georgina said.

'You didn't come here to talk to me about a present for Sybbie at all, did you?' Sally accused.

Georgina blew out a breath. She'd had the bright idea of coming here today and talking to Sally in the hope she'd open up and it would help Colin, because the case had stalled; but instead she'd just interfered and really messed everything up. 'No,' she admitted. 'I wanted to talk to you about something else, but I wasn't sure how to bring it up.'

Sally frowned at her. 'I don't understand.'

'Remember how Bert uncovered a skeleton at Sybbie's friend's house, last year?' Georgina asked. At Sally's nod, she continued, 'He did the same at the lighthouse.'

The colour drained from Sally's face again. 'Bert found a skeleton?'

'At Hartington, I managed to find out who the skeleton was and – well, bring some closure to the situation,' Georgina said. With the help of Doris, though she wasn't going to complicate matters even further by trying to explain the unexplainable to Sally. 'Ryan Everett went missing from Summerstrand in the 1960s. His family's never been able to find out what happened to him, even though they reported him missing, they've searched for years, and they've got a website page up about him. He just vanished into thin air. And it's his niece who owns the gallery and sculpts the bronzes.'

'Why did you want to talk to me about him?' Sally asked.

'I think Ryan Everett was the one who made that sketch of your collie,' Georgina said. 'Because he'd...' She raked a hand through her hair. 'There isn't a tactful way to say this, and I apologise in advance. I talked to Niamh, the sculptor, about her brother. She said after her dad threw Ryan out, he came to live with his great-aunt Joan in Summerstrand.' She met Sally's eyes. 'Ryan used to write to his older sister. He sent the letters care of her best friend, so his dad wouldn't get rid of them before she could read them. And he told her he'd met someone special in Summerstrand. He didn't give her a name, just an initial.'

'"M",' Sally said dully. 'And that's the photo you didn't want to show me just now. You gave that sketch to Colin, didn't you?'

'The photograph of it, yes,' Georgina said.

Sally closed her eyes for a moment. 'I lied to Colin when he showed the portrait to me. I denied knowing who he was.' Her voice was hoarse. 'I denied my own brother. Even though I knew it was Martin. That picture made me want to cry, seeing my brother look so happy and knowing it all went so badly wrong.'

Georgina held her breath for a moment. Did Sally know what happened to Ryan? Was she going to confide in her?

Sally hunched forward, wrapping her hands round her coffee mug. 'At the time, I was eight. I just thought Ryan was Martin's new friend who'd moved to the village and was good at art. Martin had one of Ryan's sketches of Cracker – I think he must've taken it with him when he left, or else Dad burned it.' She grimaced. 'Dad had a bonfire and burned everything of Martin's that I couldn't rescue.'

'Do you think...' Georgina's mouth felt dry with strain. 'Could the skeleton have been Martin?'

'No. It wasn't him.'

'Sorry to ask, but how can you be sure?' Georgina asked.

'Dad had been on at Martin all week, saying he'd have to give up all the nonsense about football because he wouldn't allow it. Martin had to be the next lighthouse keeper. The Armitages had been the lighthouse keepers at Summerstrand for generations, and that's the way it was going to be. If he didn't like it, he'd just have to lump it.' Sally bit her lip. 'Martin used to go out when Dad started getting at him. He'd run on the beach, as if he was training for football, and he'd run and he'd run until he'd stopped being angry, and then he'd walk back through the dunes. Sometimes he met Ryan – I think he liked having someone to talk to, someone who understood what he was going through. Except I think Ryan had told him that he didn't have to put up with Dad. That Martin could leave Summerstrand, go to London, and maybe lie about his age. That he could follow his dreams, and he didn't have to beg for Dad's permission.'

Georgina waited, not wanting to interrupt.

'There'd been a huge fight between Martin and Dad that night. Martin told me he was going to the dunes. I knew that meant he was going to see Ryan.' She closed her eyes. 'If only he hadn't told me where he was going. Dad had been drinking, and he was a mean drunk. I was doing my homework – late, because I'd helped Dad in the lighthouse earlier, polishing the brass. He shouted at me for being up late when I ought to be in bed. And then he asked me where Martin was. I told him I didn't know, because I didn't want him to find my brother and have another fight with him, but he knew I was lying.' She swallowed hard. 'He hit me. Then he asked me again. I still said I didn't know. He hit me and asked me again, saying that next time I'd get the buckle end of his belt. And – God forgive me, I was so scared and I just wanted him to stop hitting me.' Her voice cracked. 'So I told him. I told him Martin was in the dunes. And it's all my fault.'

Georgina pushed her chair back, walked over to Sally and wrapped her arms round the other woman's shoulders. 'Sally, it wasn't your fault. You were eight years old, and you were in an impossible position. Your father threatened you. He *hit* you until you gave him an answer. How could anyone blame you?'

'*I* blame myself,' Sally said. 'Dad sent me to bed. I didn't dare leave my room. I heard the door slam behind him, and I knew he was going to find my brother. Even if I disobeyed him and left the house and ran as fast as I could, I knew it was too late. I wouldn't be fast enough to reach Martin in time to warn him.' Another tear trickled down her cheek. 'My door was an old-fashioned plank one. There was a tiny knothole you could just about see through. When I heard someone come up the stairs, I looked. It was Martin. He had a black eye starting, and there was blood all over his face. Dad had obviously hit him, too. I wanted to go to him and tell him I was sorry, but I was too scared Dad would hear me and hit me again.'

'It wasn't your fault, Sally,' Georgina repeated.

'I couldn't get to sleep, that night,' Sally said. 'And I heard something outside. Stupidly, I looked out of my bedroom window. It was Dad, and he was taking soil off a heap and putting it in a hole. He looked up, saw me peeping through the curtains, and beckoned for me to come down.' She bit her lip. 'If I didn't go, I knew he'd come and get me. He'd drag me down the stairs by my hair. So I went down. There was something in the hole underneath the soil he was shovelling in. I think it was an old blanket, and I was sure it was wrapped round a... round a *body*. And Dad said that seeing him by the hole, seeing what was in there, made me an accomplice.' Her words hitched. 'He said if I ever told anyone what I saw, I'd end up in prison. And he made me... he made me take the shovel and put soil on top of the blanket. I nearly dropped the shovel, because it was so heavy, and he slapped me and told me not to be clumsy. Then he told me to go back to bed before he lammed me again.' She rubbed the tears from her eyes. 'The next day, Martin was gone. And Dad put a patio down, all concrete and pebbles. And I...' She gave another sob. 'I knew there was someone under there. I knew Martin had come home that night, and I'm sure I would've heard if there had been another fight. Plus he was bigger than the body under the patio, so I didn't think it was him. I didn't know who it was, though.'

'Couldn't you have told the police?' Georgina asked.

'Who were they going to believe, an eight-year-old girl or her dad, who'd fought in the war and helped rescue people from shipwrecks?' Sally asked. 'And if I told... even if I wasn't an accomplice, he would've found a way to move the body so when the police dug up the patio there wasn't anything under it. And then...' She shivered. 'He might've killed *me*, next. So I kept quiet and I did what I was told, and I tried not to make him angry. I worked so hard at school, because my mum was obviously never going to leave him – back in the sixties you didn't leave, you just told people you'd walked into a door as a warning not to interfere and make it worse – and I knew education was my only ticket out of Summerstrand.'

Georgina hugged her more tightly.

'It was part of the reason I became a doctor, and why I've been involved with a women's refuge. So that I could help people and make up for the bad thing I'd done,' Sally said. 'When the lighthouse came up for sale, I was going to buy it, to make sure nobody ever took the patio up. But then Manson gazumped me, and I heard he was going to remodel the lighthouse. I looked up the plans on the county's planning permission portal and I could see he was adding an extension. That meant he was going to take up the patio – and he'd find what was underneath it. And for weeks now I've been torn between dreading it and relief that it'll finally be over.'

'That *what* will finally be over?' Ben asked, walking into the kitchen.

EIGHTEEN

Georgina had been concentrating on Sally's words and hadn't heard the door to the pub's flat open. And Sally had clearly been so focused on her tale that she hadn't been paying attention to sounds outside the kitchen.

Horrified, Sally stared at her husband.

Equally horrified, Georgina stared at him, too.

'That what will finally be over?' Ben repeated.

'I...' Sally buried her face in her hands and sobbed.

Ben went over to her and rested his hands on her shoulder in a gesture of comfort. 'What have you been saying to her?' he demanded, narrowing his eyes at Georgina. 'Look what you've done! My wife's in bits – and she wasn't like this when I left for the wholesaler's.'

'I'm sorry, Ben,' Georgina said. 'This wasn't supposed to happen.'

'I think you'd better go,' Ben said. The usually genial pub landlord suddenly looked menacing, and Georgina was aware of just how big he was. Tall, muscular and, despite being in his sixties, very capable of throwing troublemakers bodily out of his pub.

'No – stay,' Sally said. 'It's not Georgie's fault, Ben. It's stuff that happened years and years ago.' She drew in a faltering breath. 'Stuff about Martin.'

Ben dragged the nearest kitchen chair so it was right next to Sally's and sat down, his arm going round her. 'Martin?' He shook his head. 'Love, you did what you could to find him. Nobody could've tried harder. It wasn't your fault he died in London before you could see him again.' He fixed Georgina with an accusing gaze. 'Why did you have to come and stir all this up? She hasn't been sleeping properly for weeks, as it is!'

'Ben, it was always going to come out,' Sally said. 'The body... under the patio, next to the lighthouse. My dad buried it.'

'What?' Ben looked at her in shock. 'Your dad *buried* someone next to the lighthouse? And you knew about it?'

She nodded miserably. 'I didn't know who it was. Not when it happened. I was scared it was our Martin, except I'd seen him come home. There was blood all over his face. When he was gone, the next morning, I thought...' She closed her eyes. 'Well, I *hoped* he'd run away.'

'He did. He went to London. You found his grave,' Ben reminded her. 'So... whose is the body?'

'We think it's a man called Ryan Everett,' Georgina said quietly.

'Who was he? Why did he end up...?' Ben shook his head as if to clear it. 'I don't understand.'

'I'm an *accomplice*, Ben. I saw Dad putting soil back into the hole he'd dug.' Sally's voice shook. 'He looked up and saw me looking out of my bedroom window. He made me go downstairs and put some of the soil in the hole, so that made me part of what he'd done. An accomplice. He said I couldn't tell anyone now – because if I did, he'll tell them I'd helped him bury what was in the hole and I'd go to jail.'

'Sally, you weren't an accomplice. You were a *child*,' Ben

said. 'And your father was a violent bully. If he wasn't already dead, I'd want to kill him myself for what he's done to you. Of course you wouldn't have gone to jail.'

'I believed it, all these years,' Sally said. 'I know I'm winding down to retirement and I only work a couple of days a week, now, but I'm going to have to resign from the practice. I'm tainted.'

'You're not tainted at all,' Georgina said. 'You're the village's favourite GP, because you listen and you make things happen. All this happened nearly sixty years ago, and you were a little girl at the time. Your father coerced you into helping him, and you were below the age of legal responsibility. Plus you weren't responsible for anything your father did.'

Ben's stare was a little less hostile when he looked at her. 'She's right, love. Whatever happened, it wasn't your fault.'

'I think you need to talk to Colin,' Georgina said. 'Tell him what you told me.'

Sally sagged against Ben. 'All the *damage*. I can't fix this.'

'Yes, you can,' Georgina said, keeping her voice gentle. 'You can tell the truth about what you saw and what your dad forced you to do. Get justice for Ryan, and closure for his family.'

Sally's eyes were wide and pleading.

'Colin's like you,' Georgina said. 'He listens and he doesn't judge. He'll help you, Sally.'

Ben gave a single nod of agreement. 'He's all right, Colin.'

'But – we've got to open the pub,' Sally protested.

'We can close it,' Ben said. 'Or I'll call in some favours and get someone to cover.'

Which would take time. The longer they waited, the more likely it was that Sally would start to lose her nerve.

'I can drive you to the police station,' Georgina said, 'while Ben sorts everything out here, and then he can come and join you. That way, you don't have to worry about what's happening here, and you won't have time to get nervous about talking to Colin. Because it's just a chat about things that happened a very long time ago, when you were a little girl,' she emphasised.

'She's talking sense, Sal,' Ben said.

'All right,' Sally said.

'Look after her,' Ben said to Georgina, when Sally was sitting in the passenger seat of Georgina's car with the window down.

'I will,' Georgina promised.

And she kept the conversation light all the way to the city, though she was aware of Sally tensing as soon as she pulled into the entrance of the car park and pressed the intercom by the barrier.

She'd sent a quick message to Colin while Sally was getting her things together, letting him know that she was bringing Sally in to talk to him about Ryan Everett. As she'd hoped, he'd had a word with the front desk; as soon as she said, 'Georgina Drake and Sally Forrester, here to speak to Colin Bradshaw,' the barrier lifted.

'I feel sick,' Sally said as she climbed out of the car.

'Of course you do,' Georgina said. 'Anyone would. But I promise you, Colin isn't going to clap you in handcuffs and drag you to a cell. He'll take you to a quiet room, probably with another member of his team who can take notes for your statement, and he'll offer you coffee. It's actually drinkable coffee, too.'

As she'd hoped, the gentle teasing made Sally give her a reluctant half-smile.

Colin himself came into the reception area to collect them.

'Thank you for coming, Sally,' he said. 'I appreciate you taking the time to help me out with my case. I've got an interview room booked, so we've got somewhere quiet to have a chat. I'll introduce you to my colleague Larissa, who'll be joining us to take notes.'

'Ben's getting someone to cover the pub while I'm here,' Sally said. 'Do we – can I...?'

'Do you want to wait for him?' Colin asked.

She swallowed miserably. 'I want to get it over with.'

But she clearly didn't want to be alone.

'Do you want me to stay with you until Ben gets here, Sally?' Georgina asked.

'Would you?'

'Of course,' Georgina said. It was the least she could do, considering she was the one who'd broken Sally's resolve not to tell her father's secret.

'Come with me, and I'll organise some coffee,' Colin said. 'I'm afraid I can't do biscuits, because everyone's in league to stop me eating them. They say I have to listen to our practice nurse.'

'Pre-diabetes?' Sally asked.

Colin groaned. 'Another eagle-eyed medic. Yes. Though on the flip side it means I really enjoy my one slice of cake per week.'

'As long as it's only one slice, and you're switching from refined carbs to wholegrains as much as possible, that one slice will do you good,' Sally said.

Georgina could see what Colin was doing: making Sally relax because she was thinking as a medic and a friend rather than worrying about what she was going to tell him about her past. That would hopefully reassure Sally, too.

Once they were settled in the interview room with coffee and after he'd introduced Sally to Larissa, Colin said, 'Just so we're clear, this is a witness statement you're giving me, Sally. You can stop at any time, and we're not judging you.'

'Even though I'm... I was... an accomplice?'

'What year did the events happen?' he asked.

'1965,' Sally said.

'Do you mind me asking how old you were, then?' Colin continued.

'Eight,' she said.

'Then, whatever happened, you couldn't have been an accomplice,' he said. 'In 1963, the Children and Young Person's Act set the age of criminal responsibility at ten years old. You were too young.'

A single tear trickled down Sally's cheek. 'All these years, I believed...' She scrubbed the tear away.

'Tell me what happened,' Colin invited gently.

Sally was halfway through telling Colin what she'd told Georgina in her kitchen when there was a knock at the door. 'Mr Forrester has arrived, sir,' the young policewoman said.

'I'll leave you now, then,' Georgina said. She squeezed Sally's hand. 'You're doing the right thing. And it's going to be fine.'

Ben was standing outside when Georgina left the room. 'Thank you for staying with her,' he said gruffly.

'It's the least I could do,' she said.

'I always knew there was something she wasn't telling me,' he said. 'I knew there was a reason why she was helping at a women's refuge, and I knew it wasn't her first husband because Robert really loved her and Vicky. He was an emergency doctor, and he would never have laid a finger on her.' His jaw clenched. 'Everyone in the village suspected that Dennis Armitage hit his wife when he'd been drinking. But back then people also thought you'd made your bed so you had to lie in it. The only thing my dad could do was refuse to serve him more than four pints and hope he didn't have a stash of spirits at home.' He shook his head. 'Why the hell didn't her mum leave him and take the kids?'

'Even now, it takes a lot of courage to admit something's wrong and be ready to leave a tough situation. Back then, it was even harder,' Georgina said. 'I think Sally's worried that you're going to judge her.'

'Never,' Ben said feelingly.

'I'll leave you to it,' Georgina said. 'If there's anything you need, you know where I am.'

'Cheers,' Ben said, and went into the interview room.

Through his job, Colin had seen much of the darker side of human nature. But Sally's father sounded like a really nasty piece of work.

Surely it couldn't have been a secret in the village that Dennis Armitage was mistreating his wife and children? Surely a social worker – a welfare officer, as they would've been known back then – would've been called in? Or one of Sally's teachers might've been able to do something?

Then again, he'd seen enough cases where someone had refused to press charges against their partner, whether from fear of further reprisals or a mistaken hope that this time they'd change.

'Did you think your brother might have been closer than just friends with Ryan?' he asked gently.

'It never occurred to me,' Sally said, 'until years and years later. In fact, not until I finally managed to track Martin down.' She closed her eyes for a moment. 'I was too late to see him again. He died from AIDS. The sad thing is, I would never have judged him for being gay. He was my big brother, and I loved him. I missed him. I was angry with him for a while,' she admitted, 'for leaving without a word. I resented the fact he never managed to get a message to me or our mum that he was all right.'

The way that Ryan had written to his older sister, Colin thought.

'But mostly I loved him,' she continued, 'and it's my biggest regret that I never got to tell him I was sorry for telling Dad where he was, that night. If he hadn't left when he did, when I was a bit older I probably would've realised he was gay, but it wouldn't have bothered me.'

'Do you think your father knew about Martin's sexuality?' Colin asked.

'I don't know,' Sally said. 'And I don't really know what happened when Dad found him. I assume Martin was with Ryan, but whether they were just talking or doing something more, I don't know.' She bit her lip. 'Maybe Dad heard Ryan telling Martin to defy him and leave for London anyway. Or maybe he saw them together and realised they were both gay. Either way, my guess is Dad lost his temper and hit out.' She looked at Colin. 'I assume you've had a forensic bones specialist looking at the skeleton?'

'Yes.'

'Do you know... how Ryan died?' she asked hesitantly.

If he told her the truth, it wouldn't give her any comfort. But if he didn't tell her, her imagination might supply something worse. 'There's some evidence,' he said.

'I need to know, Colin,' Sally said, her eyes beseeching. 'I need the truth.'

'Some of his ribs were broken; they hadn't healed, so we think the injuries happened in a fight.'

'Maybe Dad knocked him to the ground and then kicked him while he was on the floor,' Sally said. 'Ryan was slender. But broken ribs don't kill, unless they puncture the chest wall and cause a pneumothorax – a collapsed lung,' she added.

'The hyoid bone was also broken,' Colin said.

Sally winced. 'Dad must've kicked him and strangled him – probably in front of Martin. My brother was limping when he came upstairs and he was covered in blood,' she recalled. 'I'm sure he would've tried to stop Dad kicking and strangling Ryan. But if Dad had already punched him hard enough to knock him out, or wind him, he wouldn't have been able to help Ryan.'

'Why didn't Martin call the police?' Colin said. 'You said he was ten years older than you. Being eighteen meant that he was still a minor, yes, but he was old enough for people to believe what he said.'

'At a guess, he was probably in shock. And if he'd said anything, Dad could've retaliated by saying he'd caught Martin and Ryan together. In court, he would've been up on a charge of gross indecency. Martin would've got a jail sentence, and Dad would've found a way to sweep the rest under the carpet. He'd say Martin was lying to try and cover up what he'd done. And which of them would be believed? The teenager who was angry because his dad wouldn't let him try to make something of himself, or the local hero?' Sally shook her head. 'I'm not surprised Martin ran away. He probably knew Dad would've come after him again, maybe to silence him for good. And now I understand why he never made contact with me. He couldn't take the risk of Dad finding him.'

'I'm sorry,' Colin said. 'We'll never know precisely what happened, unless Martin wrote it down at some point or told a friend. But what you've said would fit the evidence.'

'Now what?' Sally asked. 'Dad's dead. He can't stand trial for what he did. Do you arrest me?'

'No,' Colin said. 'You didn't kill Ryan, Sally. I can't officially say the body's his until we get the DNA results back, but what you've told us fits in with the body we found being his.'

Sally closed her eyes for a moment. 'I'm so sorry that my dad killed him – and his poor family never knew what had happened to him.'

Georgina was halfway back to Little Wenborough when her phone shrilled. The screen on her dashboard told her it was Jodie. She pressed the button to answer hands-free. 'Morning, Jodie.'

'Georgie!' Jodie's voice was shrill with panic. Georgina had never, ever heard her sound like that before.

'What's happened?'

'It's Harry.' Jodie took a shuddering breath. 'He's gone missing.'

'*Missing?*'

'And Robbie. Oh, my God. I hope they're together.'

'Where are you?' Georgina asked.

'The George and Dragon, in Summerstrand,' Jodie gabbled. 'Vicky and me were helping Claire today, before the painters come in.'

Of course. Sally had told her that, earlier, but after Sally's revelations about her father it had slipped Georgina's mind.

'Harry and Robbie were playing with Archie, Claire's boy. Then Archie came downstairs to see us. He said they'd been playing hide and seek, but he couldn't find Harry and Robbie.

He got bored looking for them and went to play something on his console, but that was half an hour and they still haven't come back, so he thought he'd better tell us.' Her voice was audibly shaking. 'What if something's happened? What if...?'

Georgina could remember losing track of Will in a shop once when he was small, and panicking about what might have happened to him – if he was hurt, or if he'd been snatched. It had been the longest three minutes of her entire life. 'I'm on my way,' she said. 'I'll help you look for them.' She remembered the missing-person search she'd helped with at Hartington Hall, the previous summer. 'You, Vicky and Claire need to work out a search plan – list all the rooms in the pub, plus the garden, then list the roads round the pub. We'll tackle them one by one, methodically, and tick them off as we go. Try not to worry. We'll find the boys,' she said.

When Jodie ended the call, Georgina dictated a message for Colin into her phone via the car's hands-free system, to let him know that Robbie and Harry had gone missing at the George and Dragon, and she was going to help with the search. She ended asking him to tell Sally and Ben, because of course they'd want to know that their grandson was missing.

By the time she got to the George and Dragon, forty minutes later, Jodie, Vicky, Claire and Claire's mum Tracey had already searched the flat above the pub.

'There's no sign of them,' Claire said. 'But they can't have vanished into nowhere, can they?'

'We were playing in the flat,' Archie said. 'It was my turn to seek, and they were hiding. But I couldn't find them anywhere. Not in a wardrobe, not under the bed, not behind a door.' He shook his head. 'I don't know where they went.'

'What about down here?' Georgina asked. 'Is there anywhere they might've hidden down here?'

'We weren't supposed to be down here, because Mum and

Auntie Vicky and Jodie are getting ready for the painters,'
Archie said.

'I don't remember seeing or hearing them come down,'
Claire said.

'Me neither,' Jodie said.

'Nor me,' Vicky added.

Children didn't have the same sense of time that adults did,
Georgina thought. It was possible that the boys hadn't realised
how long they'd been hiding. On the other hand, Archie said it
had been half an hour. Surely Harry and Robbie were bored
with the game by now and were starting to get hungry?

Then she remembered something else. 'When I first met
you, Claire, Frank told me about Black Shuck and the smugglers' tunnels leading from the pub. Could the boys have found
the tunnels?'

'That's a *story*,' Claire said. 'I grew up here. I don't
remember anyone talking about any tunnels.'

'Not tunnels,' Tracey said, 'but there used to be a priest's
hole.'

'A priest's hole?' Jodie asked.

'A tiny little space where someone can hide,' Tracey said.

'A lot of the big houses in Tudor times had them. When
Elizabeth I was on the throne, Catholic priests would be impris-
oned, tortured or even killed – but some of the old families were
still secretly Catholics, and they had secret hiding places built
into the walls where a priest could hide from search parties,'
Vicky said. 'There's one at Oxburgh Hall. We sometimes take
classes there on a school trip.'

'And there's a priest's hole here?' Claire asked. 'I didn't
realise the pub was that old.'

'Bits of the building date from the late 1500s,' Tracey said.
'Ben was going to block it up, years ago.' She rolled her eyes.
'But you know what your dad's like, Claire. He promises to do
things and forgets.'

'Whereabouts is this priest's hole?' Georgina asked.

'In the cellar,' Tracey said. 'I can't remember where, exactly. The whole cellar's full of panelling. The hole's behind one of the panels.'

'Stay here, Archie,' Claire directed, 'in case Robbie and Harry were in the garden and come back. Call us if they turn up. We're going in the cellar to see if they're down there.' She led everyone else down the narrow stairs.

'If we knock and wait a few moments, we'll be able to hear if there's an answer,' Georgina suggested. 'Well, everyone else will be able to hear. I might not be able to pick it up,' she said apologetically, gesturing to her hearing aids.

'Good idea,' Tracey said approvingly.

'If they managed to open the priest's hole in the first place, it's got to be somewhere accessible, which means it's not likely to be one of the panels behind the kegs or the crates,' Claire added. 'That narrows it down a tiny bit.'

'I just want my Harry back,' Jodie said quietly.

Georgina squeezed her hand. 'Try not to worry. We'll find the boys.'

Claire walked through the cellar, tapping on each panel as she reached it and waiting, listening for a sound.

Silence.

Finally, she reached the end of the room. She banged on the last panel. 'Harry! Robbie! Are you there?' she called.

The silence echoed for a moment more.

And then relief spread over Jodie's face and Georgina realised the boys must have shouted something she couldn't quite hear.

'Tap on the wood in front of you, so we can hear you,' Claire called.

Georgina stood back, letting Jodie and Vicky home in on the sounds – the direction of sounds was something she struggled with.

'I think it's this one,' Vicky said eventually.

'Mum, how did the mechanism work?' Claire asked.

'I can't remember,' Tracey said, shaking her head. 'You'd better ring your dad and ask him.'

Claire had to go to the top of the cellar steps before her phone could get a signal. She came back down, grimacing. 'No answer. I left him a voicemail and a text, and Archie's got my phone. As soon as Dad returns my call, he'll ask him how we get in the priest's hole, then come and tell us.'

'A lot of priest's holes had trapdoors,' Vicky said. 'They were usually hidden in something else, like a chimney or the bottom of a closet. The one in Oxburgh is in the floor of the garderobe.'

'I don't remember the entrance being in the floor, but it won't hurt to look. Maybe we can see if one area looks a different colour, or has different bricks,' Tracey said, tapping her phone to switch the light on.

Between them, they examined the floor, but nothing looked darker or lighter than another area.

'Or if they weren't in the floor, the entrances would be really low down,' Vicky said. 'The idea was they should be hard to find, so the priests could avoid the search parties. There couldn't be anything that would give them away, like a keyhole or a handle.'

'If there's no handle, maybe the mechanism would work by pressure,' Georgina said. 'Like modern soft-touch cabinets.'

Jodie dropped to her knees in front of the panel and began pressing on the wood, working methodically along it in the hope of finding the mechanism.

Finally, there was a creak, and one end of the panel popped free, like a door just coming ajar. She stood up, pulling the panel open as she did so.

Immediately a boy Georgina assumed was Robbie crawled through the gap, followed by Harry. Both of them were filthy, both of them had tear-streaks on their faces, and both hugged their mothers very, very tightly.

'I'm sorry, Mum,' Harry said. 'We didn't mean it.'

'Sorry, Mum. Sorry, Auntie Claire. Sorry, Nan Tracey,' Robbie echoed, looking from one to the other. 'Harry, I think we're in trouble. No console for a month.'

'You're not in trouble,' Jodie said, stroking her son's hair and blinking back tears. 'We're just glad you're both all right. I thought maybe you'd been' – she gulped – 'snatched.'

'We were only playing hide and seek,' Harry said. 'Archie was counting to a hundred, upstairs. Me and Robbie were going to hide behind the kegs, except that was too obvious. We were messing about, shoving each other and that, and Robbie fell over. I didn't mean to push him that hard.'

'I fell against the wall,' Robbie said. 'And that door opened. Harry shone his phone torch in to see what was behind the wall, and it looked like a brilliant place to hide. Archie'd never think of looking there.'

'So we did,' Harry said, taking up the story. 'And we heard Archie come down here. He was really fed up with us. He said f—'

'We don't need to know that bit,' Jodie said hastily, cutting him off.

'He didn't find us,' Robbie said. 'But then he went. And he was gone for ages.'

'He got bored of waiting for you,' Jodie said, 'and he was on his console.'

'We got bored, too. And we tried to get out,' Harry said. 'But the door was stuck. We shouted and shouted, but nobody heard us.'

'Because we had music on while we were cleaning,' Claire said. 'Why didn't you ring one of us?'

'We couldn't get a signal on our phones,' Robbie said miserably. 'There's a tunnel back there, but we didn't know where it went, and we didn't dare go down it in case we got even more stuck.'

'Well, I'm glad the pair of you showed *some* sense,' Tracey said. 'But don't ever do anything like that again!'

'And you two have to do *everything* Archie says for the rest of the day,' Claire said sternly.

'But – but he might tell us to eat worms and stuff, like the celebs do in the jungle!' Robbie said in horror.

'Or spiders. Crunchy ones,' Harry added, not to be outdone.

Georgina hid a smile. 'I should let Colin know they're both safe and sound, too, and we're not going need a search team.' Leaving the boys to their reunion and to be fussed over by their mums and grandmother, she headed for a quiet part of the pub and called Colin.

'I was just about to ring you,' Colin said. 'Are the boys still missing?'

'No. Panic over,' Georgina said. 'They were playing hide and seek. It seems there's a priest's hole in the cellar. Claire's mum – Ben's first wife – came over to help with the search. She remembered about the secret door, and eventually we found it. The boys had hidden there and couldn't get out when the door jammed. There's no phone signal, so they just had to wait for us to work out where they were. They're both trying to be brave, but it's fairly obvious they were scared to death when they got stuck.'

'As long as they're safe,' Colin said. 'I hadn't actually told Sally and Ben, yet.'

'OK,' Georgina said. 'But the boys said something else. It's not just a priest's hole. You know those tunnels that history teacher told me about and Claire said were just an old story? I think they really do exist. The boys said the tunnel went back behind them, but they didn't go down it in case they got lost.'

'Don't *you* think about going down there, either,' Colin warned.

'I'm not stupid. If anyone does decide to see where they go, they need to have someone with them for backup. As I said, there's no phone signal down there, so you wouldn't be able to call for help if you got into trouble,' Georgina said.

'Tunnels,' Colin said thoughtfully. 'Smugglers' tunnels.'

'I doubt they'd lead to the beach,' Georgina said, 'because the cliffs at Summerstrand are really low and made of sandstone. There's a lot of erosion on the coast here; any cave wouldn't last long until the cliff above it crumbled.'

'But the tunnels might start somewhere *near* the beach, somewhere that the smugglers would land their goods,' Colin said. 'And they'd lead to someone who benefited from the old smugglers and their brandy – which I think would be the local manor house, and the local inn, and maybe even the church.'

'Near the beach. A house, or maybe the lighthouse,' Georgina suggested.

'And these tunnels had been forgotten about?' Colin checked.

'Not necessarily,' Georgina said. 'Claire was as surprised as anyone else when we found the door. But her mum – who came to help look for the boys – said she remembered there being a priest's hole in the cellar, and Ben was supposed to block it up years ago and never got round to it.'

'So there's a good chance Ben knew about the tunnel,' Colin said. 'And Ben had history with Manson – who'd treated his stepdaughter badly. And we know now that Manson buying the lighthouse had upset Sally because of her dad killing and burying Ryan under the patio, so it was all going to come to light. Ben obviously didn't know about that, but he knew that something was giving her sleepless nights, and they'd started after Manson bought the lighthouse so there had to be some kind of connection. That's motive and opportunity.'

'But when would he have been able to use the tunnel?' Georgina asked. 'Plus we don't know for sure where it goes.'

'I think Ben and I need a chat,' Colin said. 'But first, I need to find out where that tunnel leads. I'll find out who's free here to be my backup. In the meantime, can you ask Claire and her mum if they can draw me a really rough map showing the pub at the centre, the streets, and the rough locations of the local manor house, the lighthouse, and any particular building that's got historical links to smuggling. It would also really help if they can mark where north is.'

'OK. I'll get that sorted,' Georgina said.

TWENTY

Forty minutes later, Colin arrived at the George and Dragon and introduced himself and Larissa; he'd already met Claire when he'd collected a handwriting sample, but Georgina introduced Tracey.

'Has anyone ever told you that you look like Mr Darcy?' Tracey asked.

Colin simply smiled politely; the comment had worn so thin over the years. 'How are Harry and Robbie doing?'

'We've cleaned them up a bit and given them something to eat, so they'll be OK,' Claire said. 'Look, it's lunchtime. Can I get you and Larissa a sandwich or something?'

Colin shook his head. 'Thank you for the offer, but I'd really like to check out the tunnel.'

'We've done the map for you – well, Mum did, because her drawing's better than mine,' Claire said.

'So you knew about the tunnel before today?' Colin asked Tracey.

'I knew about the priest's hole, but I never went in it.' She shuddered. 'I hate to think of the mice and spiders that have been there. Ben's dad said there was an old storeroom behind the priest's hole. When it stopped being illegal to be a Catholic and priests didn't have to hide anymore, the room was used to store stuff to avoid taxes. That's where they'd keep all the little tubs of smuggled gin.'

'How big were the tubs?' Colin asked.

'A half-anker – which is about four gallons.' Tracey clearly did some rapid mental calculations. 'Fifteen litres. They'd easily fit through the priest's hole door.'

'Fifteen litres doesn't sound as if it was worth trying to avoid the tax,' Colin said.

'The stuff in the kegs wasn't drinkable,' Tracey said. 'It was raw spirit – about seventy points over proof. You'd have to dilute it quite a bit before you put it in bottles and sold it.'

'I had no idea you knew that much about smuggling, Mum,' Claire said.

'Between your granddad and Frank Burton, I got to learn quite a lot,' Tracey said dryly. 'Ben's dad said there was a hole in the wall. There were rumours it was a smuggler's tunnel, but he thought either someone started trying to dig it out and realised it'd be too hard to hide all the earth from the excavations and gave up, or else the tunnel was blocked up years ago, because you couldn't get through it.' She shrugged. 'Mind you, just about every pub on the coast that's old enough has got a tall story about a secret tunnel and smugglers. The same as every church is meant to have a tunnel in the vaults leading to the local nunnery. And then, when anyone asks for proof, the story-teller says that the tunnel was blocked up years ago and nobody knows where the entrance is.' She rolled her eyes. 'Half the time, the stories are made up just to entertain the tourists.'

Colin made notes. 'What do you know about the priest hole?'

'Ben's dad researched the pub's history when he retired,' Tracey said. 'He reckoned the local gentry were Catholics, owned the pub and used it to hide priests from Elizabeth I's spymasters. He had a photocopy of the pub's deeds; they were all written in Latin and dated that far back, so he might be right.' She looked faintly annoyed. 'Ben was supposed to make sure that door was made safe so none of the kids could accidentally get trapped – like Robbie and Harry were today. But obviously it was on his list of things he meant to do and never quite got round to them.'

'Can you show me the entrance?' Colin asked.

'Sure,' Claire said. 'It's in the cellar.'

The door to the priest's hole in the cellar was almost invisible. The only reason Colin could see the tiniest gap on one side of the panelling, where the door opened, was because he knew it was there. Blink, and you'd miss it.

Claire pressed on the panel, and the door opened.

Colin put on the hard hat he'd brought with him and went in first; he had to crawl through the gap. Although he'd expected the space behind it to be narrow, it actually opened out into a low-roofed room.

'I think Ben's dad might be right. It might have started out as a priest's hole,' he said to Larissa, who'd followed him through into the room, 'but then it became a place to store the smuggled goods.' He paused. 'If, as I suspect, the tunnel leads to the lighthouse, we need to take it slowly and check for evidence that someone's been through it recently.'

'All the footprints here look about the right size for an eight-year-old,' Larissa said, shining her torch on the beaten earth floor.

'Maybe that will change when we get in the tunnel,' Colin said. He switched on the headlight attached to his hard hat, checked the map Claire's mother had drawn, and looked at the small magnetic compass he'd brought with him. 'The entrance is heading south.'

'Which means the lighthouse,' Larissa said, looking over his shoulder. 'Unless the tunnel starts twisting and turning.'

'It's manmade,' Colin said. 'Two hundred years ago, our smugglers would be bringing barrels and packages through. They'd probably be using a cart. They'd want to keep the tunnel as straight as possible to make it easy for themselves.'

'Good point, guv,' Larissa said.

Colin took a couple of photographs of the room. He shone the torch on the ground at the entrance of the tunnel; again, there was a flurry of small footprints which were likely to be those of the boys. He shone the torch up at the ceiling, but there was nothing of note. After the last couple of photographs, he said, 'Let's go.'

Once in the tunnel, he had to stoop; clearly men in the early 1800s weren't as tall as they were today. There was a dank smell, like the crypt of an old church; it was cold, and the air felt clammy. Hopefully the tunnel was sound and wouldn't be flooded.

A short way in, the tunnel suddenly narrowed. A quick sweep of his torch showed bricks stacked at the sides.

'It looks as if Ben's dad was right and someone bricked up the tunnel, at some point,' he said.

'And then someone opened it up again,' Larissa agreed.

A little further on, there was another opening. 'It leads north,' Colin said, consulting the compass and the map. 'I think it goes along the main street, towards the manor house.' He shone the torch upwards; the roof was boarded and beamed. 'I'm guessing the tunnels went under the houses rather than under the street, and those boards might be floorboards in a cellar. Someone would've seen a signal from the ship earlier and passed the word round, so people would be waiting to hear a knock; they'd lift a floorboard and the smuggler would hand up a package of tea or a bladder of Dutch gin, and they'd hand down the money.'

'It's the sort of network that could be used for drugs, today,' Larissa said thoughtfully.

'We'll get the county lines team to do a proper check, and see if any of the boards look as if they've been lifted in the recent past. For now, I want to concentrate on our case and check if my theory's right, and this bit of the tunnel ends at the lighthouse,' Colin said. He continued shining the torch as he went, checking for footprints or a bit of fabric caught on the rough wood. He stopped just in front of an area where water had obviously leaked through during the recent heavy rain; there were a couple of clear footprints. 'We'll get Alexsy's team to come and check this,' he said. He took photographs and measurements, made notes on his phone, and he and Larissa both made sure they avoided compromising the footprint as they made their way through the tunnel.

Finally, the tunnel came to an abrupt end.

'We're about six hundred metres away from the pub,' Colin said, checking his fitness watch. 'So I reckon we're near the lighthouse.'

He looked up to see an obvious trapdoor in the wooden section above them.

'It'd be possible to pull yourself up,' he said, 'if your upper body strength is good enough. Which mine isn't.'

'Give me a leg-up,' Larissa suggested. 'And I'll use gloves, so I don't add fingerprints.'

Once she'd pulled on her gloves, he lifted her up. She pushed at the trapdoor, and it opened with a crash, but no light came down from whatever was above them.

'What can you see?' he asked, aware that she was using her phone torch.

'It looks as if I'm in a cellar.' She paused. 'I can't hear anything. I don't think anyone's here.'

'Is there a ladder or anything?'

'No,' she said. 'I'm going to take a look around.'

'Not on your own,' he said.

'Well, how else are we going to know where we–? Oh, hang

on. Have you got the find-a-friend thing with Georgie on your phone?' she asked.

'Yes,' he said. 'Though only so I can find her if she's out somewhere with Bert, trips in a rabbit hole, sprains her ankle and needs rescuing.'

'And she's got you on her phone?'

'Yes.'

'Hand me your phone,' she said, 'and I'll call her and ask her to check where we are.'

'Good idea, but tell her to go somewhere she can't be overheard, first,' Colin said. 'Right now, I don't want anyone else at the George and Dragon knowing where we are. Ask her not to mention it to them.'

He heard Larissa talking, then laughing. 'OK, see you in a bit.' She passed the phone back to Colin. 'You can let me back down, now. Georgie says we're in the lighthouse.'

Colin gently lowered her back to the floor. 'This is all starting to connect. Ben Forrester has the motive to wish Manson harm, because of the way Manson had treated Vicky and gazumped Sally, bringing back her bad memories of the lighthouse. Manson was Ben's former son-in-law, so Ben would know what he drank; and Sally told us that Ben's on blood pressure medication.'

'So he's got the means, too. And he knew about the tunnel,' Larissa said, 'which gives him the opportunity. Do you think that footprint might be his?'

'Forensics can tell if it's a match to his shoes,' Colin said. 'I'll talk to Alexsy and ask him to get his team to check it out. We need a chat with Ben Forrester.' He frowned. 'And with Sally. She lived in the lighthouse, so did she know about the tunnel entrance in the cellar?'

'Which could mean they were possibly both involved in Manson's murder,' Larissa said.

'Let's head back,' Colin said. 'At least we know how far we

have to go this time. And we need to be doubly sure not to compromise that footprint.'

Back at the pub, Colin and Larissa crawled back out of the priest's hole.

'Where did the tunnel lead? Do you think it was the smugglers who made them?' Archie asked, his eyes wide.

'You are absolutely *not* to go anywhere near those tunnels, Archie,' Claire said. 'I'm getting that hole blocked up for good.'

'I don't want anyone in there at all,' Colin said. 'Because there may be evidence there, linked to a couple of cases I'm working on. If that evidence is compromised, whoever is responsible will be in serious trouble. *Really* serious.'

'Thank you,' Claire mouthed to him.

Larissa taped off the panel. 'Official police tape. Nobody goes through without Colin's say-so. And that means *nobody*,' she said.

'Claire, can we have a quiet chat, please?' Colin asked, knowing that Larissa would keep an ear out on what everyone else was saying. 'Somewhere private?'

Claire took him into the pub kitchen. 'Will this do?'

'It's fine,' he said. 'Can I ask you, when did you last see your dad or Sally?'

She thought about it. 'Sally, the Monday before last because she and Dad came over for lunch. I saw Dad on Thursday when he came to pick up my paperwork – he does that every week because he likes to keep everything up to date for the accountant,' she said.

'When, on Thursday?'

'Mid-afternoon. Why?'

'Just getting something clear in my head,' Colin said blandly. 'So you really knew nothing about the tunnels?'

'Really,' Claire said, 'which makes me feel very stupid.

Though, when I was a kid, Mum used to tell me the cellar was full of spiders. Obviously it isn't, because of hygiene inspections, but the idea of spiders was enough to put me and my friends off the idea of playing there. And we never sneaked into the cellar when we were teenagers to pinch some bottles of beer or cider, because someone would've seen us go down the stairs and told Dad. Even when I was old enough to work behind the bar, I only really went into the cellar to change a barrel, or to grab a crate of something.'

All the physical signs were that Claire was telling the truth; but, by the end of their conversation, Colin was no further forward.

'I think we're done, here. We're going back to the station, now,' he said. 'Georgie, I'll catch up with you later.'

'OK.' She smiled at him. 'I'm heading home in a little while.'

'What now, guv?' Larissa asked when they were back in the car.

'We'll go to see the Forresters. I'll talk to Ben; you talk to Sally,' Colin said. 'We want to know if Sally was aware of the smugglers' tunnels in Summerstrand as a whole – then narrow it down to whether she knew about the entrance in the cellar of the George and Dragon, and the entrance in the lighthouse.'

'Ben obviously knew about the one in the pub,' Larissa said.

'He might even have been the one who unblocked the tunnel,' Colin said. 'But what I don't get is the timing. If he did use the tunnel to get into the lighthouse and spike Manson's whisky, to get rid of him for good... why now? He was angry about the way Manson treated Vicky, but surely he would've wanted to do something at the time, rather than wait years?'

'They say revenge is a dish best served cold,' Larissa said. 'Maybe that's why.'

'Maybe,' Colin said. 'We still don't know who wrote the note to Manson suggesting the meeting in the lighthouse on

Thursday night, or who wrote the anonymous letters to Tara – and we don't have any of the letters, either.'

'I think, guv, this is one of *those* cases,' Larissa said. 'We just need a break.'

'I've been thinking,' Georgina said to Jodie. 'That anonymous note we found. Supposing Tara saw it first, and she thought it was from the woman Manson was cheating with? It sounded a bit like an ultimatum.'

'Ye-es. But she couldn't exactly go and lie in wait for them at the lighthouse, could she? She was in London.'

'Maybe,' Georgina said, 'she asked a private detective to watch him and take photos – so she had proof he was cheating on her.'

'Meaning he couldn't do to her what he did to Vicky, claiming she was the one having the affair and taking everything from her when they split up?' Jodie asked. 'Maybe.' She paused. 'Or maybe she took the photos herself.'

'How could she do that, when we know she was in London at the time?' Georgina asked.

'She bought one of those pet cameras,' Jodie said. 'I forgot about it, but it arrived on Monday last week, when I was doing her cleaning. She said she really missed Philip and wanted a kitten. She hadn't told Manson yet, but she'd got stuff organised with the cat rescue centre. And she'd bought a pet camera so she could keep an eye on the kitten when she was in London and make sure it was all right. She knew she could ask me to pop round and feed it when she was away.'

Georgina frowned. 'Surely you'd get the kitten first – or at least know when you were bringing a kitten home from a rescue centre or a breeder – before you bought a pet camera? And you'd buy the bed, bowls and toys first?'

'Tara had her own way of doing things. She said she was

sorting it out and getting most of the stuff from the rescue centre. She'd bought toys, too. Unless the camera wasn't really for the kitten,' Jodie said. 'She was using her doorbell to find out who sent the anonymous letters, so maybe she was using the pet camera in the lighthouse. Maybe she thought after seeing the note that he was meeting someone there on the Thursday night and decided to film the meeting.'

'We need to talk to Colin,' Georgina said. 'If we're right, where would the footage from the camera be stored?'

'Same as the doorbell – on her laptop and her phone,' Jodie said. 'We know her laptop's missing, but her phone was in her handbag. So if Bethany can remember Tara's password, Colin can unlock her phone and see it for himself.'

'I'll ring Colin, and you ring Bethany,' Georgina said.

Colin answered within two rings. 'Hey, Georgie. You're on speakerphone and Larissa's next to me.'

'No smutty talk from me about Mr Darcy in the pond, then,' she teased, and was rewarded by a peal of laughter from Larissa.

'*Not* funny – and not a word about that in the office from *you*, Larissa,' Colin grumbled. 'I'm about to do some interviews, Georgie. Is it important?'

'It might be.' Georgina explained to Colin the theory she and Jodie had worked out. 'Jodie's ringing Bethany now.'

'Bethany said she can't remember the passcode to Tara's phone, and the other day she wasn't willing to guess in case she got it wrong and the phone wiped all the data,' Colin said. 'She doesn't want to lose any of the photos.'

'Which is understandable,' Georgina said. 'But you asked her on the day when she learned about her sister's death, and she was probably too upset to think straight. She's had a few days to start to come to terms with what happened. And maybe her best friend can help her think about what the passcode might be.' She paused. 'Who are you going to interview?'

Colin sighed. 'I can't discuss that with you.'

'Then Jodie and I will meet up with Bethany and call you later,' Georgina said.

He sighed again. 'I'll meet you at Bethany's after the interview. Don't do anything until Larissa and I get there.'

'All right,' Georgina agreed.

TWENTY-ONE

Barbara Cox had made a pot of strong tea and poured a mug for everyone. 'This isn't going to wipe everything off our Tara's phone, is it?' she asked, looking worried.

'No. You get six attempts before it locks you out for a minute,' Jodie said confidently. 'Me and Bethany looked it up.'

'And we've been thinking about the most likely numbers she would've used, on our way here,' Georgina said. 'Starting with her birthday – day, month and year.'

Bethany tapped the numbers in. 'No,' she said. 'Maybe it's your birthday, Mum.' She tried the combination and sighed. 'That's a second no.'

'Your birthday?' Barbara suggested.

'That's the third no.' Bethany sounded nervous. 'What now? The day she went to London and that agent signed her?'

'That's in the public domain, isn't it? Like her birthday?' Colin asked. 'So maybe she thought that would be too easy to guess.'

'So's her own birthday. I wish I hadn't tried that one, now,' Bethany said. 'We've only got three more guesses before the phone locks us out – and only three more after that before it's bricked. We can't do that.'

'Could it be Philip's birthday?' Harry said. 'She said she really missed him. That's why she was going to get a kitten.'

'Though we don't know Philip's actual birthday, because we rescued him – didn't we, darling?' Bethany asked, making a fuss of the ginger cat.

'Gotcha day, then,' Harry said.

'You know,' Barbara said, 'I think Harry might have the right idea. It's a special day, so she'll remember the numbers, and it's not something that's going to be easy to find on the internet.'

'What's the number?' Jodie asked.

'We brought him home ten years ago, on May Day: 010514,' Bethany said, and took a deep breath. 'I really hope we get it right, this time, because I can't think of anything else.' Slowly, she tapped in the numbers, her fingers trembling slightly. And when she pressed the final digit, the phone unlocked.

'Oh, my God. Well done, Harry!' Jodie said, hugging her son.

'There's like a million messages,' Bethany said. 'But they can wait. What are we looking for?'

'A pet camera app,' Georgina said.

'There's one here,' Bethany said, and clicked into the app. 'It's saved just the bits where there's movement.' She glanced at Colin. 'I guess you need to see this first, don't you?'

'Strictly speaking, yes,' Colin said.

'But could you treat this as part of an interview, and ask us to promise not to talk about it to anyone else until you tell us it's OK?' asked Jodie.

'We won't talk to anyone,' Barbara said. 'We just want to know who killed our Tara, and see them get locked up for it.'

Colin looked at the phone. 'One screen, seven of us. We're not all going to be able to see it at the same time.'

'We can if you can make the phone play on the telly,' Harry piped up.

'How?' Bethany asked.

'I'm not the world's best with technology,' Colin admitted.

'I can do it,' Harry said.

'We don't know what's on the footage. It might not be the sort of thing your mum would want you to see,' Colin said, trying to be as tactful and gentle as he could.

'I don't want you having nightmares,' Jodie said.

'But you need me to make it play on the TV,' Harry said.

Jodie shook her head. 'I know how to do that. I think you should wait in the kitchen.'

'That's not fair,' Harry said.

'Your mum's right,' Barbara said. 'But, as long as your mum says it's OK, I happen to know where you can find some chocolate biscuits in the kitchen.'

'Mum? Please?' Harry begged.

'All right,' Jodie said. 'But no more than two.'

'And you can give Philip some treats,' Barbara added.

While Barbara found the biscuits for Harry and the cat treats for Philip, Jodie sorted out the TV. A couple of minutes later, they were all sitting in front of the television – apart from Harry – watching the footage from Tanya's pet camera.

'That's the inside of the lighthouse,' Georgina said as the room came into view. 'You were right, Jodie. I thought maybe she'd got a private detective to follow Manson, but Jodie remembered the pet camera Tara said she'd bought for the kitten she wanted.'

'It looks as if she's wedged it behind one of the boards on the windows,' Colin agreed.

Tara herself appeared, next, walking from the front door of the lighthouse over to the table, and then doing a circuit of the room.

'She's checking the camera's working,' Bethany said. 'Look. She's looking on her phone to make sure it's positioned right.'

'So we should get to see who wanted to meet Manson in the lighthouse, that night,' Georgina said.

'The woman he was having an affair with, if the anonymous letters were telling the truth and it wasn't just Manson making it up so she'd stop working in London,' Jodie added.

Tara left by the front door, and the footage stopped.

The next bit of footage appeared to be timestamped in the afternoon and showed a door opening – but not the front door. The person who walked into the room was obviously using their phone's torch to help find their way, given that the boarded-up windows didn't let in any light, but the infra-red made his identity clear.

'Hang on. Isn't that Ben Forrester from the Feathers?' Barbara asked.

'Yes. But he didn't come through the front door of the lighthouse,' Colin said. 'If the door he came through leads to the cellar...'

'... then he must have come through the trapdoor. The one you lifted me through,' Larissa said. 'He wouldn't have needed a key. All he had to do was go through the tunnel from the George and Dragon to the lighthouse.'

'What's he doing?' Barbara asked.

'It looks as if he's doing something to the heater,' Colin said grimly. 'Which is maybe why it was pumping out carbon monoxide.'

'He's doing something else, too,' Bethany said. 'He's taking the lid off the whisky bottle and putting something in.'

They all watched in silence as Ben screwed the lid back onto the bottle, shook it, peered at it, and set it back down on the table.

And then he simply walked back through the door he'd used to enter the room.

'I'd say that was pretty conclusive evidence,' Larissa said.

There were a couple of very short snippets of video.

'Mice, caught by the infra-red, I'd guess,' Colin said.

The next section seemed to go on for a very long time. Manson arrived, sat at the table and poured a slug of whisky into the glass. He'd brought a battery-operated light with him, clearly not trusting the electrics in the lighthouse. He added the cola to the whisky, and took a sip. Satisfied that the drink was to his liking, he fiddled with his phone; Colin assumed he was playing some kind of game. Every so often, he glanced at his watch and took another sip of his drink. Finally, he muttered to himself and stomped round to the paraffin heater.

'Whoever he's meeting is obviously late,' Bethany said.

Manson sat back in the chair and continued fiddling with his phone. He poured himself a second drink, then a third. Still nobody came through the front door, or the door that led to the cellar.

'Let's play it speeded up,' Jodie said. 'Then we can stop it again when someone else turns up.'

But nobody else turned up.

Eventually, Manson propped his elbows on the table and rested his chin on his hands. A little later still, and he slumped onto the table and the footage stopped.

Jodie paused it, and Colin checked the timestamp. 'One in the morning. Smack in the middle of when the pathologist thought he probably died.'

'I know he'd upset a lot of people and he hadn't behaved well, but it's really sad, anyone dying like that,' Georgina said.

The footage started up again, with the front door opening and Manson's secretary Phoebe walking in, freezing in horror and screaming. The door opened wider, revealing Colin.

'We'll need to retrieve the pet camera from the cottage,' Colin said, stopping the video. 'But we all saw what happened, and all the video recordings are date-stamped.' He looked at

Barbara. 'I need to take Tara's phone with me, as evidence, but I'll make sure I return it to you personally.'

'Thank you,' she said. 'It still doesn't tell us who killed my Tara, but I suppose some good's come out of it. Maybe Ben Forrester will tell you what he was doing in the lighthouse – why he killed Manson – and that'll help explain what happened to Tara.'

'I hope so,' Colin said.

<h1 style="text-align:center">TWENTY-TWO</h1>

'I wasn't expecting to see you again today,' Ben said when Colin and Larissa walked into the Feathers.

'We need a quiet word,' Colin said.

Ben frowned. 'What about?'

'Thursday last week,' Colin said.

Ben's frown deepened. 'You've already talked to me about last Thursday evening. I was here, working – and you know that's true because I served you myself.'

'It's not the evening I want to talk about. It's Thursday afternoon,' Colin said. 'When you went to collect the paperwork from Claire.'

'What about it?' Ben asked.

'I really think we need to do this in private,' Colin said. 'And you're going to need to close the pub or get cover for the bar for the rest of today, at least. Shall we?'

Reluctantly, Ben spoke quickly to the girl behind the bar, then ushered Colin and Larissa through to the flat. 'Does Sally have to hear this?' he asked. 'She's lying down, having a rest. It's been a rough week.'

'We can talk to her later and break the news to her,' Colin

said. 'Ben Forrester, I'm arresting you on suspicion of the murder of Eliot Manson on Thursday 15 April. We have evidence that shows you may have been involved, and your arrest is necessary to question you about your involvement.'

Larissa finished the rest of the caution, and they led him out to Colin's car. Ben was silent, as if he could hardly believe this was happening.

'You can call a solicitor of your choice,' Colin said, 'or you can use the duty solicitor.'

'I... The duty solicitor will do,' Ben said, clearly shaken.

Back at the station, once the duty solicitor had arrived, they went into the interview room. Colin set the tape running, stated the names of everyone present and the time, and repeated the caution. 'Ben, we need to go through the events of last Thursday afternoon. I believe you went to collect paperwork from your daughter, Claire, at the George and Dragon in Summerstrand.'

'I like to keep my accounts up to date,' Ben said.

'That isn't all you did,' Colin said. 'You went through the smugglers' tunnel in the pub's cellar.'

'Smugglers' tunnel?' Ben rolled his eyes. 'It sounds like you've been listening to Frank Burton. He's a nice old boy, knows a lot of the history in the area... but he's obsessed with smugglers and Black Shuck.'

Nicely deflected, Colin thought. But not quite well enough. 'Actually, no – Georgie was the one who chatted to Frank on the previous Friday,' he said. 'It was Tracey who told us about the priest's hole.'

Ben paled. 'Tracey? As in my ex?'

'As in your ex. Apparently, your dad knew a lot about the smugglers' tunnel, too. He's the one who used to talk to Frank about it, but he said it was blocked up. She asked you to block the priest's hole up years ago, and you never got round to it,' Colin said.

'And Robbie found the entrance today when he was playing

hide and seek with Archie and Harry,' Larissa chipped in. 'The younger two thought it was a great place to hide – until the door jammed and they couldn't get out.'

Ben's concern seemed genuine. 'Oh, my God! Are they all right?'

'They were hungry, thirsty and a bit scared when they were found, but they're fine,' Colin said. 'Larissa and I checked the tunnel out, though.'

'We went all the way through to the end,' Larissa said. 'And found we were in the lighthouse.'

'I don't see what this has to do with me,' Ben said, glancing at his solicitor.

'Tara Cox. Someone's been sending her anonymous letters,' Larissa said.

Ben put both hands up in a 'stop' gesture, crossing his hands rapidly. 'That wasn't me.'

'Anonymous letters,' Colin continued, 'saying that Manson was having an affair.'

'Still not me,' Ben said. 'Though I wouldn't have put it past him. He cheated on Vicky. Though he covered his tracks well. She was the one who got the blame for the marriage ending, in the judge's eyes – even though he was the first one to have an affair, and she left him before she started seeing Dan.'

'Maybe Tara knew that,' Larissa said.

'Someone sent Manson an anonymous note. This one,' Colin said, showing Ben the photograph. 'For the benefit of the tape, I'm showing Mr Forrester a photograph of the note. Can you read what it says for me, Ben?'

Ben stared at the photograph, then Colin. Then he mumbled, 'Meet me at the lighthouse on Thursday night. We'll sort things out for good.'

'Tara assumed this was from Manson's lover,' Colin said. 'So she decided to set up a pet camera in the lighthouse – the camera she'd bought for the kitten she was going to get – and catch him red-handed.'

Ben didn't meet their eyes. 'I still don't see what that has to do with me.'

'Manson wasn't the only one she caught on the camera,' Colin said. 'She set it up in the lighthouse on the Wednesday, and went to London for her photoshoot on the Thursday. But before Manson arrives, the footage shows someone else in the lighthouse. The infra-red means we can see that person very clearly – but he puts the light on his phone. So we see him even more clearly. And we see him,' he continued inexorably, 'do two things. Firstly, he does something to the paraffin heater; and secondly he adds something to the bottle of whisky on the table. Would you care to tell us what you actually did, Ben?'

Ben's face turned an odd shade of grey. 'I...'

'What did you put in the whisky?' Colin asked.

Ben stared at him for a long, long moment, and Colin wondered whether the other man was going to deny it. But then he slumped back in his hair. 'Beta-blockers. The ones I take. I thought... I thought they'd make him feel dizzy and faint.'

'And what did you do to the heater?'

'I just changed the settings,' Ben said. 'If he was careless enough to put a paraffin heater on in a room and not ventilate it...'

'A paraffin heater that was pumping out carbon monoxide,' Colin said. 'He felt woozy. The footage from the pet camera shows him slumping on the desk – from a combination of carbon monoxide, alcohol and beta-blockers. A deadly combination. Why did you do it, Ben?'

'For Sally,' he said, his voice cracking. 'That man's done so much harm to her.' Ben's face was filled with a mixture of anger and anguish. 'He was a terrible husband to Vicky, having affair after affair – but he was clever about it. When he finally drove her into Dan's arms, he managed to make out that *she* was the one who'd caused the end of her marriage. And, even though we can't prove it, we *know* he was involved in that hit-and-run that killed Dan, Robbie's father. He's hounded Vicky ever since. And he gazumped Sally for the lighthouse.' He shook his head. 'I knew *something* happened when Sally was a kid – until she told you today, I didn't know what exactly, just that it was bad. She has bad dreams. She talks in her sleep. It's been so much worse since Manson bought the lighthouse. I just wanted it all to stop – to protect her.'

'So you killed him?' Colin asked.

'I wrote the anonymous note to him. With my left hand.'

Which explained why Colin hadn't seen the similarity with Ben's handwriting in the sample.

'I knew he'd guess it was me, because I'd said I wanted to sort everything out for good, this time. We'd crossed swords a couple of times before, when he was following Vicky about and I'd... Well.' He grimaced. 'In bar work, sometimes you have to deal with someone who's had a few too many and started throwing their weight around. You learn to handle yourself. I'm not proud of myself, but I threatened to break a few bones, and he knew I could do that if I wanted to. It made him back off.'

'What would make him know it was you?' Colin asked.

'Like I said, it'd be sorting everything out for good, this time. I knew he'd be there, just because he'd be curious what I'd offer – whether I'd try to buy him off, because obviously if I was going to beat him to a pulp I would've done it before now. And I could've paid him off, bought the lighthouse from him. I've made some good investments over the years.' Ben blew out a breath. 'I knew he'd sit and have a drink while he was waiting for me. More than one. I had no intention of turning up; I thought a couple of big glasses of whisky, laced with the beta-blockers, would knock him out. And he'd put the heater on and be careless about it, so he'd wake up with a hell of a headache in the morning and know that I could do a lot more if he didn't back off.'

'They were your beta-blockers,' Colin said. 'And your wife is a GP. You know that drinking alcohol and taking an overdose of beta-blockers can slow your heart to dangerous levels. I think you intended to kill him.'

'Not kill him – *nearly* kill him,' Ben said. 'To warn him that if he tried to hurt Sally or Vicky again, next time I'd finish the job.'

'Which isn't the same as sorting everything out for good, like you said in your note. You finished the job, this time,' Larissa said. 'And you didn't realise that your actions had been caught on camera.'

'I didn't realise Tara had seen the note and put a camera up to catch Manson being unfaithful,' Ben said. 'Not until...' He swallowed hard. 'Not until she called me, saying she'd got the footage of me in the lighthouse cottage on her laptop and she knew I'd killed Manson.' He shook his head. 'She was trying to blackmail me. I went round – not to hurt her, but to get her to delete the footage. He was a bastard. That sort never change the way they operate. He'd hurt Vicky and he would've done the same to Tara eventually. She deserved better.' He rubbed a hand across his eyes. 'She didn't see it that way. We had a struggle. She fell and hit her head on the coffee table. It was an *accident*.'

'She *fell*,' Colin said. 'Why didn't you ring an ambulance? You could've called nine-nine-nine anonymously and they could've saved her.'

'No, they couldn't.' Ben shook his head. 'It was already too late. I checked her pulse, and there wasn't one. Blood was pooling round her head. I panicked. I rummaged around a bit, finally found her laptop and left.'

'What did you do with the laptop?' Larissa asked.

'I wiped everything off it and disposed of it,' Ben said. 'Look

– Sally had nothing to do with any of this. Claire didn't have anything to do with it, either. Or Vicky. Just me. Don't arrest them.'

'We're going to have to question them,' Colin said. 'But you killed two people, Ben, whether you meant to or not. I'll need to keep you in custody until the Crown Prosecution Service decide to charge you formally in front of a magistrate.'

TWENTY-THREE

A week later, the DNA results were back, showing that the skeleton was Niamh Webster's uncle. Colin, Georgina, Sally and Niamh were standing on the shore at Summerstrand, having left the almost-deserted beach car park. The sea was dark pewter, reflecting the sky; but the waves were relatively calm, merely lapping at the sand. In the distance was a lone walker with a dog.

'I'm so sorry,' Sally said. 'I didn't know your uncle well. And at the time I thought he was just my brother's friend who was good at art and drew gorgeous pictures of our dog.' She dragged in a breath. 'It wasn't until many years later that I realised my brother was gay, and he'd loved Ryan. I just wish they'd been able to have the life together that they deserved. The happiness.'

'That was the plan,' Doris said softly in Georgina's ear. 'They were going to London together. Ryan had friends who would let them stay until they found a place of their own. They'd both lie about their ages; Ryan would go and work in advertising, to earn money, and Martin would get his try-out at the football club or, if that didn't work, he'd train as a PE teacher.'

Except, on the eve of Ryan and Martin leaving for their new life, Dennis Armitage had killed Ryan.

'It's not your fault, Sally,' Niamh said.

'Oh, but it is. If I hadn't told my father where Martin was, he wouldn't have found them together.' Sally closed her eyes briefly. 'They could've been sitting six feet away from each other, and he would've lashed out anyway because he thought Ryan was telling Martin to defy him and be a footballer. But I think maybe Ryan must've had his arms round Martin, comforting him after the argument. And my father...' She shuddered. 'I'm ashamed to say he was a product of his time.'

'Ryan was in the wrong place at the wrong time,' Niamh said. 'And his father – my granddad – shared your father's views on gay men. If he hadn't thrown Ryan out in the first place, Ryan might never have come to Summerstrand and met Martin.'

'Or maybe Martin might've run away to London, made it as a footballer, and met Ryan at a party. Fallen in love with him when the world had started to become more accepting, to realise that love is love,' Sally said.

'When Colin realised what had happened, Ryan remembered everything,' Doris said. 'I was coming to tell you that it's all worked out. They're together again now. And they're grateful for that.'

Not that Georgina could tell Sally and Niamh, though she was glad to hear that Ryan and Martin had finally found happiness.

'I brought you something,' Sally said. 'It's a photograph of Ryan; I found it in one of Martin's books.' She gave a wry smile. 'I managed to rescue some of his stuff before Dad burned it.'

'Thank you,' Niamh said, accepting the envelope. 'And I have something for you. A sketch Ryan made of "M".'

'Thank you,' Sally said. 'And that's really generous, because I know you can never forgive my family for what my father did – and for what I covered up.'

'You were a *child*. Back then, nobody would've listened to you,' Niamh said. 'Look, we're burying Ryan, next week. If you'd like to come to the service, you'd be very welcome.'

'I'd like that,' Sally said.

'Let's walk,' Niamh said. 'Look at the sea, listen to the waves, and remember they loved each other.'

Sally slipped her arm into Niamh's, and together they walked along the flat golden sand.

Colin and Georgina hung back slightly, giving them space.

'At least this part of it's settled, with Ryan's family finally having closure,' Georgina said. 'But what's going to happen to Ben?'

'The magistrate's sitting tomorrow for the preliminary hearing,' Colin said. 'I'm not sure whether they'll keep him in custody until the trial.' He sighed. 'I'm not sure whether Sally's going to stand by him. After all, he thought she might be capable of murder; and he's a double murderer.'

'She's definitely not going to buy the lighthouse. Not now the truth is out about what her dad did,' Georgina said.

'Maybe the local history society can raise the money to buy it and turn it into a museum, but focus on the positive stuff,' Colin said. 'Frank's trying to persuade Claire to make the tunnel into a tourist attraction, but she's told him it'll be a health and safety nightmare. She's going to let him walk through them and take photos, though – once we're done with the forensics.'

Georgina smiled. 'He'll enjoy that. And I wouldn't mind betting that Archie drives Claire potty until she agrees he can go with Frank.' She paused. 'Sally's retiring officially, now. But she's also planning to buy a house that can be used as a women's refuge.'

'To give people the same help that she, her mum and

Martin needed and never got? I can understand that,' Colin said. 'The only thing I haven't managed to find an answer for is who wrote the anonymous letters to Tara.'

'I'm leaning towards Bethany's theory,' Georgina said. 'Manson didn't like Tara being away from him. He thought that, if he could make her jealous, she'd stay rather than go off for a photoshoot. The letters always arrived the day after she was on a shoot – but she didn't get one on the morning after he died. And maybe she never spotted anyone delivering it on the doorbell camera because they were never put through the letter box in the first place. I bet if your computer forensics team looked at his computer, they'd find something.'

'You're probably right,' Colin admitted. 'But it's not going to make a difference, and the manpower's better used elsewhere.'

'But some good's come out of this. Niamh's family has closure. And, although Sally's going to have to face what Ben did, at least she can finally stop reliving the nightmare of her past and stop thinking it was all her fault,' Georgina said.

'Secrets are always better out in the open, where they can't fester,' Colin said.

'Mmm,' Georgina said, thinking of the secret she was keeping from him. It wasn't something that could fester, exactly; but it could definitely drive a wedge between herself and Colin.

Somehow, she'd have to find a way to tell him the truth about Doris...

A LETTER FROM THE AUTHOR

Huge thanks for reading *The Body in the Lighthouse*; I hope you enjoyed Georgina, Doris and Colin's journey. If you want to join other readers in hearing all about my new releases and bonus content, you can sign up for my newsletter!

www.stormpublishing.co/kate-hardy

If you enjoyed this book and could spare a few moments to leave a review that would be hugely appreciated. Even a short review can make all the difference in encouraging a reader to discover my books for the first time. Thank you so much!

This series was hugely influenced by three things. Firstly, I grew up in a haunted house in a small market town in Norfolk, so I've always been drawn to slightly spooky stories. (I did research it when I wrote a book on researching house history, but I couldn't find any documentary evidence for the tale of the jealous miller who murdered his wife. However, I also don't have explanations for various spooky things that happened at the house – including the anecdote about Sybbie's dogs in *Rookery Barn*, which happened in real life with our Labradors and a tennis ball.) Secondly, I read Daphne du Maurier's short story *The Blue Lenses* while I was a student, and... I can't explain this properly without giving spoilers, so I'll say it's to do with how you see people. Thirdly, I'm deaf; after I had my first hearing aid fitted, once I'd got over the thrill of hearing birdsong for the first time in years, my author brain started ticking. The du Maurier story gave me a 'what if' moment: what if you heard something through your hearing aids that wasn't what you were supposed to hear? (The obvious one would be someone's thoughts; but that's where my childhood home came in.) It took a few years for the idea to come to the top of my head and refuse to go away, but *what if you could hear what my heroine Georgina ends up hearing?*

And so Georgina Drake ends up living in a haunted house in a small market town in Norfolk...

The Body in the Lighthouse comes from my love of the sea and my fascination with hidden tunnels (the ones that intrigue me most are the alleged ones under Norwich Castle, but that's for another book!). Summerstrand is a completely made-up place, but the North Norfolk coast is one of my favourite places in the world, especially on a winter's day. I also highly recommend the snowdrops at Walsingham. They are stunning!

I've borrowed a local legend about the day that Black Shuck visited Bungay and Blythburgh in 1577. (The pamphlet, *A Straunge and Terrible Wunder*, was written by Abraham Fleming in London, the following year.) My theory is that it was actually a lightning strike (the parish registers refer to the terrible storm that day), and the folk tale was later used by smugglers to keep prying eyes away. But, y'know, how could I resist using the 'true story' of a spooky dog?

Little Wenborough isn't a real place, but the name is a mashup of the town where I grew up and the river where I walk my dogs in the morning. But Norfolk is an amazing place to live. Huge skies (incredible sunrises and sunsets), wide beaches (aka my best place to think, and the Editpawial Assistants are always up for a trip there), and more ancient churches than anywhere else in the country (watch this space!).

Thanks again for being part of this amazing journey with

me and I hope you'll stay in touch – I have so many more stories
and ideas to entertain you with!

All best

Kate Hardy

ACKNOWLEDGEMENTS

I'd like to thank Oliver Rhodes and Kathryn Taussig for taking a chance on my slightly unusual take on a crime series; Emily Gowers for being an absolute dream of an editor – incisive, thoughtful and a wonderful collaborator as well as being great fun; and Shirley Khan and Charlotte Fry for picking up the bits I missed! I've loved every second of working on this book with you.

Gerard, Chris and Chloe have been particular stars with location research (aka beach walks). Thanks to Chris for pointers on chemistry (any mistakes are mine).

Special thanks to my family and friends who cheer-led the first Georgina Drake book, made useful suggestions about theatres/cake/ghosts, and are there through the highs and lows of publishing: in particular Nicki Brooks, Jackie Chubb, Siobhàn Coward, Sheila Crighton, Liz Fielding, Philippa Gell, Rosie Hendry, Rachel Hore, Jenni Keer, Lizzie Lamb, Clare Marchant, Jo Rendell-Dodd, Fiona Robertson, Michelle Styles, Heidi-Jo Swain, Katy Watson, Ian Wilfred, Susan Wilson, Jan Wooller and Caroline Woolnough. (And apologies if I've missed anyone!)

Extra-special thanks to Gerard, Chris and Chloe Brooks, who've always been my greatest supporters; to Chrissy and Rich Camp, for always believing in me and being the best uncle and aunt ever; and to Archie and Dexter, my beloved Editpawial Assistants, for keeping my feet warm, reminding me when it's time for walkies and lunch, and putting up with me photographing them to keep my social media ticking over while I'm on deadline.

And, last but very much not least, thank *you*, dear reader, for choosing my book. I hope you enjoy reading it as much as I enjoyed writing it.

9 781805 087519